the page 3 murders

Kalpana Swaminathan has lived most of her 48 years in Mumbai. She finds the proximity of twelve million lives an inexhaustible source of enchantment. Her most recent novel is *Bougainvillea House. Jaldi's Friends,* an adventure about Mumbai's vagrant animals, was written in the aftermath of 6 December 1992. Writing with Ishrat Syed as Kalpish Ratna, her articles on books and science appear in many periodicals. Their first book together is a submarine murder mystery, *Dr Wrasse of Crystal Rock.* They have also authored *A Compendium of Family Health.*

aLALLI
mystery

the
page 3 murders

Kalpana Swaminathan

IndiaInk
ROLI BOOKS

India**ink**

© Kalpana Swaminathan, 2006

First published in 2006
India*ink*
An imprint of
Roli Books Pvt. Ltd.
M-75, G.K. II Market
New Delhi 110 048
Phones: ++91 (011) 2921 2271, 2921 2782
2921 0886, Fax: ++91 (011) 2921 7185
E-mail: roli@vsnl.com; Website: rolibooks.com
Also at
Varanasi, Agra, Jaipur and the Netherlands

Cover design & photograph: Arati Subramanyam
Layout design: Narendra Shahi

ISBN: 81-86939-19-9

Typeset by AGaramound Roli Books Pvt. Ltd. and
printed at Syndicate Binders, New Delhi

FOR MY PARENTS, ON THEIR
GOLDEN WEDDING

Acknowledgements

This book was inspired by the many dispossessed men and women who rebuilt their lives on the pavements of this sheltering city in the decades following the liberation of Bangladesh. Their stories of exemplary courage and fortitude have little to do with the story in this book, but I have borrowed some of their unquenchable relish in life.

Most of my friends and acquaintances have unsuspectingly contributed to the cuisine in this book, and I expect reprisals.

The exposition of Raag Jinjhoti, I owe to my aunt P. Saraswathi who generously imparted the essence of its meaning to one who has a poor ear for music.

Ardeshir Villa was designed by Shubha Pachigar who invested her considerable skills as an architect in making my castle in the air not just habitable but luxurious – and then remodelled the interior to accommodate the author's eccentricities.

Tarok Ghosh's millennial menu cannot be blamed on any chef or historian, but the average cook can conjure it up without tears.

Cast of Characters

FELIX REGO: The Food Critic

Our Food Correspondent's greedy column has a penchant for murder...

ALIF BEY: The Genius

The brilliant recluse turns mean when his Muse displays her feet of clay...

RAFIQ KHAN: The Dancer

His Shiv Tandav unleashed chaos. Will his next performance restore order?

Dr HILLA DRIVER: The Hostess

This house party is her way of exorcizing the past, but something goes horribly wrong...

CHILI: The Model

What can be better for a girl's complexion than a vitamin pill? Only, this one turns her livid...

TAROK GHOSH: The Cook

This footpathia turned gastronome uses his superb cuisine to winkle out secrets. And then he ventures on one recipe too many...

LOLA LAVINA: The Survivor

From victim to crusader was a natural progression, but this woman of substance has set her sights on what lies ahead...

RAMONA: The Debutante

The weekend promised to be all she'd dreamed of. But she had reckoned without murder...

UJWALA SANE: Femme Fatale

She has the men on a leash. But in her book, cooks aren't gentlemen...

LALLI: The Sleuth

She collects curiosities: and this weekend seems to get curiouser and curiouser...

THE NARRATOR

She complicates her narrative by falling madly in love...

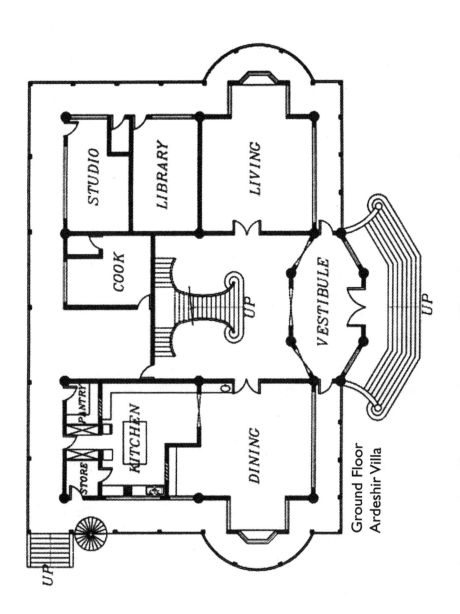

Ground Floor
Ardeshir Villa

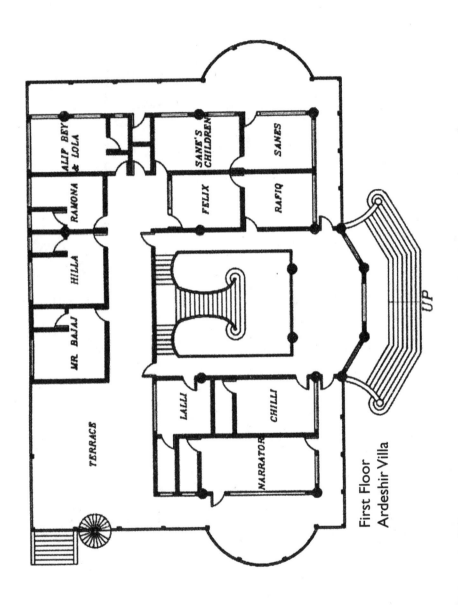

First Floor
Ardeshir Villa

1

I had spent all morning with a corpse. It loomed on the speckled granite of the park bench, bloating in the sun.

A year ago, the modest success of a slender volume of stories had spurred me on to a novel. I was between jobs – or was I? 'You're thirty-two and creaky at the wrist,' my publisher said, 'You'll be teaching dead poets to dyslexics for the next thirty years unless you let go now.'

I hated him, but he was right. 'Plumb the sewers of the soul,' he advised, with some relish. It took a year and a hundred thousand words for me to realize the plumbing had sprung a leak. The book stank.

This morning I had dragged it outdoors thinking an al fresco reading might help. Nada. The book was good and dead and fresh air did nothing to revive it.

Let me begin at the beginning.

I lost my career, my boyfriend and my library all within twenty-four hours, surely a record in the annals of unnatural disaster. One of the worst things a junior lecturer can do is defend a maligned student. I did it, too, at nine-thirty in the staff room, with all the major players in the subtle game of academic pimping listening in avidly.

There's nothing subtle about professorial ire. It hit me before the day was out.

All that week I was inundated with memos, eased out of lectures. My card was refused in the library, my access code invalidated. The staff room emptied the moment I stepped in. On Friday morning the matter was brought to a quick surgical finish.

At eleven a.m. my boyfriend said we had a respiratory problem, he could no longer stand the air I breathed. Oh well – he had a doctoral thesis to submit, didn't he?

At eleven-thirty I was led in, without premed or blindfold, for the beheading. My letter of dismissal lay on Professor Sandeha's desk, as yet unsigned. Her hand hovered over the bright array of plastic ballpoints: acid pink or bilious green which would deliver the coup de grace? Eventually she ignored them all.

She reached for her handbag. I was flattered.

Clearly, this was to be a Mont Blanc moment.

One brutal slash with that black Mozart Meisterstucke, and it was all over. I walked out, freed of my cobwebbed career.

A little before noon I went up to my room to clear out my things. My books were gone. *All* my books.

The career and the boyfriend could be replaced. The library, not. The boyfriend, needless to say, took the books.

In the next twenty-four hours I acquired a typewriter, a new address and an aunt.

A year later, I still have all three.

The typewriter is a Brother portable, with a crooked finial on the T.

The address is 44, Utkrusha, Adarsh Road, Vile Parle East.

The aunt is Lalli.

Let me tell you right away that she is not a generic aunt. Her auntness is accidental. The accident is my father who recently, and for reasons both private and worrying, reclaimed this extremely peripheral twig of the family tree.

When I went home that afternoon, having jettisoned career, boyfriend and library, I found my family splintered in chaos.

The next morning, Lalli arrived. I had no idea where she had sprung from, or who she was, or why her presence was such a solace to my bewildered parents. It was a bewildering time for me, too. I was excluded from their anxieties on the premise that I already had too much to grapple with.

But I'm not ready yet to tell that tale. Enough to say here that I drew as much comfort from Lalli's presence as they did. Although in my case the comfort came more from her complete lack of curiosity in my recent upheavals. When the dust settled, my relieved parents had moved to Lonar to grow roses, and I had moved in with Lalli.

We share a roof, but little else. She has her space, I have mine. We have a tacit agreement to keep out of each other's hair. (In Lalli's case, a silvery tumble of curls. Mine, since you ask, is straight as a plumb line, and twice as boring.) Over the year we have progressed from mutual wariness to mutual tolerance.

When I move out, as I soon must, I'm going to miss Lalli more than I've missed anything else in my life. And that's unnerving – considering how little I know about her. She's sixty-three, five foot six barefoot, a hundred and ten pounds on the bathroom scales. An actor's face, lined, mobile, expressive. Eyes, black and gleaming when quiescent, but with a blaze like a blowtorch on occasion. Hair, as I mentioned earlier, a silvery froth. She moves with a swift economy easily mistaken for grace till you realize it's discipline. *Then* you think stealth, speed, agility. She has square, surprisingly hard hands for a woman who spends most of her time reading.

Till I moved in here, she lived alone, or almost. I haven't asked, but I don't think she's ever been married. There is, for certain, a crowded life within her that has nothing to do with the one she visibly leads. I have surprised moments when the day falls away from her and she turns edgy with expectation. She looks up, listening for a footstep or a distant note of music. Alert. It never lasts for more than a moment. Then the thin flush pales, and her eyes turn inward and opaque.

Our living room has a constant stream of visitors. At first, their variety dazzled me. They turned up at all hours. Sometimes they stayed all day in a daze, going through the motions of politeness while meals were served and cleared away. Some were bounced by Lalli with a terse command: 'Please leave. Now.' These, I noticed, were usually very well dressed and brought with them the ineffable aura of money.

In my first week in Utkrusha, I answered the door to one of these callers. He had an appointment, he said. His name was Surendranath Shah. Lalli was out, spirited away by a phone call, and I felt obliged to keep my visitor company. I brought him the customary glass of water and offered him a choice of tea or coffee, handed him the newspaper and prepared to return to my typewriter, when something made me linger. We got talking, and Mr Shah, I discovered, was an astrologer – not so much by choice, as by inheritance. By the time Lalli returned, we were deep in discussion over Egyptian funerary symbols. I left with some regret.

Later, when he was gone, I asked Lalli if his predictions were reliable.

'I don't know about his predictions,' my aunt said. 'I'm waiting to discover if mine are.'

I was surprised. Lalli seemed too rational to rely on star power.

'I predict that he will soon give himself away,' Lalli continued. 'You two seemed to have a lot to talk about.'

'He has a keen interest in Egyptian symbolism.'

'No. *You* have.'

'Oh I do, but I know next to nothing about it. He's an expert.'

'And how did you reach Egypt? What exactly was the opening gambit?'

Her tone was unnecessarily cynical. He seemed such a harmless rabbit. A tad shabby, but essentially bechara, pavam.

'He's an astrologer,' I said firmly. 'All his family has been for the last six hundred years.'

'And he told you this the moment you opened the door?'

'After I made him comfortable with a glass of water and the newspaper, yes.'

'Aha. And the newspaper was exactly the way you left it after you finished your second cup of coffee?'

'How ...'

'Never mind. Which means it was the City section, open on Page 2 and folded vertically with the coffee stain just beneath *The Stars Foretell* column.'

I was about to protest indignantly when I caught sight of the paper, stain and all.

'But that wasn't all, was it? You've been worrying the Egyptian motif for a week, wondering how you could sneak it into your book. Yesterday you considered setting a scene in a pyramid. This morning you had shifted your loyalties to the Sphinx. These things *show*.'

'How? Did he read my mind?'

Lalli laughed. 'He read his surroundings. Look around.'

I did. I saw nothing.

'Look at the bookshelf.'

That was easy, it's harder to look *away*. Other rooms have walls. Lalli's living room has books. I need a stepladder for the top row.

'Which is the book you last read? It's easy to tell.'

I noticed then, one thick scarlet volume stood a little out of step. It was too high up for the title to be easily read, but the spine bore the unmistakable squat geometry of a pharaoh's tomb. I had been reading it last evening

'Not so quick,' I countered. 'Firstly, that's Norman Mailer's *Ancient Evenings*. Mr Shah does not look like the kind of man who reads Mailer. Secondly, why should he think *I* was reading that book? It could have been you!'

'Certainly, it could have been me. But with the added evidence of the cartouche doodled next to the crossword, clearly made with the pencil that even now lies where you put it down, and which you were probably holding when you opened the door – Mr Shah was quite logical in concluding you were interested in ancient Egypt. And as for your idea that he doesn't look like the kind of man who reads Mailer – how would you know?'

'He couldn't possibly have noticed all that. Nobody ever notices things of that sort.'

'I do.'

'You have a low criminal mind.'

'So has Mr Shah. He's a keen bigamist who has asked me to trace his missing wife. I rather think he's murdered her.'

I laughed.

And sobered up quickly when I saw her face.

She was dead serious.

'Wait a moment,' I said slowly. 'He wanted you to trace his wife? What are you, a missing persons bureau?'

'Among other things. I collect curiosities. I agreed to find Mr Shah's wife because I find him curious.'

My jaw had dropped to my waist by now. Still, there remained one last vital question. 'But why?'

'Why did he go to all that trouble of cultivating you?' Lalli smiled wickedly.

I shuddered. Surendranath Shah, given more time, might have got his act together, and leapt nimbly from kundali to kundalini.

After that, I remained wary of Lalli's visitors for a while.

But gradually my squeamishness wore off. Today I proudly number among my acquaintances a counterfeiter, an embezzler, several prestidigitators who pick pockets for a living, and a modest collection of impostors. As for Mr Shah, he's awaiting sentence. The missing wife was traced quite easily. She was found in a truckload of fruit, evenly distributed in convenient bits between layers of alphonso mangoes, ripening on her way to export.

There are files from Homicide every week. It took me some time to realize Lalli had spent the last thirty years in the police. She isn't my idea of a policewoman, or even a hotshot detective squinting at bloodstains. I learnt of my aunt's celebrated past through one more serendipitous encounter.

This time it was a uniformed policeman with a whole rainbow on his shoulder, and a grin of anticipation that faded when he saw me. 'Lalli please,' he snapped. 'If she is not at home, I will wait.' And before I knew he had slid past me and made straight for the beige sofa.

I tried to keep my voice calm while my head swam with all the lurid tales of police harassment I'd heard from NGO pals. 'What do you want with my aunt?' I barked. 'You cannot badger her like this. We are well aware of our rights. The uniformed police may not visit a householder without prior notice ...' I took great comfort in that *prior notice*. It struck the right note. I made a rapid inventory of people who would rush to my aid, and junked the list. I would have to do this on my own, and I seemed to have all the right words. My eloquence was wasted, though. He wasn't listening. He was punching his cell phone feverishly. Probably calling for reinforcements.

No, I was being handed the phone. 'I'm still at Colaba,' Lalli's voice said. 'It'll take me an hour or more to get home. Don't worry about Balu, he won't bother you. He's one of my boys.'

Balu! I narrowed my eyes. The plastic tab on his uniform said Balkrishna Jadhav. He grinned happily at me. 'Uniformed police can visit fellow officer at residence. Even if retired.'

'I – I didn't know Lalli was in the police,' I stammered stupidly. 'You didn't know the *Ramayan* was about Ram?' he laughed. He tapped the thick file he'd parked on the coffee table. 'See how thick this is? If Lalli doesn't see it this week, it'll grow thicker.'

In a daze I opened the file.

I shut it hastily.

I needed to sit down. I needed a glass of water.

Our apologies collided. 'Sorry, I shouldn't have opened that.'

'No, no, my fault, I should have stopped you. It can be very – shocking.'

It was.

There were photographs in the file. Brutal, nauseating pictures. Worst of all, I had recognized the face. I'd seen it on the front pages all of last week, as had the rest of Bombay's seventeen million.

Sarika Doshi. Sixteen, and killed in the safety of her own home in broad daylight. The murder had stunned the city. Tabloids had never had it so good, printing doublespread interviews with wiseacres who had never been within screaming distance of the girl. (*Senior citizens are regularly murdered in the city, but the death of a teenager cannot be ignored* began one unguarded report.)

Nothing in the angelic calm of those newspaper photographs of the victim had betrayed the horrific assault on her body. Now I recalled details.

She had been battered with an iron dumb-bell and slashed with a knife. Both weapons belonged to the household. Her father, a fitness fiend, worked out with dumb-bells everyday. The knife came from the kitchen. The girl had let the murderer into the house. He seemed to have found the weapons quite easily. The kitchen knife was a cinch, but what about the dumb-bell? There were no signs of struggle. Both parents were at work when the girl was killed.

Multiple injuries, the reports said, but that glib jargon had blocked *this* out. *This* was more than rage or desperation. *This* was hate. This could not be imagined. This had to be seen. When I opened the file I had had one split-second glimpse of that instant of hate. It punched my eyes in. It cut off air. I blacked out.

Balkrishna Jadhav got me a glass of water from the fridge and switched on the TV. India was playing New Zealand at Ahmedabad. We watched numbly as Dravid and Sourav kept the bridge. Sourav's dazzling sixer fetched no more than a perfunctory cheer.

'Forensic report,' Jadhav said suddenly. 'By now public is used to bodies. You see Discovery Channel, no? Body Farm? You've seen that one?'

I wanted to say *That isn't real. That's happening somewhere else. That's on the box, this is down the road from us, for godssake ...*

He pushed the file away angrily. 'The whole day I stare at this, then I go home and what do I get? Children are having dinner and watching Body Farm.' I could imagine the scene. Two or maybe three eager little Jadhavs counting maggots over varan bhat. 'So much forensic expertise, so many tests, so many expensive kits. What's the use?'

'We don't have these skills here?'

'Of course we have them. You want PCR, we got PCR, you want STR we got that also, we got every thing from A to Z, and what's the use? No DNA match. And today I get memo, we have exceeded budget, why no result? So naturally I come here.'

'Naturally?'

He pushed back an errant lock of hair and shook his head ruefully. 'When I first met your aunt, I used to call her Madam. One day she says, Balkrishna, I also have a name, you can read, no? On her tab like this, only one word, Lalli. Then I feel ashamed, how I can call her like that, not even full name, something like pet name? So I say, please, madam, what is your full name. She points to the tab again. So I ask people, they also say madam is Lalli, we are all calling her like that from beginning. But I am too worried. So one day I am digging up her file. There also, same thing, Lalli. No surname. Then I am thinking Tamil people have only initials, village name, father's name, my good friend R.C. Ramanathan, Rayavaram Chandrashekhar Ramanathan, like that. Not like Maharashtrians. We are keeping first name, middle name father or husband and after that surname. But there also – no. No initials for Lalli. Real dilemma. By this time, I am also calling her Lalli, but tell the truth, I am not comfortable. One day I tell this to Fernandez. Very senior man, Fernandez. He laughs. "Nowadays we are supplying initials also," he says, "We are calling her L.R. Lalli because she is our 'last resort'." For many years now, she has been L.R. Before we close a file nowadays we have one extra form to fill. Unofficial, because she is officially retired. We keep at end of file always, one blank sheet of paper with initials L.R.'

When Lalli returned, I was about to excuse myself, but she stopped me. 'Stay if you can bear it,' she said.

'She is not able,' Balkrishna offered. 'Fainting just now.'

Lalli broke into my indignant protest. 'A common reaction to the unexpected. She'll cope.'

Yep. I'd just have to factor in a lot of blackouts if I planned to stick around with Lalli.

'How far have you got with Sarika Doshi, Balu? Forensics?'

No DNA match, Balkrishna Jadhav repeated gloomily. No fingerprints either. Assailant used gloves. Nothing on the dumb-bell but the father's prints, as expected.

'And the knife?' Lalli asked.

'Nothing. Wiped clean.'

'The post-mortem report says no evidence of rape. I find that difficult to believe.'

Jadhav looked uncomfortable. 'There is some confusion. The pathologist says victim was leading active sex life, second opinion of gynaecologist also is intercourse before death. But forensics is negative. I had a talk with them, they are using very advanced techniques.'

'Since my time you mean, Balu?'

'Every week some new test. How are we to know all this ABC and SNP? But they have not been able to find any sperm, they say.'

'And this is the father? Recent photograph?'

'Yes, yes, police photo, after the murder.'

'Sarika was an only child. How old are the parents?'

Balkrishna glanced at his notes. 'Fifties. Early fifties. Child was born after many years of marriage. They are now completely broken. Their full life was this girl.'

'A sixteen-year-old, still at school, leading a very sheltered life, yet sexually active.'

'Of course parents are saying it is impossible. Mother became hysterical, father became violent when we gave them facts.'

'Of course.'

Lalli placed the photograph of the parents on the table. 'You'll need lots of verification, but here's your answer. The case is clear enough.'

'Clear? We have nothing! Girl let the murderer into the house. She knew him. Maybe she was expecting him. Murder is premeditated. He brings gloves.'

'Oh no, the gloves were in the house.'

'No gloves in the house. Why should there be? And how would he know there were gloves?'

'You have just made the most important statement in this case, Balya. Now go investigate.'

He blinked at her stupidly, and so I suppose, did I.

Lalli sighed impatiently. 'There were no gloves in the house! *Why* were there no gloves in the house?'

I didn't get it. Gloves are scarcely necessary in a 1BHK conservative nuclear household without a garden or a contagious disease.

'Did you notice the father's hands, Balu? I suppose forensics didn't take a look either.'

'His hands? No.'

Lalli threw up her hands in disgust. 'No dye stains? Then he used gloves. He's recently dyed his hair, not too long before this picture was taken. Ask yourself why a fifty-five year old man should want to dye his hair and his moustache and work out with dumb-bells. Get inside his mind. And find those gloves. Check his medical history and you'll know why forensics turned in a negative report. Talk to Mrs Doshi, Balya! Find out how long the Doshis were trying for a baby before Sarika was conceived. Go back sixteen years, go!'

It made no sense to me, but Balkrishna Jadhav almost ran out of the flat. Lalli sighed: 'Oh the blind faith they have in technology! They just look at the report, positive or negative, and the matter's over. If you don't find sperm, ask why!'

'Why,' I asked obligingly.

Lalli smiled, 'I keep forgetting how strange all this must seem to you. One possibility that should be considered when there's no DNA evidence is that the rapist – or consensual partner, we can't tell here – has a low sperm count, or has been sterilized.' I reeled a bit as the coin dropped at last. 'You can't mean ...'

'Let's find out why Mrs Doshi took so long to conceive her first baby before we jump to conclusions.'

'That – that's too dastardly.'

I protested feebly.

Lalli shrugged, her face a mask of stone. 'Happens everyday,' she said.

The following week the papers said Mangesh Doshi was helping the police with their inquiries. 'He's confessed,' Balkrishna said. You would have thought that enough to make the guy happy, but no. Both he and Savio looked gloomily across at Lalli.

'It won't do,' Savio said, biting savagely into a biscuit. 'He'll get away, Lalli.'

'You've got a confession, what more do you want?' I demanded. All three glared at me. 'The confession was made in police custody,' Savio said. 'That's not admissible.'

That was the craziest thing I'd heard so far, but evidently they were resigned to it. Lalli said, 'Oh he won't get away. Go find those gloves. Then let's see what forensics has to say.'

Eventually, Savio found the gloves, but it was Lalli who knew where they'd be.

Savio – ah, Savio.

He's the third member of our menáge, and quite frankly, I can't imagine why.

He doesn't live here, not officially, though it's the rare week when I don't wake up to his legs sticking out of the beige sofa as I walk through the living room to the kitchen. A man his size has no business sleeping on sofas. I first met him a fortnight after I'd moved in, just as I was getting over seeing those photographs in Jadhav's file.

I bumped into his legs as I sleepwalked to the kitchen at six a.m. for my first cup of coffee. Not a propitious meeting. I screamed. He leapt. We glowered – and have kept at it since then.

Savio is a six foot two slab of dense muscle, dense being the operative word. How exactly he happened on my aunt I haven't the faintest, but once he did, he stuck. He has the run of the place, though I must admit he's neat as a cat. He's evidently a protegé of hers. In the world outside he's Inspector Savio D'Sa, but everybody forgets the D'Sa. I stay out of his way, and he stays out of mine. In this case, mutual wariness has stayed mutually wary. He is not a naturally talkative man. We're the same age, thirty-three, and I can't see what business he has hanging round a woman of sixty-three. He seems to have no life of his own, and makes up for it by throwing the occasional tantrum at Lalli over her health and suchlike. She bakes biscuits for him. They are good biscuits.

From time to time girls turn up at our doorstep demanding to see Savio. Lalli gives them tea. They come here to talk about Savio, but stay to talk about themselves instead, till Lalli gently prises them away. 'All they need is a good listener,' I've warned Lalli, 'that's why they find Savio so irresistible.' I can't think of any other reason.

For the last month we have been free of Savio. He is away, training. In what? When I asked Lalli, she said, of all things, self-defence. I laughed, but apparently the Man Mountain has been raised to turn the other cheek. Before he left he asked me how my book was coming along. I was surprised. I had no idea he knew I wrote. But then I didn't know he read, either.

He has been a rather numbing presence in the excitements that make life with Lalli so tumultuous. I sometimes wonder if I would have grown so blasé over murder and mayhem if Savio were less phlegmatic. His flat feet never leave the ground. His skull is practically soundproofed against screams. He temporizes the outrageous, dampens the curious, and wouldn't recognize a hyperbole if you handed it to him on a plate. Savio's idea of heaven is probably a padded cell.

In the sensational Sant Baba affair, the one where Lalli grappled with a miracle, and the press thundered for copy, Savio simply made his arrest without comment. Then there was the Varsha Khot murder that shocked respectable Parlekars out of their sceptic wits as they watched a body being exhumed from the Khots' backyard. Savio worked into the night restoring the turf, transplanting saplings, raking and pruning as if restoring the garden would also restore normalcy by noon. I've seen him lose it only once – in the Raja Ravi Varma case. He got clumsy while slipping on the handcuffs and bent the murderer's wrists a little too far back. We heard the bone crack.

In the midst of such urgencies, it's a little difficult to

concentrate on the leaden lives of the people in my book. Besides, I had got into the habit of tagging along with Lalli. I found myself pitched very far from the bookish ambit of academic life, and I wasn't complaining.

This morning Lalli, aware that my typewriter had been silent all week, asked, 'So how far has that rough beast slouched yet?'

At that I had made myself a snarling cup of cafe noir, hauled out the manuscript, and knotted my eyebrows over it. Finally, irate, claustrophobic, and utterly disgusted I had stormed out of the house dragging it with me.

And now here I was at high noon wondering how to best dispose of the body.

A fine rain powdered the lawn.

The clever thing would be to walk away quickly now and let the rain soak it to a pulp. It would pour soon, the sun glowered behind a dirty wadding of cloud. It would rain hard, hammering the bench with malignant persistence through the afternoon, leaving behind a sodden bundle rinsed of failed words.

I did it too. When the rain came down, I ran. Or perhaps I floated, lighthearted in the pelting rain.

By the time I reached home, my elation had drained away. My head throbbed with too little sleep and too much coffee. I craved solitude like drink. Thankfully I didn't have to socialize on the lift. The ubiquitous Raos were not about, and neither mercifully, was Patherphaker. As I stepped out, I heard voices.

Lalli was back and we had company.

It was Hilla.

Dr Hilla Driver is my favourite among Lalli's friends. Most of them are interesting, but in a purely clinical way. Hilla is *nice*.

She's a paediatrician, a few years younger than Lalli, and as unlike her as possible. She's more like one of her patients, plump, pink and liable to go from sunny to doleful in the space of a heartbeat.

She was being doleful now. Her voice rose in comic dismay, 'I really cannot bring myself to cry!'

As I entered, she looked up from the man-sized handkerchief in which she had buried her face.

'It's my uncle Framroze,' she wailed. 'Lived a recluse, walled up in that bhoot bangla of his for the last forty years, whose fault is it that nobody knew he was dead!'

I listened with relish. This was going to be good. Hilla's stories generally were. Cadaveric uncles have promise. Maybe the vultures had quite literally, come calling, and the neighbours gatecrashed the party. 'Why me, I should have asked when his neighbours called me. Why call me? Family? *Of course* he's family. He's been the family spectre for two generations! I should have told them that. But did I?'

'No,' we said gravely. It seemed expected of us.

'Exactly. No. "Oh my," I say when they tell me Framroze Vakil is dead. "I'm sorry to hear that." That's what I say.'

'A mechanical response,' murmured my aunt.

'Mechanical be damned. Stupid response. I should have put the phone down. Wait till you hear the story. He'd been dead four days or more before the bai found him. The lawyer sounded as though *I* was responsible for the delay, being his niece and all, I should have smelt it earlier.'

Hilla's face darkened. For some minutes she scrutinized her toes. When she looked up, her face was suffused with rage. She spoke in low deliberate tones, very different from her usual breezy lilt.

'I'll tell you about Framroze. Listen. Have you ever been inside the old chawls at Parel? Not the new concrete blocks. The old, really old buildings with tiled roofs, bulging and sagging over the shop fronts on S.V.Road? I grew up in one of them. During the day it's so dark indoors you can't see your feet. At night, when the street falls silent, you begin to hear the sounds of mortality. Creak. Snap. Thud. You can feel the walls crumble, the wood rot, the tiles slip and slide out. Rats on the rafters gnawing so busily, you're surprised to find so little sawdust on the floor next morning. You lie there with your heart thudding because you know the house is cracking up and there's no place else to go. And in the morning, sure enough, you read in the papers: 4 killed in house collapse. And the whole family smiles with relief because it wasn't *your* house. Not yet.

'All through my childhood a figure blocked the grimy window that overlooked the street. My father. He was there before we woke, he was there when we returned from school, he sat there watching the darkening streets day after day. All the light we got indoors was through that little window, and he blocked off most of it. This was long ago, mind you, when I was about ten. Later he could no longer make it to the window, he huddled in a corner and coughed. Some days he never got out of bed.

'This is what Framroze did to my father.

'My grandfather was a very rich man. Framroze cheated him, ruined him. On their wedding day, my parents discovered they were paupers. Grandfather shot himself with his hunting rifle. My father became an outcast overnight. Shame and scandal clung to him like an odour. Very soon there was no money, no house, no job, and a child on the way. That was me.

'Grandfather's creditors finished what Framroze had begun. Mother's family disowned her. Finally Papa found a job. He became a mazdoor in a cotton mill.

'My earliest memory of Papa is his cough. Today I know it was the cotton that did it – turned his lungs into thick rubbery bogs that wouldn't aerate him. Those days we called it asthma.

'It broke him before he was forty. It hurt him to walk up the stairs. It hurt him to talk to us children. There were five of us. I was the clever one. My sisters helped Mother make pickles and papad. She kept the house going, selling these from door to door.

'After his forty-fifth birthday, Papa never left the house. He sat in that dark room mumbling useless prayers, watching Mother helplessly. Sometimes he helped with the pickles and papad. Long before he died, we kids had forgotten him. To us he was only a shadow.'

Hilla blew her nose and glared fiercely at us.

'I've never spoken of this to anyone. Not even to my husband. After Papa died, we never spoke about him. There was more light in the house without him blocking that window, that's how we noticed his absence. Mother never mentioned him, either. But after she died, I found among the treasures in her old box, her wedding sari. And between its folds, their photograph. How young he was, how handsome and gallant and vulnerable! Ardeshir, bold, intrepid, valiant, righteous leader of men! Those were the first tears I shed for my father. Later, I burnt that photograph. I could not live with the memory of that face.'

Lalli touched her shoulder gently, then drew back and let her sob till she was exhausted. I made tea. The biscuit tin was full, safe from Savio.

Hilla gave me a wan smile over her teacup. 'It's difficult to imagine such happenings in a sane world like ours – or is it?'

'Now tell us what you really came here to say,' Lalli said.

Hilla laughed in one of her lightning transitions of mood.

'It's really rich,' she chuckled. 'The bastard's left me all his money!'

2

Hilla was not being entirely accurate. Framroze Vakil did not believe in liquid assets. Most of Hilla's fortune was designed to bypass her, tied up in worthy trusts that could be bequeathed, but not tapped.

'Untouchable,' Hilla pronounced with a Brahmanical sniff. 'Time enough for that when the vultures gather. But he's left me enough for a bit of fun. There's the house, the jewellery. And the Rolls.'

Lalli and Hilla laughed at my stricken cry.

'I didn't know you had a thing for cars,' Lalli remarked as we waved off Hilla's dented Maruti 800 to a jerky start.

'A Rolls is not a car,' I said coldly.

That red Maruti 800 with its crumpled rear was just Hilla's style. She would never keep the Rolls. She would sell it for mere pelf.

'And quite a lot of it,' Lalli completed my thought aloud. I hate it when she does that. Gives me goosebumps.

Morosely, I wondered what model it was. For all his evil ways, the late Framroze had taste.

The only Rolls on *my* shopping list is the Phantom 2003 – rear-hinged rear doors, for the first time in automobile history a boon for the tibially challenged celebrity. (Can't you guess? Five foot one, and no, I absolutely won't wear heels unless they're lucite Manolo Blahniks with the right degree of toe cleavage. Till then, it's chappals.)

You know the way it is sometimes, things simply won't quit on you. The Rolls came up next morning again.

It was raining, of course.

August, what else could one expect?

Raining with unrelenting malice, thin steely needles poking past crevices, buckling into puddles on the floor. When I'm a millionaire, I shall have windows that are vacuum sealed. I staggered to the kitchen, hefted my first mug of coffee, groped for the newspaper and collapsed in a boneless heap at the table where Lalli, crisp as toast, was halfway through her day. Seven o'clock indoors. Timeless purgatory outside.

Mornings like these, I'm a glutton for punishment. I begin the day with a masochistic rite.

I read Page 3.

Don't tell me you don't.

Everybody, but everybody, reads Page 3. You do too, unless you're an extraterrestrial with stalked eyes and twenty tentacles. Even then you probably would – if simply to view the competition.

You look at Page 3 because it jumpstarts the day. It's sand in the sugar, grit in the eye, the sly pin slid deep in the nail's quick. Your brain revs up with a roar of outrage. Ten seconds later you've done the evolutionary leap from mollusk to *T. rex* and are now equipped to take on the day.

It's basic ethology. The aggressiveness of the city on the move, the elbow-in-your-eye-I-get-in-before-you-do stampede at the station is wholly and unconditionally attributable to Page 3.

I said as much to Lalli.

'Work on it,' she said. 'Some small-town American university will reward you with a Ph.D. one day.'

I hardly heard her.

I was staring at the paper.

Stretched across Page 3 was about six yards of leg, at the far end of which, distant as a brontosaur's head, bobbed the pouting face of a popular bimbette. Usual Page 3 fare.

Except for one thing – she was draped over the gleaming bonnet of a deep blue Rolls. *Stretch of imagination*, said the caption. *Leggy lass Sonia Sorabjee checks out the merchandise. Bidders beware!*

A 2-cm wedge of print beneath informed us that the vintage model auctioned yesterday belonged to Dr Hilla Driver, and was sold to an unnamed bidder. *When asked what it finally sold for, the good doctor permitted herself a smile. 'Satisfactory,' she averred.*

Lalli wrinkled her nose. 'I can't picture Hilla *averring*, can you?'

'No. But I can picture her in mauve catsuit, stripy pants and pointy dark glasses. Captioned "The Phantom Rolls Again". That's a Phantom V – no, wait a minute, it's older, it's the Silver Dawn. Oh my God – A drop-dead drop-head royal blue Silver Dawn and she's *sold* it.'

'For riches unimaginable. You should have suggested the catsuit to her. Hilla would have loved to perch on the bonnet wearing it.'

'That would have been an improvement on Sonia Sorabjee. Just look at the creeps that turn up on Page 3, will you?'

Lalli sighed. I was off on my morning rant about the inane, the inapt, the inconsequential, the inchoate. 'All right. Out with it. What's it this morning?'

I grinned at Felix Rego eating spaghetti in profile. The photographer had wickedly managed to make him look like a marionette with limp strings appended from his weak chin.

'Isn't that the crime writer?' Lalli asked over my shoulder.

'*Macabre Macaroni*. Don't tell me you've read his stuff.'

'No. But you have.'

'In a purely investigative spirit.'

'Naturally.'

I hate her when she purrs.

'It's really vile stuff,' I hastened to assure her. 'The khoon-asoo-pasina school of writing.'

'Aha. Bestsellers. And what are those girls, Beauty Queens?'

Six vacuous faces stared glassily at me. They believed in inner beauty, every one of them, arranged flowers and dreamed of becoming astronauts. This year the operative word was *untainted* – all six stated an unequivocal preference for this strange quality. (Last year it was *holistic.*) They were all below twenty and ripe for disaster. It was terribly depressing.

Then I caught sight of something that quite banished my grief. The photographer had frozen a voluble American in mid-spate. '*Feminist lauds India,*' I read. '*I'd heard of India as a place where they burn widows', says American freelancer Meg Connolly. 'When I come here, what do I find? A widow, of foreign birth, who's running for prime minister – and she isn't even burnt!*'

'You made that up.'

'I did not! But I admit it's a bit extreme even for Page 3.'

The phone rang. It was Hilla. I bit back my words when she demanded if we'd seen the paper. 'Of course you've seen it,' she said smugly. 'What are you doing this evening? Cancel it. You're coming with me to see the house. Four o'clock, then. Tell Lalli.' She rang off before I could react.

Hilla's red Maruti had a new dent. 'Oh, just a dimple,' she dismissed it with a wave, hurrying me into the sagging back seat. I could well believe she hadn't felt a thing parting with the Silver Dawn.

The drive was thrilling if you go in for thrills of that sort. Hilla's the kind of driver who makes Formula 1 look like a sack race. We scraped the paint off a Santro and cracked a headlamp or two before we zoomed into the highway as the lights turned red.

'Relax,' she laughed. 'Traffic cops love me.'

Framroze would never have left her the Silver Dawn if he'd seen her drive.

We turned off the highway at Malad. As we turned west, I smelt the sea and dreamed of a vast private beach so sacred the coconut palms had never ever been scaled. There was a little boat to sail in all night as dolphins sang to the moon. Silver bells and cockleshells led up to a house as exciting as a sandcastle.

Hilla turned into a slushy lane that ended in a thicket. To my surprise the car leapt into the foliage with practised ease. The bushes parted, and we found ourselves on a rough road. On either side were towering trees matted with creepers. Inquisitive tassels of thistle stuck their heads in at the window as we slowed. Any moment now mushrooms might spring up between my toes, breaking past the car's rusty floor.

Somehow the car found the road. By this time I'd begun to suspect the thing had grown a brain of its own for sheer survival. Not only did it find the road, but *it stayed on it* (a feat Hilla on her own could never have accomplished) taking steep curves con brio as we wheezed up the hill. It was a cliff, really, and the road looped around it. We practically had to cut our way through the vegetation.

Hilla pulled up right in the middle of this rainforest and flung open the door.

'You're joking!' I cried

By way of answer, Lalli hurried after Hilla who seemed to be in imminent danger of walking into a tree.

Predictably, there was a wall. An angry red wall, more than six feet high, and thick enough to keep out an army. Its glass teeth glinted, bloodied in the sun. Embedded in its bulk was a small door, that Hilla squeezed through. We followed. Hilla hadn't mentioned her late uncle was a midget, but I failed to see how he could have used this entrance otherwise. I was rueing my grazed elbow and freeing my dupatta from the thistles when I turned – and gasped.

Against the changing evening sky, loomed a mammoth cube of red brick, Framroze Vakil's bequest. The rear view was incredible enough, I couldn't wait to see what the front looked like.

Of course there was another approach to the house – he must have used the Rolls *some* time – but that was blocked now by the large road roller we saw as we hastened round the house.

It was a dark red one-storeyed house, built by some crazed architect enamoured with Bombay's colonial Gothic. It had a high-shouldered shrug of tiled roof and any number of windows. Over all that, like a fool's hat stuck askew, was a truncated cone on which swung a creaky weathervane. The windows, of which I counted thirty-four, were of some timeless wood painted black, and paned with pebbly bottle-green glass. In the gathering dusk the building took on a quality of menace. It drew in the clotting hues of sunset till it seemed to throb, a morose stain beneath the leaching sky.

Lalli gasped.

Hilla beamed.

I couldn't repress a shudder – incredible that anybody could beam over *this*.

'Aha! Tongue-tied at last. No, I don't want to hear a word! Come on in!'

We followed her up the steep sweep of stairs.

'I'm building a ramp for wheelchairs,' she called over her shoulder.

'Do you expect to be here that long?' Lalli asked, but Hilla was out of earshot.

Miraculously, the house was lit (from the outside one expected bats). Even before Hilla switched on the lights, a rosy light suffused the walls. It only served to heighten the desolation of the tall rooms. The house was very airy too, being totally devoid of furniture. That Scrooge had probably sold every stick from his deathbed. What did he die *in*?

'He left you an empty house?' I found myself whispering. One simply had to whisper – and even that echoed.

'All the furniture's in storage. You ought to see how he's kept the stuff. Looks as if it were bought yesterday. A grand piano, imagine, and really brothelly beds, all mirrors and gilt,' Hilla marvelled. 'I've never lived in a flat with more than two rooms, and *that* was luxury!'

'Are you converting it into a hotel?'

'A hospital?'

'Nonsense! I shall live in it.'

I was awed. Hilla had courage.

'I wanted you to see it before the jewellery and the Rolls have walked through it,' Hilla explained.

We peered into the large rooms on the ground floor and followed Hilla up the sweeping staircase. The view was breathtaking from the verandah upstairs, and I didn't follow them on their tour of the rooms. I found the thought of Framroze a little chilling and wondered what was in the locked room we'd passed downstairs. Hilla didn't take us to the back of the house. It was mostly kitchen and utilities, she explained. There were rats.

We were silent on the drive back. Lalli said one or two encouraging things, but we couldn't entirely keep the doubt out of our voices. Hilla drove with a grim smile.

I felt we'd let Hilla down. Lalli though, had no such qualm.

'Hilla's found a way to express herself,' she said, surprising me with that Women's Page idiom.

It wasn't till late August that we discovered exactly how Hilla would choose to express herself.

3

Hilla's windfall that had all the charm of a fairy tale while the weather held us in thrall, dwindled to a polite item of interest by the end of the week when the sun was actually sighted for more than ten minutes. Sunshine called a truce to depression. I plunged joyously into work, losing track of the day. Lalli was kept busy with a forgery, so neither of us had much time to speculate over Hilla's bhoot bangla.

About a fortnight later, stopping by for the afternoon paper at a kiosk, I was confronted by a familiar chubby face. She wasn't wearing a Phantom catsuit, but it was Hilla all right, beaming at the world from the cover of *Inns & Out* (Rs 150 a copy). Finances being what they were, I walked past quickly.

As I let myself in, Lalli looked up from the tattered tome of Hans Gross' *Criminal Psychology*, her idea of light reading. 'Hilla ...'

'I know! But it's one-fifty and I can't afford that!'

'... has invited us to a house party.'

I took my time digesting that. 'In that mausoleum? Wait! She must have made something spectacular of it or she wouldn't be on the cover.'

'Sit down for heaven's sake and tell me what you're ranting about. I've said yes to the party. For both of us.'

I told Lalli about *Inns & Out* distractedly. I was aghast at the thought of a house party. There's nothing I loathe more than enforced propinquity. It makes me claustrophobic. Hilla's tolerable in homeopathic doses, but – a *house party*! The entire concept is ridiculous. An alien, colonial, contrived situation for a madhyavarti working woman to be caught in. Decidedly declassé!

'I know,' Lalli agreed (I hadn't said a word). 'But this is a big thing for Hilla, and I'm going to indulge. You can phone your excuses. Better do it right away. And no, it won't be friends and relations. She's "just throwing people together", she said. That's usually interesting, explosions do occur. She mentioned a variety of – not quite the butcher, the baker, the candlestick-maker – but nevertheless, trades. And that old bore Alif Bey. Call her and beg off, give her time to find a substitute.'

I pulled a face at my devious aunt. 'At last a chance to wear my cadmium capris. When does the balloon go up?'

'Next week. It's a long weekend. I wouldn't waste those capris on Alif Bey. I've met him. He's a fat hairy self-important ape.'

'Who cares? He's a genius!'

I marched out in high dudgeon.

For years I had idolized Alif Bey, but the man was a mystic, as secretive as his name. He was seldom interviewed, never photographed. From time to time he bewailed in print the recent trend among publishers to hawk authors before their books got written. He hadn't published a book in ten years, and for the last five it had been rumoured he had just completed his masterpiece. In my opinion, Alif Bey is the only writer to have achieved the perfect sentence in the last fifty years.

There's nobody quite like him.

His looks had nothing at all to do with his prose. Neither did these cadmium capris I bought last week in a fit of temporary insanity. When you're five foot one on a good leg day, you do NOT wear pants that pretend your knees are six feet above terra firma. I made some fresh coffee and settled down to prune my adjectives.

Hilla expected us on Thursday evening.

Tuesday saw Lalli seized with a fever to shop. We went to one of the glitzy new malls that seem to clone themselves every week. Lalli is a total loss as a shopper. She never seems to know what she wants. I enjoyed watching her agonies of indecision. It was a rare thing in my usually brisk aunt. She bought silver earrings for Hilla, delicately enamelled in meenakari, and a rather more flamboyant pair for me. They were not as dangly as the ones I'd promised myself to go with the Rolls and the Manolo Blahniks. Still, they made a promising start in that direction.

My finances ran to a burnt orange dupatta for Lalli, the sort that the Fashion page assures you makes a statement, without telling you of what. It complemented the elegant bronze silk I knew she'd pack for the weekend. For Hilla's house, with great misgiving, I purchased a pot. Finally, we made it to the billing counter – almost.

One moment she was queued patiently beside me. The next, she had vanished.

This kind of thing puts me in a panic. The abyss yawns. I suddenly remember that all sorts of low life might be out on parole, gunning for my aunt.

I had to tour all four floors twice over before I glimpsed her silver halo at the perfume counter. I raced up and found her dithering over two sample strips, eyes tightly shut in either concentration or ecstasy. Both perfumes smelt green to me. Cut grass and mint. Lalli opened her eyes and shook her head sadly at the salesgirl. 'It's not the same,' she said.

The girl shrugged. 'Maybe you can't remember what it smelt like, exactly. It was long ago, you said. Maybe you don't remember.'

'I will always remember,' Lalli said tartly, turning on her heel.

The mystified salesgirl shrugged at me.

I took my place in the queue at the billing counter and found myself ogling a life-size cutout of Pierce Brosnan. He was no comfort at all. I was worried about Lalli. Something at the perfume counter had touched a nerve. In 007 parlance, she was shaken, not stirred.

'My! Look who's here!'

A vaguely familiar voice, an entirely unfamiliar face – but I did know her from somewhere.

Luckily, the dormant part of the brain that takes over when memory fails, came up with a name. 'Meenal.'

'I thought you didn't recognize me!'

I hadn't. The last time we met, she was thin, elegant, coiffed and faintly decadent. She had grown since then. Her hair was a cheery mop of pepper and salt. She bulged in a khadi kurti, worn over dirty white salwars. Gone were the strappy shoes. Now she wore mojdis. She was missing a cigarette, but was otherwise the very picture of compulsive feminist chic. Right on the nail, she rummaged through her grubby knapsack and brought out a pack of cigarettes. She lit up and began the interrogation.

'So what are you doing?'

'Oh this and that.'

'Still teaching idiots?'

'No. Not that. And you?'

'Oh me!'

She rolled her eyes. I knew I was about to be given the Revelations, chapter and verse. My alarm may have showed because she said rather abruptly, 'We must catch up. I've got to go now. Bye!'

I wondered if I'd seemed rude. I had never liked her.

'Friend of yours?' asked Lalli.

'I used to know her. But she's changed drastically.'

'What do you expect?' said Lalli.

I didn't get that.

We picked up our bags and prepared to dive into the rain.

Almost at once, I walked into a man.

He stepped aside hastily and apologized. I looked up, but his gaze had travelled over my head to Lalli who was by now dodging puddles and braving it to the parking lot.

Then he turned to me.

A curious light leapt in his eyes, as if with that flash he had a snapshot of my soul.

And then he was gone.

I didn't turn around.

I knew I would never forget that look.

I got into the car in a fussy flap of wet clothes and carry bags.

'Something's happened,' Lalli said.

'What?'

'To you.'

I shrugged dismissively, but something *had* happened.

Lalli waited, her eyes expectant.

'There was this guy. He looked so strangely ...'

'He looked odd?'

'No, no. He looked okay.' He had a nice face. Lined, fortyish, somehow *lit*. 'It was the way he looked at me.'

Lalli smiled, infuriatingly.

'It's not that,' I snapped. 'I'm an old hand at spotting that. He looked – how shall I say it – as if he were staring right into my soul.'

She wasn't listening. Her eyes were lost in the distance.

The Fiat leapt forward, startled like a stray dog shaking off the rain.

Thursday came quicker than expected. I had a deadline to meet. My finances had recently got a fillip with the arrival of Lulu, my goofy 27-year-old ephemerist. She fretted over all the things I was dismissive about. I got enough copy out of her woes to sustain a column, and the editor, for once, didn't quarrel over it. *Lulu's*

Logbook was currently paying my bills. A 600-word update on her career was due every Thursday morning, and that week it wasn't done till noon. Lalli was still taken up with her forger, and though I was packed and ready by four, we only left an hour later.

We reached Hilla's place in the gold slant of late evening. This time we approached it in style, driving down a road parallel to the beach, then snaking up the satiny road, turning our backs on the sea. Framroze's domain probably extended to the foot of the hill, that explained the road repairs.

The tall wrought iron gates were the same, but the zinc sheeting Framroze had nailed across to keep out voyeurs had been removed, the gaps in the iron lace lovingly restored. The walls, no longer fanged, were painted a neutral cream, relieved by flaming cascades of bougainvillea in terracotta and yellow. The effect charmed me into forgetting that those walls made an impenetrable bastion of the house.

The house itself had acquired a delicacy of line I could not have imagined. Its squat proportions had been soothed by the intelligent use of paint. Cleared of that intimidating crimson, the grey walls looked nacreous in the evening haze. Gone were those squinty windows with their murky cataracts of glass. Tall French windows promised rooms drenched with light. A large bay suggested a window seat, deep and cushioned. Darn. I hadn't packed any books. Dormer windows caught the last rays of the sun in a sudden rush of fire.

At the gate a bronze plaque (phonily aged) read *Ardeshir Villa* – Hilla's tribute to her father. It's difficult to sweep up the drive in a Fiat that groans in second gear but, you understand, it was a drive of that sort. The hairy hill of our last visit was barely recognizable. In the parlance of the *Homemaker's Supplement*, it had been landscaped. A neatly razored lawn showed between spurts and spumes of vegetation.

The doorway, which I remembered as grotesque now looked perfectly gracious. Its columned facade was not in the least ostentatious. The shelled hood, which seemed comic at my last visit, looked less clunky in the evening light. By night, cleverly lit by an antique lamp, it would enchant with a porcelain fragility. My misgivings vanished. There was a prickle of expectation in the air.

The door flew open and Hilla's niece burst out.

'Did you bring the ice?' she shouted, and stopped short at the sight of us.

'Sorry, I thought you were the ice,' she explained. 'The cook's ordered tons, I thought I heard a truck.' Her eyes travelled past us to Lalli's Fiat wheezing after its climb. She commandeered my decrepit aunt, hauling her up those steep steps by an elbow. When I returned after parking, she called from the top of the steps, 'Can you manage? There ought to be a lift.'

After a day in Ramona's company Hilla generally looks as if a typhoon's hit her. I was beginning to see why. Ramona is one of those well-meaning teenagers to whom the average adult appears senile.

'Out of breath?' she asked kindly as I ran up the steps, wishing I were barefoot to feel the sun-warmed stone. I got a glimpse of a stained glass fanlight as she whizzed me through the door. A little later the sun would throw a rich carpet of colours on the floor – if the fanlight was genuine glass, that is, not the pebbly plastic you find everywhere.

The octagonal vestibule we entered glowed with the light I remembered from my last visit, but there was nothing sinister about it today. Tall planters with some kind of dark green herbage spilling out in fronds flanked the arched entrances on either side to a generous verandah that appeared to ring the house. The slender pillars that formed the octagon had fluted capitals with a tulip flare that heightened the soaring loft of the ceiling. The small room was buoyant with light. I would have been content to camp right here through the weekend, but Ramona was busy organizing our lives. 'Hilla Aunty shouldn't have given you rooms upstairs,' she said. 'Running up and down these stairs is going to tire you dreadfully.'

'I'm a mountaineer,' Lalli lied with dignity.

'Didn't your aunt tell you?' I asked. 'We're just back from Kanchenjunga.'

Ramona giggled, shrugging off the hostessy manner, restored to the flagrant insanity of seventeen.

The staircase rose in a subtle curve from a spreading ripple of wide steps. The delicate balusters were balanced by a simple newel post. The rose window at the landing had an oculus of clear glass. Beyond, the staircase bifurcated, leading to a verandah like the one downstairs.

Ramona ran on ahead, abandoning us sherpas. 'Second and third to your left,' she yelled. 'Hilla's with the cook, I'll tell her you're here!'

As I turned into the corridor, I bumped into one of those ghastly midget Laughing Buddhas that always give me the creeps. Framroze seemed to have bought them by the dozen. I could see another one exulting evilly at the end of the passage.

My room was delightful. The west-facing window caught the sunset and drew deep violet shadows on the floor. There was another door that I hoped led to the terrace. But it was too early to explore.

There was very little of old Framroze in the rooms Hilla had given us, but the architect had steered clear of nouveau kitsch. Our rooms were furnished neither in phony Belle Epoque nor early Mohenjodaro.

I had expected ethnic chic: clay walls, Warli motifs on faux tempera of gobar, bamboo screens, straw matting and short-legged birthing chairs from Tilonia Bazaar. Instead, the floor was a beautiful old mosaic, undisturbed from Framroze's time. The ivory dado had roses in bas relief. There was a desk in my room, with a block of paper and a choice of two pencils and three ballpoints. The bookshelf, invitingly close to the bed, held a fair selection. Hilla had provided a handsomely bound edition of *The Thought Cyclist,* Alif Bey's masterpiece. It was inscribed to Hilla by the author, and was clearly unread.

Ramona burst in as I was sorting out the jewels in the first paragraph.

'Do you think I should order tea?' she demanded.

Tea? Were we going to be done out of dinner, then? It was nearly eight.

'Order? Isn't there a kitchen?'

She regarded me with pity. She gathered both my hands and dripped benevolence. 'I want you to forget all about cooking and washing up and all that sort of thing for three heavenly days. Just laze!'

'You'll make the tea?'

Her face hardened. She dropped my hands. 'We have a cook. A chef, actually. Do you want tea or not?'

'Not. Who's coming, besides Alif Bey?'

'Oh him! He's not important! Guess who's going to be here – Rafiq Khan!'

It was nice hearing her real voice again, gushing with the hero-worship of seventeen.

'Rafiq Khan the dancer? Jazz and break dance and that sort of thing?'

'They're not the same thing at all. He dances fusion. Very creative, he's got this crazy rhythm thing that puts elastic in you, takes your muscles just way out – I've got this fabulous outfit with sequins and all. Want to see it?'

Of course I did. She obligingly trotted off and returned with a pair of cutoffs in some silvery material, and a white bustier with sequins and diamanté.

'Mummy made me put sleeves on it,' she said sadly. Folded back like wings in reserve were two gauzy wisps of lace.

'Do you think I should wear it?' she turned troubled eyes on me. 'It isn't too ...?'

'Of course you should wear it,' I said a little too heartily, thinking of the cadmium capris. 'And you can have this if you think it will go with your dress.'

I dug in my purse for my tiny filigree butterfly. I had bought it when I was about Ramona's age, and for a similar occasion.

She squealed her pleasure and pinned it on the bustier immediately. 'Oh but don't you want to wear it yourself? Look at its eyes! It's so *cute*!'

It was, actually.

'It's a bribe. Tell me about the guests now, the complete inside stuff, mind!'

She giggled and settled herself on the bed.

'First there's you and Lalli – you're friends.'

'Thanks.'

'Rafiq Khan I already told you. He's into dance therapy, you know? For handicapped kids? Then there's Dr Sane. You don't know him? He was Jimmy Uncle's friend. I didn't know Jimmy Uncle too well, I only grew up after he died.'

Hilla's husband Jamshed had died in a car crash ten years ago, with no life insurance and several rash debts.

'Dr Sane isn't too awful, I've met him. But his wife is supposed to be a real wow! Glamorous and all that. I haven't met her before. They're coming tonight, with their two kids. I hate kids. Not babies, I love babies, but these are BIG kids. They get all over you.'

Ramona paused to darkly consider her impending doom. I had to prompt her several times before she continued.

'Then there's Felix Rego – heard of him? He writes bestsellers?'

She stopped in some embarrassment at having touted a celebrity before a dismal non-starter. 'Thrillers. I haven't read them.

You know how it is, two hundred bucks yaar, who's got that to throw on a *book*?'

Well. Not for *Mystic Murder*, perhaps. Or *Bloodstains and Bacardi*. Or *Sewers of Success* and other gems of the guts-and-gonads school.

'Then there's Mr Bajaj. His wife called yesterday to beg off because there's some urgent meeting she has to attend in Calcutta. But he's coming. Jimmy Uncle's friend again. Frightfully rich, horses and all that. That's all I know of them.'

'Alif Bey. Tell me about Alif Bey – the author.'

'Oh he isn't an author! Not like Felix Rego! Nobody reads him. I don't know why Hilla invited him. Probably asked him out of pity, you know Hilla Aunty – because his shirts are darned or something.'

I wondered in which category I fitted. The butterfly probably blurred the issue for the nonce.

'And there's Lola Lavina. You know her.'

'No I don't. Nobody, Ramona, has a name like Lola Lavina. It's a made up name. Is she a model?'

'No. That's Chili. You know Chili. We've put her next to you.'

Certainly, I knew Chili. Who didn't. She made the average leg look like a tree stump. She was svelte, sinuous, and drop-dead gorgeous. My heart sank as I thought of those cadmium capris.

'Aunty says she's nice. But then Aunty says that about everybody till she's in a mess, and then she simply runs away! That's what Daddy says,' she added, to quench any whiff of disloyalty. 'Anyway, Chili's on.'

With a leggy model, a jazz dancer, a cook, a domesticated doctor, a greedy columnist, a reclusive writer and the mysterious Bajaj, the weekend wouldn't lack for variety. That only left Lola Lavina unexplained.

'She's a feminist,' Ramona said. 'Hilla says she's a woman of substance.'

Hilla seemed to have seriously adopted the idiom of Page 3.

She joined us now, breathless and agitated. 'Here you are, thank

God. I've been on a last-minute scrimmage for booze. You know how I hate the stuff. I won't have it in the house I said, but would the cook listen? Luckily he's low on the hard stuff, but wines he must have. Moselle. Chardonnay. Never heard of these things before. We're going to be very cultured m'deah and appear on Page 3, sipping wine and nibbling cheeses, and if you think that's plain Amul or Kraft, take a sniff at what he's ordered. Yuck. Smells like feet. The cook is going to make a fondue. He says it has news value. Didn't I tell you? Felix Rego's "Our Food Correspondent". Do you know I'm already beginning to loathe the idea of a house party? I just have a few hours left to misbehave in. The Sanes arrive tonight. "Lateish," she said, I imagine that means midnight.'

'Really, Hilla, isn't that inconsiderate? Why don't they stay home till morning?'

Hilla shrugged dismally. 'Come, let's find Lalli and be miserable together before the enemy arrives! Ramona, take the booze to the kitchen, it's in the verandah, and don't let me find you drunk on the stairs.'

Ramona fled, giggling. Lalli had her usual soothing effect on Hilla, and we lounged on the lovely blue and white namda in her room, gossiping contentedly.

'Now tell me why you need a food correspondent?' I demanded. 'And why such outlandish foods? Why do we so aspire to Page 3? We're not exactly Page 3 material.'

'You think I'm trying to acquire class? Like the feverish nouveau riche in their homes away from home in Khedegaon East?'

'For that you need a jacuzzi. And it's hard to beat the late Framroze for class. I bet he gnashed his spectral teeth when you sold the Rolls.'

'It's the cook,' Hilla explained. 'He wants to put this place on the food map.'

'Through Page 3?' I was incredulous. 'What or where is this food map?'

'The cook has it in his head. He thinks we're projecting a phony food culture, particularly in food columns. He says newspapers lampoon serious eating. The only foods they consider digestible are those with a price tag running into three, maybe four figures – or those served at some modish rat hole. He turned down truffles on principle, though Felix didn't take kindly to that. He said it's morally depraved to eat a fungus that sells at 15,000 bucks a kilo.'

'A colourful cook,' murmured Lalli.

'Yeah. He's some guy. Insists on being called cook, not chef. Won't mix with the guests, that was the proviso. Look at the French, he tells me, see how they respect their cuisine. Why can't we? '

'I don't know about the French, but this cook sounds a complete phony to me,' I said. 'Why fondue? That isn't part of our food culture. And I have it on good authority, it tastes exactly like baby puke.'

Hilla rose hurriedly.

'I'll tell him to make very little of it. Just enough to feed Felix Rego, since he's asked for it. I hope the rest of Felix's list isn't so bad, considering it runs into two pages.'

'And this tapeworm is going to eat his way through the entire list?'

'We will too! He says it's the only way to test the cook. That's necessary if I'm to fall in with what the cook wants.'

'Which is?'

'To turn this place into an inn for serious Indian food. You know, home stuff.'

'You're besotted with your cook,' Lalli said crisply.

'Wait till you meet him, he's fun. But you won't have much chance to talk to him with Bajaj and Felix and Alif Bey around. And Ujwala Sane – grrrr! You got to meet that one.'

'And Chili? What's so special about her, Hilla?'

'Oh Chili's one of my babies. All my babies are special to me.'

I mentally gifted Chili with some irremediable childhood

illness, something perilous and chancy, without being exactly life-threatening. It was surprising how much nicer she seemed after that.

'And Lola Lavina? Why a genuinely false name like that?'

Both of them looked at me blankly.

'But you know her!' they reproached with one voice.

I threw up my hands in despair. Everybody seemed intent on foisting this psuedonymous feminist on me.

'I saw you talking to her on Tuesday,' Lalli said. 'When I got lost at the perfume counter.'

Good heavens! *Meenal!*

'She's changed her name!'

'Naturally.'

'But why Lola Lavina?'

'Why not? Lavina is her mother's name.'

'You know her?' I was surprised at Lalli.

'No. Of her.'

'So what is it that I don't know about Meenal?'

'Never mind. You'll have to hear it all from her anyway, several times over, she seems that sort,' Lalli said, rather cruelly, I thought. 'Now Hilla, tell me, why did you have to do this at all? Why this house party?'

Hilla's face grew stern. 'I owe them, Lalli. You've guessed right, I can't stand any of them except the boys, Rafiq and Felix and of course that sweet kid Chili. But I owe them, and I can't live that down.'

It seemed a strange explanation, but I saw a flash of intelligence in Lalli's eyes.

'The cook's idea isn't bad,' I said. 'People pay madly to swallow any swill in a fancy place, so why not dress up decent food instead? It's bound to be a good investment. And Hilla, the house is beautiful.'

'Isn't it? The Rolls and the jewellery, don't forget.'

'I'm glad, Hilla,' Lalli said quietly.

To my surprise, Hilla's eyes filled and she abruptly left the room. I suppose this sudden luxury had revived the memory of her parents' suffering with fresh bitterness. This was a different Hilla from the mercurial woman I knew. Her distress was something deeper, more central.

A little later, Hilla took us downstairs to see the house. I thought the dining room rather grand with its long table and elegant upholstered chairs. At this hour the curtains were drawn across the large bay window, but it would be pleasant in the morning.

There were plenty of windows everywhere. The architect seemed to have punched in the walls and glazed them wherever she could. It was clever, the way that had transformed the building's stolid, rather suffocating dimensions. 'Ria Negi, you must have heard of her? Quite the buzz these days,' Hilla enlightened us.

'At least she didn't go vaastu on you' I said, 'Or feng shui, with wind instruments and bonsai bamboo to match those jokers in the corridor.'

'She's smart,' Hilla conceded. 'But don't remind me of the bills. It's once in a lifetime, what the hell, I can spend that miser's money. He had all the furniture in storage, lived in one miserable room upstairs, can you imagine?'

The living room was surprisingly comfortable, after the rather pompous dining room. The only boudoir touch came from a chaise longue, a muted gleam of gold fleur-de-lis showing against its rich blue. That, Hilla said, was a Framroze original though the piled cushions of grey velvet and gold lamé were part of the new look. 'She said the living room ought to be worked around that couch, whatever that meant. Blue, but not bedroom blue she said. What's bedroom blue I asked her. I tell you Lalli, she looked at me with pity. Didn't answer, as though I'm past bedrooms by now and why should I care? This blue here, you know what she called it? Van Gogh blue. Can you imagine?'

Actually, I could. Tonally, Starry Night. Blue turning unwillingly to violet caught up in a blur of gold. Yes, I could live with that.

We followed Hilla round the house, passing a locked door that she said was the library. 'All his books. Ancient. I'll open it in the morning, we've left it practically untouched,' she shrugged. The verandah at the back of the house was empty of plants and other obstacles. It was a grand place to pace in. There were some chairs at the far end. We passed what Hilla called the studio, a large empty room with a parquet floor meant for Rafiq Khan. Then came a brightly lit window, with the curtains drawn. Hilla said it was the cook's room. She whispered this, actually, past the hum of the AC. She seemed in awe of him. His was the only room with air conditioning. The kitchen, at the end of the corridor, was locked. Dinner was waiting for us, though.

A buffet had been set out in the small pantry adjoining the kitchen. The cook did not appear. The serving hatch above the table remained stubbornly shut. We carried our plates to the verandah and ate watching the rain. The wrought iron chairs, at first sight reminiscent of medieval torture, turned out surprisingly comfortable.

The fare was simple, but delicious. Dhaba food of the sort I'd last eaten off the highway in Ludhiana ten years ago. Baingan bharta, urad daal, roti, lassi. You couldn't ask for better. (I leave to Our Food Correspondent his surreal adjectives. I will merely say the brinjal spiritedly defended its smoky flavour against a faint bickering of spice.)

Hilla had recovered her spirits, and ragged her niece about her new boyfriend, much to Ramona's delight. The kid almost forgave present company for being so geriatric, and was halfway convinced that death doesn't begin at thirty.

'If only you hadn't invited Chili, everything would be just perfect!' she blurted.

I could have added Lola Lavina to the blacklist, but what the hell, I could afford to be generous, with an entire weekend of Alif Bey ahead of me.

For some unaccountable reason, the man I'd bumped into on Tuesday haunted me. The memory of that look I'd surprised in his eyes gave me a shiver. Was it pleasure? Was it dread?

Conversation petered out.

We lingered in the mesmeric hush of rain.

It wasn't yet ten when we trooped upstairs.

'The cook will let the Sanes in,' Hilla yawned. 'I'm in the wing that leads from there. She pointed to the end of the corridor where the Buddha reared, black and huge like Wordsworth's peak, with voluntary power instinct.

Ramona announced she had put off her project of washing and styling her hair tonight.

'If he doesn't like it the way it is, he can lump it,' she said superbly.

Even a jazz dancer gets told his place sometimes.

4

I woke inconveniently early. This always happens to me in a new place, and leaves a vague cobwebby headache clinging to me all day. I squinted at my watch in the faint grey wash of light. Five-thirty. I shut my eyes with resolution and tried to block out voices left over from a dream. But they kept on, and tired of fighting them, I gave in and listened.

'What is it you want?' Sullen. Male. Middle-aged.

The other laughed. 'Oh I want nothing! Why not forget we've met before. Let's be strangers here.' Also male, rough, amused.

'No, no. It doesn't have to be that way. Anything I can do, I'd be glad to. It will be a pleasure.'

'I'm not on the market.' The voice had turned lean, and dangerous. There was anger in it now, and hurt pride.

'Look, that's not what I meant. I'll be frank with you. I can't risk anything now. It could destroy me.'

Silence stretched, tense, implacable. Then the other man said, the contempt in his voice biting like acid, 'Just put it out of your head. As far as I'm concerned, Doctor, it never happened. It doesn't matter to me any more. Those that mattered to me are dead. It's over. You've never seen me before.'

At this point the dream dissolved and sleep claimed me – an uneasy slumber that I shook off at first light.

It was nearly six. A hot shower in the small oyster-coloured bathroom was just what I needed. In the shell-shaped mirror, my early morning face looked better than it ever had.

I emerged vivified in a scarlet shirt to shake a fist at the elements. It had rained all night and the morning wore a sodden look, grey clouds hanging low like badly laundered sheets.

I cautiously nudged the door I'd left unopened last night, hoping it didn't lead into another room. It opened onto the terrace. I ran out in delight. The wide terrace was paved with flagstones. The balustrade enticed. Its delicate tracery of wrought-iron was topped by a sensible railing that looked sturdy enough to sit on. The flags, deliciously uneven and chilly, moulded to my bare feet. The sea lurched directly beneath. I perched on the balustrade, high above the lashing waters. Palm fronds brushed the railing, their swish echoing the tormented breath of the sea.

'Good morning!'

I turned, irritated at the intrusion. And gasped as I recognized him. It was the Tuesday man.

He must have seen the flash of recognition, for he said, 'Not entirely a surprise. I expected you.'

That was a surprise.

We chatted banally about the rain.

Then he said, with sudden shyness, 'I liked your book.'

Could joy be more complete? This isn't moronic modesty, but I didn't believe the guy. Had he really read it? After all, *Ladies Compartment* isn't exactly a conversation piece. What it says has been said before, and with more wit.

'You escaped sounding naive,' he said. 'Without losing your innocence.'

Neat.

I was beginning to fall in love with him. Could he be Alif Bey?

'And of its joy content, the heart luxuriates in indifferent things …'

Of course he was Alif Bey. Who else would quote Wordsworth on a rainy morning before breakfast? Would he resent it if I asked him now about *The Thought Cyclist?*

'Coffee?' He broke into my thoughts.

'Oh yes,' I bleated. 'It'll only be some ghastly instant stuff.'

'Certainly *not!*' He drew back, stung. 'Popayan. Hand-roasted. Fresh ground. Strong. Solid. Mellow, with an occasional sharp note. Filter coffee of course, with the obligatory two-inch head of froth *and* served in a steel tumbler.'

'What are you?' I marvelled lightly. He wasn't real. Nothing was quite real this morning. 'Everybody's dream man?'

He smiled wryly. 'Think again. I'm the cook.'

The cook!

The cartographer gastronomique, the fondue fusspot – *this!*

My jaw must have hit the floor for there was more than a suspicion of a sneer in his voice: 'Shall I serve your coffee on the terrace madam?' His eyes had retreated into the distance.

'You needn't be so touchy. I was thinking about the fondue, that's all.'

'So what's wrong with being a cook?' he extrapolated my voice. 'Some of my best friends are cooks.'

'None of my friends are, actually.' I moved away. 'I just made the mistake of thinking perhaps one could be.'

'Ah, come down to the kitchen and get your coffee then,' he said peaceably. 'I'm a bear most mornings.'

Who isn't?

I followed him, taking the wrought-iron staircase that spiralled down the side of the house, enjoying the occasional raindrop on my face. We stepped off onto the verandah where we had gorged on dhaba food last night. The chairs, I noticed, were missing.

'Welcome to my domain,' he said. We passed the first door, and through the next entered a short passage into the kitchen.

I drew in my breath sharply. This was a kitchen to die for. He laughed at the look on my face. The early light formed a tender haze as it flooded the French window. The L-shaped counter ran along two walls. Bright arrays of glass jars winked back and forth from high shelves. Best of all was a rough wooden bench in the centre of the room. The wood was old and grainy and knotted. There was a stool that matched, wide as a giant toadstool and just the right height.

'I'm glad Hilla saved this,' he tapped the bench. 'It's the best part of the kitchen for me.'

The coffee was excellent, though I picked a mug instead of the tumbler, disliking the sear of white hot metal on my lip.

'Wait.'

He took away the mug I held out and bewitched another out of a cupboard. This one was a brilliant royal blue, lickety-slick black within.

'Goes with the shirt.'

He filled the discarded mug for himself and we sat in companionable silence, savouring the steam.

Strong. Solid. Mellow. He'd picked the right adjectives, even if the sharp notes were more than occasional.

With the first invigorating sip, I felt an unaccountable surge of happiness. I looked up, surprising his eyes, and laughed. Life was wonderful.

Of course, he could be married.

'I'm not,' he said.

I hadn't asked.

'You're not what?' Now *I* was cross.

'Nothing, nothing. Just thinking aloud.'

Liar.

He filled my cup.

'What was that about fondue?'

'Hilla said you were going to make some.'

'And?'

I hesitated. I'd riled him with the coffee to begin with. He might burst a blood vessel if I told him I'd heard that fondue tastes like baby barf.

'A well-made fondue does not taste like puke,' he said. He'd done it again. 'It's a simple rustic dish: eggs, a third of butter, a sixth of cheese, stir to melt and bubble till smooth.'

'I thought it was cultured and French. I don't know French, and I'm not cultured culinarily.'

'Ha. The culinary culture. You need a chef for that. Chefs are cultured. And their fondue tastes exactly like puke. I'm a cook. And my fondue's good.'

'I thought you were Alif Bey.'

'What!'

'Because you'd read my book.'

'And a cook can just about spell?'

'You said it. Isn't the house exciting? The terrace has flagstones, did you notice? Isn't that wonderful? Exactly like having a vast empty pavement all to oneself.'

'Yes, I'd noticed. And no, it's not wonderful having a large empty pavement all to oneself. I've been there before.'

Ouch! Another nerve jangled.

'Only we called it footpath, not pavement. You know the stretch between VT Station and Crawford market? I lived on it for six years. From 1972 to 1978. I was a footpathia there.'

He wasn't joking. I didn't know what to say.

'You're too young to remember the Bangladesh war, I guess. Liberation! It was some kind of liberation when I got to that footpath. It was the first place I didn't hear the screams. We had been running six months when we got there, six months when all I heard was screams. And gunfire. Once I reached the footpath, street sounds began again. Traffic. Trains. Voices. Thirty-one years ago, almost to the day. It's a good word, refugee. The footpath *was* my refuge. But I couldn't get out of it fast enough. Believe me, it's not all that wonderful.'

He reached for my mug. Our fingers brushed lightly. 'I'll tell you about it sometime, if I survive being mistaken for Alif Bey!'

The moment passed.

I threw myself into *The Thought Cyclist*, glad of the distraction. 'And what a recluse he is!' I wound up after ten solid minutes. 'What's he like? Nobody even knows his name. Of course to a mind like his, the mundane is just maya.'

'Don't you believe it. He's in advertising.'

'No!'

'Sure. You know that aftershave ad that sounds like *Pippa Passes*? That's Alif Bey. Oh good morning, madam.'

Hilla was upon us, looking like death in a floral housecoat.

'Started your act, have you? Tea, if you want me to live.'

'Rungli Rungliot? Earl Grey? Family Mixture Number Eleven?'

'For godssake! Chai. Anything out of a packet.'

She slumped heavily next to me.

'For that you deserve a teabag. But seeing you're the boss, I've brewed Rungli Rungliot. Sip, don't glug.'

'I thought you were going to behave like a cook. Labour problems I have the very first day. Insubordination. Dadagiri.' She turned to me. 'I see you've met. Tarok Ghosh the cook, to get it nice and formal. I've known this guy since he was a kid of eighteen. My mother's friend. My mother's blackmailer I should say, since he wheedled all her secret recipes out of her. And now he calls me madam!'

'Discipline, mai-baap.'

'What's for breakfast?'

'Breakfast is at nine-thirty. It's now seven-fifteen.'

'Takes time to cook.'

'Not breakfast.'

Hilla, heavy with gloom, produced a slip of paper from a capacious pocket.

'I told you it was foolhardy to ask people what they want for breakfast. I'm scared to break it to you.'

'Save it. That's for tomorrow. Today they eat what I give them.'

Hilla looked doubtful.

'Mrs Sane wants breakfast in bed. Perhaps something on a tray?'

'Tell her to get up and brush her teeth. This isn't the decadent West. Give her a neem daantoon.'

'Go tell her yourself. Hey – wait! I'll take that tray.'

'No. She comes downstairs unless she's dying. Tell her the omelette will wilt.'

'Is that what we're having? What's the use of hiring you then?'

'Not for you. Only for the kids. Souffle omelette with homemade pineapple jam.'

'Better stick to boiled eggs,' Hilla said anxiously. 'They're the sort of kids who drown everything in ketchup. They might turn up their fine noses at your souffle omelette.'

Tarok Ghosh said icily, 'Children always eat what I give them.'

They did too. Prised off their mother by Hilla, the Sane kids were given breakfast in the pantry. Tarok left them unsupervised, timing his return to a nicety. They drained their mugs of milk hurriedly and left exulting over their presents – a beetroot sculpted into a rose for Arpita and a railway engine hewn from a carrot for Darshan.

'Not one word about gender bias,' Tarok warned, anticipating me. I rejoiced later to find that Arpita had swiped the engine, leaving Darshan to gnaw at the rose.

Felix Rego, Alif Bey, Rafiq Khan and Chili were expected later in the day. I went in to breakfast, curious to see if Mrs Sane had been tamed by the cook. She wasn't down yet. Lalli was sharing a table with a tubby man. I decided not to interrupt.

Small oval tables had been set out in a nook off the dining room. In better weather, it would be a sun trap at this hour. Despite the gloom a pearly light was pooled on the floor. I leaned out of the window. The lacy grille of the window box deserved something better than those fluorescent green weeds, whatever they were.

I turned, only to meet Tarok's quizzing eyes. 'The window cries out for geraniums,' I said and once again caught that fleeting light in his face.

He drew out the chair for me. I was about to protest, when I saw he wouldn't have noticed anyway. He was busy conjuring up breakfast out of thin air. The table was filling up with amazing rapidity. Finally, he set the centrepiece, a yellow African daisy in a flute of black glass, and stepped back gravely.

I almost applauded. Everything looked wonderful, but the only thing I recognized was orange juice. I sipped it with the air of an oenophile.

'I trust the bouquet is satisfactory?'

'It's a good year for oranges,' I agreed. 'Full-bodied, fruity, not too tart. Young and impulsive, yet restrained in the bass notes – heck, not bass notes. That's perfume.'

He burst out laughing, drew up a chair and set about explaining the strange foods to me. Asparagus, pale buds martyred on a rack. It seemed a kindness to eat them, dipping the delicate spears in the lemony swirls of butter clustered in an opal dimple of glass. After the first one, I couldn't stop.

He uncovered a small earthen ramekin. Pretty! A white frangipani blossom, creamy petals turned back to reveal a heart of gold.

'Oeufs en coccotte a la creme.'

I translated haltingly: baida in bartan with cream. Phooey. I could do this one. But with each spoonful it tasted as no other egg ever had, creamy, buttery, luxurious to the point of decadence. I nibbled at fragrant ovals of toasted French bread with relish. He looked pleased. And before I could guess what he was up to, he had spirited away the bread.

I was mildly irritated. I don't like my breakfast being commandeered. I had an effective speech prepared, but when he returned, bearing gifts, I forgot it all. He whipped aside a snowy napkin to reveal – a croissant. No coffee-shop croissant this, not microwaved plasticine all blebby cuticle outside and a sour knot of dough within. Aromatic, palpitant with steam, subsiding with a gasp as I tore past its flaky carapace. There was butter and marmalade, but I scorned such corruption.

When it comes to bread, I am a closet voluptuary. On the lam, I can eat my way through a boulangerie. Imagine then the austerities imposed on the soul by *sliced bread*! I would have willingly starved the rest of the weekend through for one more croissant, but he raised his hands in mock helplessness. The tall cup he placed before me had a two-inch crown of cream, not froth, faintly redolent of vanilla. Coffee bubbled up, velvet smooth, delectably fragrant, leaving a satin smudge of chocolate on the tongue.

'Mocha chocolatta. The start to a perfect holiday!'

It went to my head like champagne.

'Tarok my friend!' the tubby man who had shared Lalli's table now claimed the cook. I exchanged a look with my aunt. She shrugged with supreme indifference and returned to her coffee (*plain* coffee, I noticed). So Dr Sane was – boring, in Lalli's view. He was earnestly making a point with the cook. Tarok flashed a helpless look at me.

Dr Sane included me in his oily smile.

'I was telling Mr Ghosh he must not be upset! My wife is late, but that is a lady's privilege! Too bad she is late for this memorable breakfast. Too bad!' He laughed richly. 'Now the kids have the right idea. They ate long ago and escaped to the beach. Do what you want, I told them, this is a holiday! Enjoy!'

Tarok got himself a fresh cup of coffee. At this rate by midday his heart would be pumping out pure caffeine.

Ujwala Sane appeared at last, milky-skinned, grey-eyed, fortyish, undulant in tight white velvet pants and a halterneck blouse. The clothes sat oddly on her as though she were unaccustomed to them. As perhaps she was. She was awash with *Dune* and had dealt lavishly with rouge.

With unerring instinct she made straight for the cook and claimed his cup of coffee, brushing his fingers with insolent familiarity.

'Coffee – umm heavenly,' she grated – and immediately looked put out. She had botched her lines: remembered the carefully rehearsed opening, but forgotten to lower her voice. Her pebbly eyes skimmed the room. Me, she ignored. She acknowledged Lalli with a grave nod. She caught Hilla's eye and fluttered her fingers in greeting. She included us all in a brilliant smile and taking the cook firmly by the elbow, marched him to the window.

Dr Sane smiled affectionately. He pulled up a chair at my table and looked around. The untouched pots of butter and marmalade stared at him with reproach. He rose. He wandered. He returned with half a baguette foraged from god-knows-where. He slit it and slathered it with a slurry of butter and jam and clamped his teeth firmly down on it.

Mrs Sane too had found food. She jabbed furiously at her plate while her voice grated on and on. Dr Sane, rendered speechless by gluttony, made no demands on politeness and I was free to eavesdrop on his wife.

'So boring! So dull! No room service, no breakfast in bed, can you believe it?'

'Really?' Tarok's voice was surprisingly smooth.

'I really don't know what Hilla was talking about. Five-star luxury she said. Poor thing. All this was so sudden, she isn't used to so much. Somebody should advise her.'

'Surely somebody is?'

'Like this?'

Ujwala Sane's scornful finger described a circle around the room. Everything appeared to shrink under her scrutiny (most of the food was gone by this time). Hilla, well within earshot, was wearing her new grim smile. I was getting used to it.

'Where's Felix Rego?' Mrs Sane cried. 'He ought to be writing about this breakfast.'

'You don't like the food?' I was glad to hear a dangerous note creep into the cook's voice.

'Okay, but no variety.' She took another wolfish bite. 'Boiled eggs, bread. Butter. Jam. Servants can do that.' She gave a low conspiratorial laugh. 'Hilla asked us to choose breakfast tomorrow. Anything you like, she told me. Poor thing, she's so simple! I had no idea this cook is some local idli-dosa boy! He'll have a heart attack when he sees what I've asked for.'

'What have you asked for?'

'Continental. Crepes suzette – you know? Mushrooms. We spent last summer in Europe.'

'Ah.'

She parked her plate on a convenient chair and turned full voltage on the cook. 'Now tell me, what do you do?'

'When?'

She giggled throatily. The cook looked surprised.

Dr Sane had finished his sandwich. With a slight bow in my direction, he trundled away towards his wife. It was the cook he wanted, though.

Ujwala Sane raised her meticulously plucked eyebrows and strolled towards me. Hilla had long deserted and could be seen through the serving hatch, sitting at the kitchen counter, gulping tea like a fish.

'Hi-yee! I've heard about you.'

I forbore to ask what.

'What do you say we liven things up a bit? Before that Felix Rego gives poor Hilla a bad press. We were just discussing that. Why don't you join in too?'

'Oh. What do you think we should do?'

'Let's go down to the kitchen and frighten the cook! Let's tell him he'd better improve by lunch time. I'm very fond of Hilla. Such a good person at heart in spite of all her eccentricities!'

'Is she eccentric?'

'All Bawas are! And it must be difficult for her especially now. Menopause can be terrible!'

'Did you suffer much?'

She didn't hear me. Ramona had chosen this moment to burst in, and Dr Sane had intercepted her with rather more warmth than strictly necessary. Ramona smiled politely and got away as soon as she could, making a beeline for Lalli with some urgent need. I'd noticed already, Ramona had awarded Lalli some kind of glamorous past and was quickly making an ally of her.

'Hilla's niece Ramona,' I explained. Ujwala frowned. Clearly, La Sane was one of those women who rule the young with their petty tyrannies. She'd quench the incendiary spark of seventeen with a word as thoughtlessly as she'd stub a cigarette. I pitied her daughter. But Arpita still had a few years of freedom left before adolescence marked her as prey.

To distract Mrs Sane, I admired her bracelet. The thin silver chain bore a miniscule flask as a charm, 'It's a gift from our Swiss friends, the Schmidts.' She brightened. 'We spent a month with them last year.'

A tolerant nation, the Swiss.

She reverted to her Save Hilla scheme.

'But really we must do something for Hilla. I was telling him – handsome isn't he?' She twiddled an eyebrow at Tarok who was still entrapped by Dr Sane. 'I've seen him somewhere before.

We haven't been introduced yet. He's an industrialist. What personality! Agdi magnetic! At once, I knew. Industrialist! *Now* I remember ...'

'Oh no!' I interrupted with some malice, 'he's the cook.'

Her avid look of interest was swiftly replaced by suspicion.

'You could have told me that earlier,' she said coldly.

She walked away. The mores of Shivaji Park did not permit cooks to be gentlemen.

There was a flurry of voices outside, with Hilla's welcoming tones lilting over the rest. A cab drove away. All conversation ceased abruptly in the room.

There entered three men – and a woman.

The woman I knew. It was my friend of Tuesday afternoon, reinvented as Lola Lavina.

The first man I knew by sight. Extraordinarily lithe, he could only be a dancer or an acrobat. He was both, as much of his dancing seemed to test nerve and muscle to the extreme. Rafiq Khan. Ramona gasped and stood up uncertainly.

The gaze of the second man rested on her appreciatively. But Ramona was unconscious of everything but Rafiq Khan.

I returned to the second man, and with disappointment, recognized him.

It was Alif Bey.

But it was not as Alif Bey that I recognized him. His clever, rather cruel face was a fixture on Page 3, his opinions quoted like the punishing pronouncements of some desert God. Certainly, he'd written the *Pippa Passes* aftershave ad and several others besides. Nobody, of course, knew he was Alif Bey. In his Page 3 persona, he lived by bread alone.

Today, despite an attempt to appear sartorially challenged (crumpled kurta, dirty pyjamas, chappals), he hadn't quite lost his weekday self. I had the sinking feeling it was not the writer but his alter ego I would meet.

Still, aftershave or no aftershave, here was Alif Bey. And his unlikely squeeze was – Lola Lavina.

Evidently, they shared more than just a bed. Their clothes belonged to each other. Alif Bey was a shade hairier, but they still looked like clones or cross-dressing twins. Meenal – I would have to call her Lola from now on – cried out in either triumph or relief when she saw me, but made no move in my direction. Maybe they were conjoined twins after all. She seemed stuck to his arm with velcro.

The third man, by process of elimination, could only be Felix Rego. Our Food Correspondent was in compulsive holiday gear, a wide pair of floral bermudas, drawstrings pendant. The white T-shirt was receptively bland. Perhaps the back carried the recipe for his secret sauce. He had a small weaselly face that peered about furtively, taking notes.

Hilla did the honours. Ujwala Sane, I noticed, had disappeared.

Rafiq Khan looked ill at ease, if such a thing could ever be said of so graceful a being. He muttered something about luggage. Ramona, dazed with devotion, led him upstairs.

'Here is somebody who has a great deal to ask you about your books,' Hilla said to Alif Bey.

He took one look at me and decided I was not to his taste.

'I never discuss my books,' he snapped.

'Beast,' Felix Rego observed pleasantly. 'Nobody reads him these days.'

'They're all reading you, I suppose.'

He laughed deprecatingly, rubbing an ear in a cultivated parody of modesty. 'Alif Bey will kill you for that. His envy is pathological.'

'Suggestive of deep-seated neurosis?'

He swallowed that eagerly.

'I'm a close observer of human nature. I have to be, for my sort of work.'

I darted a suspicious look at him, but the man was dead serious.

Lola Lavina had been peeled off Alif Bey by Dr Sane. She was talking breathlessly now, and he had the rapt look doctors wear when they aren't listening. From the few words I caught – the adjectives were purely pelvic – a consultation seemed in progress.

Alif Bey was unbending over a small whisky and being attentive to Lalli, who was bored and at no pains to hide it.

Ujwala Sane now returned. She looked subtly different. There was a denser, more dangerous overlay to *Dune*. She had let herself go with green eyeshadow that threw her grey eyes into bloodshot relief.

Her arrival acted as a catalyst. At my side Felix Rego drew in his breath and stepped forward resolutely. Alif Bey spilt his whisky. Lola Lavina stopped her pelvic anecdote in mid-sentence and narrowed her eyes.

Ujwala Sane ignored everybody else and walked over to me, her back raked by Felix Rego's expectant gaze. With something of a jolt I realized Ujwala Sane was a central figure in Felix Rego's imagination. She appeared repetitively, the cat mother, possessing, devouring, she prowled his prose in various degrees of undress. She was pure Rego. I could almost hear the words pop in his brain. *Flash of teeth through black tendrils. Smooth nape offered in sacrifice – then teasingly lost as she turned, opening green slants of guile over high cheekbones. Sweat beading her temples, salt, feral. Flared wings widening at some primitive scent, hitching higher the slender column of nose. Light sculpting its pouting softness, the small red mouth opened wetly ...*

Felix opened his innings with Ujwala Sane cautiously. I left them to it and joined Rafiq Khan who had drifted in like a large leaf and stood in the middle of the room looking lost.

'What to do now?' he asked. 'Wait? Or something to eat will come?'

I offered sandwiches, but Ramona apparently, was already on the job. 'Girl is getting last half an hour.'

He looked a little fearfully at Felix now flirting with his muse.

'You are not talking like them,' Rafiq pointed out. 'You I can talk to, also Dr Hilla. Other people are like my students. All clever talk. No dance.'

'I don't dance. I don't know anything about dance.'

'No need. Don't know, never mind. But to think you know – very bad. Dr Hilla asked me to come here, I come. I can give beat, one-two, move! Bas. All these people read big books, write books even. I am not even SSC pass. Only dance.'

'I have never seen you perform live. Only on television.'

'Then tonight you see. I am dancing Shiv Tandav for Dr Hilla. In jazz. No need to know Shiv Tandav. You watch. You know.'

'Have you known Hilla long? She is my aunt's friend.'

'Aunty is beautiful lady? White hair?'

I followed his gaze to the window where Lalli stood with Lola Lavina. I read irritation, rather than beauty in her stance. But I saw what Rafiq meant. When she's very angry, Lalli retreats behind a mask, and you notice the lovely planes of her face. I watched Lalli look around, presumably for rescue.

'Other lady very famous, I think. Photo in *Mid-day* last week. Any day now she will turn up for dance class, or maybe wait till 5 kg more. But you asked if I know Dr Hilla long time. Yes, but now I hope longer.'

So Rafiq too, was here hoping. Ramona brought in her sandwich and handed it to him with the air of an acolyte offering aarti. Rafiq gave her the impersonal smile that comes with the job of ruling the roost in chickdom. 'You also, Miss, wish to dance?'

'Oh yes!'

He chuckled.

'All, all want to dance,' he sputtered with his mouth full. 'See Rafiq jumping onstage and think what is so big, I can also do. Main bhi Madonna, like Baba Sehgal.'

'No, no, I didn't mean that!'

'Not you, Miss. You are still a child, my smallest sister is as big as you. At your age, all boys and girls dance, no need to learn, the taal is in the blood. But forty-fifty years sitting like stone and suddenly because it is fashion they say teach me dance! No that is too much. To eat like elephant and hope to dance like swan. I want to tell them, go home, watch TV, have kitty party, leave me alone. I want to stop. But what to do? Question of sinful stomach.'

Perfectly on cue, Ujwala's voice floated across the room.

'Oh there's nothing like dancing for fitness! I'm going to ask Rafiq Khan to teach me. I can easily learn in a day. I'll run upstairs and change into my leotards – and then how can he refuse?'

'See?' demanded Rafiq.

5

'I've been dying to get you alone,' Lola Lavina gasped. 'But Alif is sooo possessive.'

The casual observer might have thought the shoe firm on the other foot, but who's to tell?

She looked longingly in Alif Bey's direction and when he finally caught her eye, she kissed her fingers at him. He returned the gesture. Lola asked, 'Would you like to meet him? I'll introduce you …'

'We've met, thanks. What's all this Lola stuff? You were Meenal two days ago.'

She laughed. She rummaged in the dirty denim rucksack that grew on her like an appendage and found the inevitable pack of cigarettes. 555, I noticed.

It's a gender thing. Men, no matter how brutish, invariably ask before they light up. Women never do. She inhaled deeply and shot out smoke with a faintly dragonish air.

'I didn't know you were into this sort of thing,' she said. 'Weekend parties and stuff.'

'Orgies? Raves? Saturnalia? Right up my alley.'

'You haven't changed a bit. When will you get serious?'

'You, on the other hand, have seriously changed. At least your name has!'

'Oh that. That's the least of it. After all I went through. Of course Lalli's told you all that.'

'All what? Lalli doesn't tell.'

'She saved my life.'

That was hardly informative. But she was distracted. Alif Bey, quite drunk by now, was glaring at Felix with dedicated malevolence. 'I'd better go,' she muttered. 'I'll come to your room after he's comfortable and we can have a long chat. Ciao.'

Before I could plead off, she was gone. I watched her coax a smile out of Alif Bey and talk him to the door. She certainly had him tamed.

I felt suddenly lonely in that crowded room. Like Rafiq, I too felt nobody spoke my language.

'Tis true I have gone here and there and made myself a motley to the view. What the hell was I doing here anyway?

Lalli had escaped long ago. If I knew her, she would be on the terrace, watching the sea. The thought of living through the weekend with these strangers was bizarre, and outrageous.

I fled in panic to find the cook. He was sitting on the bench, staring morosely out of the window. At my footstep his eyes crinkled in a smile and the stern set of his face relaxed.

'Do you want tea?'

'No!'

'Coffee, then? Nimbu pani?'

'Not even crepes suzette with cointreau.'

He laughed.

'Lethal, isn't she?'

'Please! Not you too. Felix is smitten already, and if I read the signs right, so is Alif Bey.'

'Oh he got over that long ago.'

'What?'

'Never mind. Hey, I've got something to show you.'

But something at his elbow distracted me.

I was enraptured by a small earthenware saucepan, exquisitely moulded, with a perky handle that just fitted my grasp. It had a neat heft. It was small, shallow, with more pout than spout and a rich red glaze I could kill for.

I should explain: I'm no cook, but I'm a sucker for hardware. My worldly goods, books apart, consist entirely of errant utensils of stone, wood, glass, enamel and unidentified alloys. Misshapen mugs that needed rescuing. Cups of great allure, proud, solitary, unmated for life, survivors of a long divorce from saucer and set.

Tarok said, 'I was right, then!' He wouldn't say about what. Instead he asked, 'Will you have tea with me? I have a surprise.'

I laughed. 'That's so quaint. To invite me to tea. All I've been doing is eat!'

'Just us, I meant. The masses will be fed in the dining room. We can escape, I know a special place.'

'And you have a surprise.'

'Five, then, on the terrace?'

'I feel as though I'm inside one of those Roman accounts of gluttony.'

'Trimalchio's banquet? Irresponsible reportage! I don't think the Romans ate like that! It just made good copy. Then, as now, it was all in the reportage.'

'Hence Felix Rego?'

'Hence Felix Rego, the world's corruption in white sauce.'

He shot a furtive glance at the stove. Time to take myself off.

'Mustn't keep you from lunch. Five o'clock, then!'

'No, don't go. I thought I saw a rat. Oh, there aren't any now, but the place was like Hamelin when they were doing up the kitchen, so I'm still leery. I keep seeing small grey shadows flit past. You came here looking for something.'

'Yep. Fortitude. The moment I leave here, Lola Lavina's going to tell me the story of her life.'

'I was planning to tell you mine over tea.'

Light words. But they gave me a rush. Things were moving too fast for me.

'Ah, there you are,' Lola said at my shoulder. 'Lalli said I'd find you in the kitchen.'

There are times when I could murder my aunt.

Lola Lavina, cross-legged on my bed, smoking like Krakatoa, frowned deeply at me. 'You've pulled down,' she said. That made me feel like a heritage site. 'I heard you had a rough time.'

I did not unbosom, so she kept at it, confident I would.

'Lost your job?'

'Got another.'

'Broke up with your boyfriend too, didn't you? Life is lousy, isn't it?'

'So you've got my news. Now tell me yours.'

She lit another cigarette.

'Where do I begin? It's been so long. Let me see – it's been a year, right?'

'Nearly.'

'I think I've lived more in this last year than I have in the rest of my life. I was married to Guru Bhagwat, you know that? You know Guru?'

'Vaguely.'

'Ha. As I did. After four years of marriage, I discovered exactly how vaguely. It all started when his mother came to live with us …'

Her misfortunes began. She found out that Guru was two-timing her. She confronted him. Mother-in-law intervened. They locked her up. Starved her. Beat her. Took her signature on documents they didn't let her read. Her parents were no help. You're married now, they told her, it's a life sentence.

She lived in daily dread of a dousing of kerosene, a flung match, an exploding stove, poison. He broke her wrist one night. Early that morning, she ran away. She went to the police. They were no help, but they lodged a complaint. Luckily for her, she had anticipated her husband. He turned up at the chowki just as she finished giving her statement. He lost it then, abused and reviled her. Right there, in the chowki, he took a swing at her and had to be restrained.

She was free. Not quite safe yet, but she didn't have to go back to the hellish place she called home.

Where could she go?

The social worker introduced her to a lawyer. He told her she had sufficient grounds for divorce. He helped her find a place to live. He was a good listener. She trusted him. In the long hours of working together on her case …

'My therapist said that I fell in love with him. That's impossible. We had nothing in common. He wasn't educated. He had his law degree of course, but no real education. It's an outrageous idea. I stopped going for therapy after hearing that. It wasn't love at all. It was drink.'

Apparently, every time he listened, he made her drink.

'I wasn't used to alcohol. My God! I'd hardly ever touched a drink, but he made me drink. Not by force, but by persuasion. By then everything he did was coercive, don't you see? He had absolute power over me.'

Every time she drank she woke up in a hotel room.

That was her life for three months.

I didn't ask her what she did between drinks, but evidently, there were a lot of drinks and a lot of hotel rooms and then she discovered every time she woke up it was in a different hotel and with a different man.

'Did he dope you?'

'With drugs? I don't know. But I was dopey all right, traumatized out of my last shred of brain. I just didn't notice things any more.'

Her horrors were not yet over. The lawyer locked her up when she protested. She smashed the toilet window and escaped, only to be trapped again. This time he shackled her to the bed and left her there for two days and nights. Finally the police broke in.

'If it hadn't been for Lalli, I would have died.'

I still didn't see what Lalli had to do with this sordid tale, unless she broke in with the police, but then that's not the sort of thing she does any more. Her fighting days are over. I was growing angrier with Lalli by the minute and didn't want to discuss her.

I cut heartlessly through Lola's account of what happened next. It was mostly complicated gynaecology anyway, better left to Dr Sane.

'So when did you meet Alif Bey?' I asked.

She smoothed her pepper-and-salt mane.

'Isn't he cute?' she cooed. 'Oh, it was tough at first, but by now I've almost got him trained. I'll tell you how it all began, you'd never guess. It started with *food*.'

'Oh?'

'Food's so erotic, isn't it. I was cooking at a friend's place when he dropped by. I knew who he was, of course, but we hadn't met. He strolled into the kitchen, and that was it. The first whiff of my basmati was enough to catapult him straight into bed. At least now he waits till we're alone.'

'And so you changed your name?'

'Had to, na? Gosh, I must run, Alif must be hungry and I'll have to get him decent for lunch.'

I gave her five minutes to clear the corridor and then knocked on Lalli's door.

She was reading Felix Rego's latest: *Avra Cadavera, the Vanishing Corpse*.

'Amazing,' she declared. 'It's a sealed room mystery. How did the corpse vanish? Our Felix has a huge magnet outside the room and Avra – she's the cadaver – she's wearing an iron bracelet. So zoom, she just floats up when the magnet moves. I thought she'd bump her head on the ceiling, but at the last moment Felix tells me there's a ventilator. Some intelligent twiddling of the magnet and the girl simply slides through. Amazing!'

I glared at her.

'Lola Lavina says you saved her life.'

She shrugged that away.

'You told me you didn't know her.'

Lalli put the book away with an impatient exclamation.

'Of course I don't. I met her for the first time this morning. What a bore the woman is.'

'So just where do you figure in her lurid tale?'

'I busted the nexus. They – the police – were squinting too close. It needed the long view. I saw the pattern. Distressed women were disappearing with amazing regularity. If they filed a complaint about rape or domestic violence they were gone, the very next morning. Then when a few of them were discovered in brothels, you can imagine the outcry, the self-righteous cant of patriarchy: *See what happens to women who are disobedient! We beat you to protect you, we burn you to save you from dishonour.* That really made me see red.'

'And?'

'I found out what was happening to them.'

'The lawyer sought them out?'

'Oh no, it was worse. *They* sought out the lawyer. It was all very clever. I haven't dealt with anything more sordid in all my years in crime.'

I felt sick and angry. I was sick of Lola's litany of disaster, angry at myself for being sick of it.

'And how does that make Lola a woman of substance?' I blurted. 'She's a survivor, but Lalli, that's not enough.'

'Not enough for you to like her, or not enough for Alif Bey?'

'Not him! He catapults into bed at the first whiff of her basmati.'

'She told you that? They deserve each other. Introduce her to Felix. He'll get a book out of her.'

'He's busy getting a book out of Mrs Sane right now.'

Lola's story had upset me more than I would concede. Not for the first time did I wonder at the courage and endurance of women whose intelligence was the absolute pits. Not only did they survive, they lived to write the tale. *Edited by a renowned victim of domestic violence* I actually saw that on a blurb the other day. Now what sort of puff is *that*?

Then again, perhaps intelligence has nothing to do with it. Perhaps the true measure of evolution is defiance.

I understood Lola's helplessness in that daze of drugs and alcohol, I understood the bewildered question that must have stung her through it all: *how did I let it get this far?*

I admired the nerve, the eggsy spit-in-your-face foolhardiness of her defiance. I admired all that. But I was damned if I was going to like her for it.

6

Lunch was a homely affair. The food was delicious, uncomplicated, plentiful.

'For this we came here, Hilla? Varan-bhat I can have at home also,' La Sane commented sharply.

Hilla laughed.

'This is to prepare your tastebuds for tomorrow. Tonight's dinner will be as simple – and early – to be in time for Rafiq's performance on the terrace. Tomorrow, and the day after, the cook comes into his own!'

La Sane pulled a face. Tarok and Felix were both missing, but hot phulkas, silky puffs of scented air, kept arriving magically. Rafiq and I ate on the steps, dangling our legs in the sun. He said the *do piyaza* was almost as good as his mother's and, with a stack of phulkas to go with it, he was utterly at peace. No conversation. Which was exactly what I needed after that overdose of Lola. The rice was basmati, with a pretty strong whiff, but it seemed to have a marked anti-aphrodisiac effect on Alif Bey. He glowered when Lola urged a second helping.

The children claimed me after lunch. Mrs Sane fell in with the rule that single women are nature's nursemaids and foisted them on me with a generous smile.

'I can trust you to keep them out of mischief,' she said. The kids looked hopeful.

'We're bored with Ramona,' Darshan said in a burst of confidence. 'We left her on the beach.'

'Very uncooperative,' Arpita used her mother's voice. 'We were burying her in sand, but she rebelled.'

I broke into a run.

'Wait!' Darshan puffed after me. 'We only wanted her head sticking out of the sand so that an elephant could stamp on it, like in the history books. You can be the elephant, if you like.'

'Fancy playing a game like that. That's for five year olds! Ramona and I are going up to the tower to look for ships. Want to come?'

Ramona was rescued, covered with sand. She pounced on them ferociously and chased them all the way back to the house.

We went up the small staircase to Framroze's eyrie beneath the weathervane. A large bay window let in the spectacular view. I felt afloat, I could have been looking down from a balloon. The old brass telescope, perfectly functional, soon absorbed the kids. Even Ramona forgot to bemoan the sand in her hair.

A lorry inched up the hill.

'Mr Bajaj,' Ramona guessed. 'Can you imagine Chili arriving in a lorry?'

'I thought Mr Bajaj kept race horses!'

'Yeah. But I think that's recent. Maybe he started with tempos and trucks.'

Darshan squealed.

'It's the ice! The iceman's come! Tarok Uncle said we could have ice cream!'

The kids clattered down the wooden stairs. We stayed, watching Tarok appear around the side of the house and drag in a huge sawdust-covered block with a hook.

'What does he need so much ice for?' I wondered idly. 'There's a fridge and a freezer.'

'He says you can't use those when the recipe says "serve chilled". It has to be stood in ice. He doesn't make ice cream in the freezer either, he's got a bucket thing for it. Hazaar tension, yaar. It's okay if you've got nothing else to do in life.'

'He'll probably keep the kids at the churn. Good!'

'They're horrible kids,' Ramona said with deep feeling.

'What do you think of Rafiq Khan?' she asked presently. 'He can dance and all that, but he's not ...'

I knew what she meant. We'd had upsets all morning, starting with the cook. Nobody, it appeared, was prepared to be quite what we expected.

'It's more fun when they turn out different,' I told Ramona.

She sighed.

'I'll never wear my bustier now. Never, never, never.'

'I don't see why not! Why don't you ask him to teach you a few steps and you and the kids can put up a show for us. Rafiq is here to dance for all he's worth, he won't mind.'

'You ask him.'

'I? I have no intention of dancing!'

She made an impatient sound. 'Obviously. I meant for me.'

I did, when we went downstairs. The studio, the large airy room behind the library, was empty of furniture, except for a mirror that covered the far wall. The parquet floor made no pretence of polish. It had been battered by dancing feet before.

Rafiq was perfectly willing to teach.

'Bring children also. First watch, then learn. Come now, I rehearse.'

The two brats ran about clearing the room.

Rafiq rolled his eyes heavenward when he noticed me make for the door, but I refused to be coaxed and ran away.

I did feel like dancing, though! Alone, unobserved, on a white beach all afternoon, in the black sand by the silver moon, dusting my hair with stars – that sort of thing.

There was a *Do Not Disturb* sign on the kitchen door. I glimpsed Lalli and Hilla on the patio, enjoying a cup of tea tête-à-tête. It was a little past four.

I went up to my room. I needed solitude like a draught of cool water. I just wanted to be still and let the endless strain of conversation rattle out of my brain. I flipped through *The Thought Cyclist*, but the words failed to beguile. I lay on my back staring at the ceiling, drifting, drifting …

The door to the terrace creaked in the errant breeze. Damn. I had forgotten to bolt it. I'm leery about half-shut doors. I was getting up to shut it when I was arrested by the sound of voices.

Ujwala Sane and Alif Bey were quarrelling on the terrace and I was not prepared to be witness. I stayed where I was, trying to shut their voices out, but the peculiar metallic clangour of her voice battered its way past the door.

'Tell me why you came, then!' A challenge: 'If you have guts, tell me!'

'I'm not going to say what you want me to.'

'Why? Why? Scared of girlfriend? Not girl exactly, huh?'

He was silent. When he spoke again, his voice was hesitant.

'I didn't know you'd be here. I wouldn't have come, if I'd known. You always were my torment, Mohini.'

'That silly name. Old-fashioned.'

'That's how I think of you.'

'Ha! Admit it. You think of me?'

'Very often.'

'So you bring this fat woman to mock me. Dangle her in my face.'

'That is a terrible phrase, Mohini.'

'Ooof! Mohini, Mohini, Mohini, I am sick of Mohini! What if my husband heard you?'

'Let him.'

Her voice changed, dropped a register or two.

'So that is your plan. That is why you are here. You want to wreck my marriage, you want to destroy my home. You want to torture me with my one small innocent … '

'I'm not interested in your life or your marriage.'

'Or in me? You want me to believe that? You expect me to believe that? How many years has it been? Twelve? Fifteen?'

'Fourteen years, two months, four days.'

'You see? You can't get over me. You can never forget. No man can. I must warn you. My husband is a very jealous man.'

'Would he be jealous of me?'

'If he knew …'

'He won't know from me. We are strangers, Mrs Sane, you and I.'

If she heard the sadness in his voice, it left her unmoved. She said bossily, 'You are come down to this level, you are picking up kachra from roadside?'

'Meaning?'

'This Lola Lola. Coca Cola. What kind of name? This Lola I'm talking about.'

'Don't. Please.'

'Why not? Everybody else is talking. Only I should not talk? Just now I came to know what kind of woman she is. I am going to tell Hilla. She does not know it yet. I am going to tell her that Alif Bey, the great writer, is spending a dirty weekend with a cheap prostitute. Isn't that what she is? Arre, deny, deny, what's the use? Everybody knows. Once Hilla gets to know, she will kick her out.'

'Please stop this. Lola is my friend, and I don't want you insulting her.'

'I am insulting her? No, the great writer is wrong. She is insulting me. She is insulting me by her presence here. Hilla is insulting me if she allows her to stay for one minute more under the same roof as a respectable lady. Being asked to share a table with a common prostitute – oof, it's too much!'

'Whatever else Lola may be, she isn't common.'

'Oh. Special Service? I have heard of such things. Blue films …'

'I'll throttle you.'

'I can call the police. My uncle is ACP Bandra. You know? Gudhade Patil? My mother's own brother.'

Alif Bey laughed. A high explosive whimper from Ujwala Sane as she burst into tears.

After a while I heard him mutter something. The answering silence told me he was alone.

Something of his torment touched me too. Mohini, the woman essence that pervaded his books was – *this*!

He saw her now as the rest of the world did. No longer backlit by memory, luminous and alluring, the wanton muse. Where would his words spring from now, towards what world would his ideas travel, and with what hope? The man was annihilated.

Not for the first time I wondered at the pitiless betrayals love connived. Always too chary for comfort, I had early found out its dross. Through book after book, I had envied Alif Bey his lifetime of infatuation with Mohini. Every line he had written sang of it. And now, like a morality play staged for me alone, it was dead, strangled in an idle hour of a drowsing afternoon.

A knock roused me.

Oh God. Tarok. I had forgotten. No time now for those capris. I splashed some water on my face and opened the door.

'You were asleep?'

Chenille marks on my cheek, I guessed. I rubbed it.

'Your eyes are somewhere else,' he said.

I was on the point of blurting out what I'd overheard, and stopped myself just in time. I countered his quizzical look by demanding to be shown my surprise.

He flushed. I realized he thought I'd forgotten our date.

We ran down the spiral staircase. This was my first view of the back of the house. Correction. Of the new improved back. I remembered the two neem trees from my first visit. The ground sloped, leading to a grassy knoll. A current of perfume prickled, spicy, sharp, from the pink and white profusion of flowers ahead. Through the arch of Rangoon creeper we walked to a small octagonal dais, paved with cracked tiles, in faded arabesques of turquoise and dull gold.

Laid out on a small table was tea for two.

From the dais, a flight of steps led down to a small round pond. And in it, as though I had arrived at the secret centre of a dream, bloomed a single purple water lily.

I had been standing with my back to the table. Now Tarok spun me around. I cried out. I had to! I had thought the pond was the surprise, but on the table was the most exquisite tea service I'd ever seen. It stung me with lust. I would have killed Tarok to possess it. It was a delicate dusky rose, the china translucent and veined, painted with a chintz of small cream flowers.

Tarok laughed at my look of absolute greed.

'Isn't it perfect? Now for the ultimate desecration. Let's drink from it.' I was in my favourite dream. It didn't taste like tea. It was lemon and mint and honey. It was mist and sunshine. It was tea.

The sun smoothed the grass in long golden stripes. Somewhere an insect droned. Our words drowsed in the silence. After a long time, after years and years I was utterly, completely content.

He nudged a plate towards me. Another surprise.

'Murukk!'

Genuine *kai murukk*, hand-plaited six-tiered spirals.

'You expected oblaten.'

'I don't know what that is, but I expected something crumbly and Danish or creamy and Viennese.'

I prepared for the worst and took one out of politeness. When it comes to a classic, I like the real thing. Not store bought stuff, greasy, heavy on the tongue with the acerbic sting of soda.

Surprise, surprise. It cracked with a definite crunch, crumbled to an aromatic melt on the tongue and sluiced me with greed.

'Do I pass the test?'

'*You* made this?'

'I like that new tone of respect. This is a bribe, though. Six should be enough to keep you here long enough to hear the story of my life.'

I took one more. Beneath his flippant manner, the man was nervous. The murukk was really good. Just salt enough, and hollow at heart. He'd even used coconut oil. Bliss.

No catering school had taught him this. He had wormed it out somehow from the specialists who run a diligent trade at weddings and upanayanams. Many of them are single women, mamis and paatis, relics of a patriarchy that allowed them this sole mode of livelihood. They might have well succumbed to his charm. Unless his mother taught him. I put my foot in it again. I asked.

'My mother didn't teach me any cooking. There wasn't enough time.'

I waited on the knife edge of disaster, but his tone changed. The pain in his eyes replaced by gentle amusement.

'Have you heard of Nataraj Iyer?'

Who hasn't?

Some remember him as that tabloid cliche, Living Legend, recycled every ten years or so. But to most he's just a name. Come wedding or upanayanam, Bombay's Tamils count on Nataraj Iyer. If he isn't available, scuttle the date. Even the planets must wait on Nataraj Iyer. Few have actually seen him. *I* never have. Which, considering I grew up in an agraharam disguised as housing society, is a bit callous. I've eaten his cooking all my life.

Year after year, at every wedding, he was the genie who conjured up the feast: a Nataraj Iyer saddi was not to be missed. Nobody waited to be invited. If there was a saddi, you went. And if it was your worst enemy being honoured there, you still stayed for lunch and enjoyed it. Of course I knew the man. He was part of memory.

But that was long ago.

Visiting the ghetto after ten years, I was at a wedding recently. The lunch was a tripartite extravaganza of Palakkad-Punjabi-Chinese grunge. Everybody ate standing up, from plates piled with everything all at once. It was gross, barbaric. There were people around me actually using *forks*.

'He hasn't been around for some time,' I said slowly.

Tarok nodded. He toyed absently with the last murukk. I took it from his fingers. His eyes were distant.

'He taught me this,' he said. 'He taught me everything I know. He took me off the footpath when I was sixteen and made a cook of me. Then he threw me out with one terse order: "Go learn every kind of cuisine there is. I couldn't do that. You do that for me".'

'And you did?'

'Some.'

The teapot was cold by now. He cast about for some distraction till he could trust his voice again.

I had stopped hearing his words long ago. I was listening to him, to all that was being said so suddenly, so wordlessly being trusted to my keeping. His silence was choked with words it would take a lifetime to spill. His fingers closed around mine. There was no more to say.

Then a voice knifed us. The moment crumpled.

'Hello!'

Footsteps, light, quick, heeled, hurried towards us.

'That must be Chili,' I said, and got up to welcome her. He looked baffled by the interruption, a man cut adrift.

I intercepted her at the bower. I simply couldn't bear the thought of anybody sharing that table with us.

She was very like her pictures, tall, slender, all eyes and dimples and whippy hair. She was dressed in cream chinos and a black shirt.

Heels, of course. (Women like her are *born* with six-inch stilletos welded on their infant feet.) Her face, devoid of makeup, looked strained and a little puffy. I liked her at once.

Our words tangled, laughingly, and I was about to lead her to the house when she froze in mid-sentence. Her smile sagged lopsided, her eyes were incredulous, horrified. I wheeled around, alarmed, but there was just Tarok behind me.

She lunged forward, stabbing the air with one gleaming purple talon.

'You!'

And with a sob of rage she hurled her bag on the grass and ran towards the house.

Tarok threw up his hands helplessly.

A vice clamped down inside me, all rusty spring-loaded teeth, tightening, tightening.

He said, 'Look, let me explain ...'

I cut him short with a shrug.

'It's really no business of mine,' I said, my eyes beginning to burn.

It couldn't have stung more if I had slapped him. And I was glad of it.

With one stabbing look he walked away, leaving the field to me with the remains of the feast, the scratchy grass prickling my ankles and the slow accretion of the gathering storm.

7

Chili's commotion was still raging when I got back to the house. Ramona hurried up and down the stairs fetching ice, hot water, tea, and biscuits by the barrel. Lola Lavina hovered with a pain balm that reeked to the stratosphere. Dr Sane stood outside, in the corridor, advising calmness, above all, calmness. His wife was not to be seen. Alif Bey called out for a stomach pump. Hilla, in the epicentre of this panic, looked as if she would make a break for it any moment.

'There, there,' Felix's voice could be heard from Chili's room. 'Pull yourself together now.'

Only my aunt, unperturbed, stood watching the sunset from the terrace.

Through all this confusion, Chili wept. Her sobs, harsh, spasmodic, guttural, were relieved by the occasional scream. There were bursts of light hammering which suggested she was stamping with those stilettos.

'Let it out, baby,' Felix sounded weary. 'Just let go.'

With this fresh encouragement, Chili let fly again. I hoped her room didn't have breakables: there was a modest menagerie of terracotta animals in mine.

Ramona whispered that just before Hilla had got here, Chili

had swallowed pills. 'Suicide,' she said in thrilled tones. 'Six tablets. Isn't she brave?'

My heart sank.

Tarok was lying low in the kitchen after bringing Chili to this pass. The least he could do by way of redemption was hold the stomach pump.

'But they were only vitamins, thank God!' Ramona finished.

'That hardly matters,' I said in my iciest voice. 'It's the intent that counts.'

'You mean she can die with six vitamins?'

'Not a chance. But she can try again. With something worse.'

Ramona, stricken, fled to the terrace to find my aunt.

I got Lola out of the way by commenting that Alif Bey might like to sample what the cook had dished up specially for him. This sent Dr Sane too scuttling in the direction of the pantry. Hilla left, giving me a look of pure gratitude. Felix, discovering they were all gathered in the kitchen without him, took flight.

My smart, if malicious, stage management had worked. Very soon now, I'd learn the worst.

I took the chair near the door and waited. Eventually, Chili's sobs quietened. She took herself off to the bathroom and returned with a brilliant smile.

'What a relief to cry! I've been wanting to do this for a week, can you believe it? I'm so totally grossed out with the whole thing. I'm like is this real, is this happening to me?'

'I know that feeling.'

'You do? Yeah. I guess. But I can't cry on my job. I mean I'm not allowed to! Puffy face, red eyes, the shoot's ruined and where am I? Can't even stay awake all night worrying because of dark circles. I've used like a kilo of potatoes since it happened.'

'Potatoes?'

'You know. For dark circles.'

'Oh.'

'What do you use?'

'Brinjal,' I said firmly. 'Big purple ones.'

'Sure. Those are good too. Where's that tea?'

It had grown a skin by this time, but she didn't seem to mind. She emptied the mug in one gulp and swept a plateful of biscuits into her lap. 'Oh God I can't stand biscuits!' she groaned, cramming her mouth with them.

'Shall I get you a sandwich?'

'No-no. I'm good. I'm good. It's just that I can't stop eating them. See. They're gone.'

They were.

'I haven't eaten for a week. Not properly. Only salads and light stuff. I just didn't remember I had to eat. You know that feeling when the day seems to go on and on for a week and maybe it'll stretch for the rest of your life?'

That I did know. I was beginning to feel it too.

'So when Hilla phoned I was like help, I'm close to a breakdown and she said come right over and have it here. I mean, it's safer, isn't it, with a doctor around. But then, you've got to call it fate, what else can it be? I hardly step in and what do I find? Him!'

Here it came now, the landslide.

'The last guy, I mean totally the last guy I want to meet. I'm like hey hello, what a great place this is, and BAM! Just like that.'

'Awful!'

'Awful! I mean who *is* he?'

'Exactly.'

'No, honestly. Who the hell is he?'

'Absolutely. The dust beneath your feet.'

'No, I mean seriously. Who *is* he?'

'The cook.'

'The cook! Nah. He's no cook. He's pretending to be a cook. It's a disguise. I know who he is. He's the messenger. That's who he is. The messenger, that's who.'

After this revelation, she slid gracefully down on the bed, slammed a pillow against her face and grew so still I began to fear she'd smothered herself. But presently I heard her snore.

I strolled out on the terrace. Ramona had left – back to dance class, I bet.

'So how's our suicide doing?' Lalli asked, a trifle tartly, I thought.

'The cook has broken her heart.'

'Nonsense.'

'I saw him do it.'

Lalli seared me with one of those laser looks of hers.

'Are you all right?'

I shrugged. 'Why wouldn't I be?'

'No reason at all. None at all. Come on, let's brave Mr Bajaj together.'

'Has he arrived?'

'A few minutes ago. Don't worry about Chili. She'll live.'

I passed Tarok on the stairs. We avoided each other. A sudden swell of sadness flattened me. I held my breath and unwillingly, it rolled away.

'You know Mrs Bajaj,' Lalli said.

'I do?'

'Lata Sandeha.'

'Good God!'

And I'd been thinking life couldn't get any worse.

This was epic disaster.

To be pursued across the city right into this sylvan retreat – talk about tentacles – even cancer had a lesser reach than Lata Sandeha. Professor Lata Sandeha was my nemesis, the woman who had altered the course of my life with one vicious slash of her pen.

I had been rehearsing that long story for Tarok. Now of course it would never be told. With brilliant illogic, that too I blamed on Lata Sandeha. At my side, Lalli remained curiously unconscious of my turmoil.

To hell with them all, the cook and the whole caboodle!

'Why did she say he was the messenger?' I demanded.

'What?'

'Why did Chili say Tarok was not a cook but a messenger?'

'She was just leery.' Lalli said promptly. 'A burnt child, you know.'

That was hardly edifying.

We found Hilla fussing over the new arrival. There was tea, and an earthenware platter heaped with small feathery crisp objects that looked poised for flight.

I had no idea what they were, and I didn't care.

Hilla, as usual, looked ready to bolt. Introductions were made. Hilla left. Lalli murmured something about keeping the children waiting, and before I knew, with nothing by way of self-defence except a teapot and a plate, I was alone with Lata Sandeha's husband.

Mr Bajaj looked nothing like the horror I expected. He was a tall craggy man in his late fifties. He gleamed with the polish of very old silver. There was a muted glint to everything about him – his hair, his grey suit, his watch and his many rings. His eyes were animated ice chips, a milky grey livened by a flash of green. He had large knotty hands. His manicured nails looked nacreous. The colourless finger that held his teacup reminded me of a lobster's claw.

'I've heard a great deal about you,' he said. 'I am an ambassador of goodwill. My wife is on a visit to Calcutta. She chose to go. It was not strictly necessary. I would have been happier if she'd had come here instead, and tried to reclaim a friend.'

Well! That was quite a burst of manly frankness. Hey, I *liked* this guy.

'Hilla tells me you're interested in the Rolls Royce?'

Mystery explained. He was being nice because he had just discovered I was a millionaire. With exactly Rs 450 and 68 paise to my name, who was I to disllusion him?

'It was in excellent condition. Hilla's uncle was a perfectionist. Even the engine parts were polished. And the interior! Fine-tooled leather. Beautiful!'

'What about the engine?'

'Perfect. Raise the bonnet, run your fingers on the machinery, not a trace of dust or grime.'

'Yes, but did it run?'

'Like the wind. Silent as a cat. Steady purr to it. I tell you, my Pajero feels like a lorry after that Rolls.'

'You drove the Rolls?'

He smiled. It was like sunset on an iceberg.

'Would you like to?'

'Would I like to what?'

'Would you like to drive the Rolls?'

My heart plummeted. So this was the man who had bought the Silver Dawn! The unnamed bidder in person. The thought of Lata Sandeha lolling on fine-tooled leather made me sick, sick, sick.

'I know the owner,' Mr Bajaj continued, my nausea having failed to register. 'A great man, only too ill to enjoy his new car. I hope, by the time the car is on the market again you would have sold your novel and become a millionaire.'

His eyes gave me the uneasy feeling that they could see straight into my bank book. 'My novel is going to make me a millionaire?' I asked stupidly.

'Of course. As they say in MTNL: Please wait. You are in queue. You will be the next Purnima Bidri.'

If he had wanted to make an enemy of me, he couldn't have chosen a more ham-fisted argument.

'Ah, I know what you young people call her,' he continued slily. 'She is a wonderful lady. A very lucky lady, of course, but talented as well.'

'Have you read her book?'

'No! Reading is the wife's field. My field is money. Ah, here is our journalist friend.'

Felix appeared, frowning over a piece of paper.

'I can't believe the menu he's drawn up for tomorrow's dinner,' he burst out. 'Here take a look.'

Mr Bajaj subtly intercepted the paper and gave it a quick once-over. He looked puzzled. He let me have it.

'Is it from a history book?' he asked.

I saw what he meant.

Every dish on the menu had a date next to it. Tarok was serving us three millennia of subcontinental gluttony – the earliest date I spotted was 1500 BC. With luck we'd have soma for starters.

'This is pushing ambition too far,' Felix grumbled. And filling his pockets with the feathery things on Mr Bajaj's untouched plate, he took himself off.

'What is this new idea of Hilla's?' Mr Bajaj rumbled. 'Who is this strange cook? If you need a chef I told her, let me get you one. Taj, Oberoi, Ambassador, name your kitchen and I'll get you the best on their staff. You just have to say the word. But Mrs Driver is a very strong-minded lady. She has always had her way! And now she must have her chef! Very well, I'll just take care she's not taken for a ride. How is the food?'

'Very good.'

'And our journalist friend is going to write about it?'

'Apparently.'

'You don't sound very enthusiastic?'

I shrugged.

'I don't know anything about food,' I said truthfully.

Mr Bajaj smiled. A glacial smile that reminded me of frosty nights and the impossible distances of stars.

'I shall have to find out for myself then,' he said pleasantly.

Felix was still pondering the menu when I found him half an

hour later on the verandah, feet propped on a wrought-iron chair. I pulled up another chair and wished the seat were slightly friendlier.

'It gets worse every time,' Felix sympathized. 'And yet they're addictive. I don't seem to be able to get up and find an ordinary chair. I might pinch one when I leave.'

'I'll warn Hilla.'

'Tarok has the nerve to say the dum pukht I wrote about last week wasn't genuine. And look at this menu.'

'Back to it, are we? I couldn't care less.'

'Oh-oh. It's like that?'

'Like what?'

'That. You'll get over it. The man's a swindler anyway. I haven't heard of half the dishes.'

'Isn't that to his credit?"

'He's supposed to be a cook not an inventor. There are rules, you know.'

'I don't. Oh, Mr Bajaj has been telling me about Purnima Mudbidri.'

'The Bidri Bitch,' he sighed. We gnashed our teeth in unison.

The Bidri Bitch, as she was popularly called, was the bete noir of every hack in the country. Like the rest of us, she wrote a book. There were a few uneasy reviews. She'd made a neat transition from Lit Crit to Clit Lit, but the thesis was pure whinge.

And then the bombshell. Her novel, *Shakuntala's Thorn* was auctioned for an incredible $4 million. Now, of course, the media found the book Chekovian, Proustian and Woolfian by turn week after week after week. Naturally, we were all sick to death of the Bidri Bitch. Equally naturally, Lata Sandeha had adopted her as the department mascot.

By now Purnima had dumped the Mudbidri for something snappier.

'Because my book was published in the UK,' she explained. 'And I thought Mudbidri is confusing. Bidri is *so* much more memorable.'

All of which only went to explain that Mr Bajaj was naive at heart and could be depended upon to drop the occasional brick.

Felix was back to Tarok's menu.

'I could kill the guy,' he muttered.

'Why don't you set your next murder at the dinner? You could call it *Millennial Murder*.'

'That is an idea – hey wait, I'm getting it – almonds, oxalic acid, arsenic ...'

' ... insecticide, mothballs, nutmeg.'

'Nutmeg?'

'Grated.'

'Really? Must look it up if you say so. I'm going to put your aunt in it.'

I boggled at the vision of Lalli garnished with grated nutmeg.

'Mystery figure, you know. Aloof. Elderly and all that. Raving beauty in her youth.'

'Lalli would love that.'

'Yeah. Sex in flashback, memories. Something about her gets me. She's deep man, real deep. What say, Tarok? Shall we put Lalli into a murder?'

I hadn't noticed him come in. Now he picked up the menu, avoiding my gaze. Felix repeated his question.

Tarok shrugged. 'In Vishnu-land, what avatar?'

Our eyes met then, and we smiled, and it was all right. I'm not too keen on Browning myself, but the quote was apt, though Felix couldn't guess that. He looked puzzled. When Tarok had moved away, Felix made his diagnosis. 'Religious chap. You never know these days, with Hindutva and all.'

We returned to the important question of nutmeg which Felix dismissed as fanciful.

'One nut is enough to conk out an adult,' I told him, remembering the strange incident that led Lalli to the solution of the Sleeping Beauty mystery.

Right on cue Lalli joined us, but she hates discussing her cases, and so I lost the argument. Felix, with the air of one conferring a rare honour, informed Lalli she was to star in his next murder.

Lalli, surprisingly, was amused.

'Am I to be murderer or murderee?' she asked.

'Oh murderer, definitely. Woman with a past. It'll be at tomorrow's dinner. Ten people. Apparent strangers, but each invited with a specific purpose.'

'Vendetta?' Lalli suggested.

'Exactly. But nobody knows that. And you – aloof, serene, traces of beauty still in your cheekbones …'

'Thank you.'

'Sex in flashback, don't forget,' I reminded him.

'Not for you,' he assured Lalli soothingly. 'Another character, not you. You sweep the room with a regal glance. Everybody is seated at the long rich table. Crystal. Silver. Chandeliers. Music. Conversation. Then suddenly – he – your lover, you know, or maybe rapist, I'm not yet sure – topples over, slowly sinks into the soup – no, better make that dessert. Raspberry mousse? Raspberry something. Red, you know. Everybody thinks he's bleeding. Only you know the truth. You smile. Oxalic acid. In the salt. Acts within seconds.'

'Why would he use salt in his dessert?' I asked

Felix dusted that off with a frown.

'Details come later. Just get the atmosphere. Lalli will be wearing purple. Purple silk. Ivory temples. Half-moon eyes.'

'Isn't oxalic acid a trifle old-fashioned?' Lalli asked. 'Surely, I can do better than that!'

'It won't be messy, that's the main thing,' Felix said severely. 'We can't have a mess at the dinner table.'

'Will I have to swing for it?'

'Oh no. Mine never do. You'll walk away with it. Give me time and I'll think up something better than oxalic acid.'

Hilla appeared on the verandah. She looked tired.

'I think Hilla's looking for me,' Lalli got up. 'Thanks, Felix, I'm sure I'll make a lovely murderer.'

'Let's put it to vote at the dinner,' I suggested incautiously.

Lalli's 'No!' was vehement. 'I never joke about murder,' she said as she walked away.

'I shouldn't have frightened her,' Felix Rego said, gazing fondly at Lalli's retreating figure and renewing my faith in the credulousness of mankind.

Ujwala Sane wandered in, plate in hand. She was eating sandwiches.

'I ask for a snack and look what I get – sandwiches! Kakdi, no chutney even. Where is that darn cook?'

The darn cook materialized. She thrust the plate at him.

'Here. Get me some sauce with that.'

'Sauce, madam?'

'Sauce. Sauce. Ketchup. Tomato ketchup. What's the matter, you don't know how to make? It comes in a bottle.'

'Easy, easy,' Felix said feebly.

Tarok took the plate from her and walked away. I followed him into the kitchen.

He tipped the sandwiches into the bin. As an afterthought, he trashed the plate as well. To keep up, I chucked in Bajaj's teacup and for weightage, threw in a spoon.

We burst out laughing, and it was impossible to be angry after that.

'Tell me,' I said. It took an awful lot of courage.

'You sure? I thought you said it was none of your business?'

'I've just made it mine.'

'Oh. Then tell me about Bajaj. You bristled.'

~ 88 ~

'I did? He's okay, really. It's not him. It's his wife. Long story.'

'I've all the time in the world.'

'Me too.'

His eyes held mine.

And of course we were interrupted.

'How long am I supposed to wait?' Ujwala Sane asked.

Deprived of tomato sauce, La Sane was bitter for the next half hour. She dragged me away with her to sympathize over 'poor Hilla'.

'What is happening to poor Hilla? It is like a curse! This girl Chili, she committed suicide? Only vitamin pills, Dr Sane tells me, don't worry, but I am thinking today vitamins, tomorrow rat poison. Better tell Hilla to hide the rat poison.'

'Does Hilla have rat poison?'

'All old houses have rats. Of course now this house is renovated, but you cannot renovate rats.'

As I digested this, she attacked again. 'Why you are carrying cups and plates for the cook? Let him do it. He has cheated Hilla. He claimed to be a five-star chef. What do we get for lunch? Varan bhat. Now maybe bhajiya. Next there is this Lola female. Really, Hilla is too innocent! She has no knowledge of the world!'

'Why do you say that?'

'Dr Sane is very upset. He wanted us to leave at once. At once!'

'Why?'

'Ai-la! You also don't know? I don't know details, but her reputation is not good.'

I was shocked, and prepared to defend Hilla to the death.

'This Lola,' Ujwala clarified. 'She is not good type. Not respectable. "I will not let my wife stay under the same roof as such a woman for one instant," Dr Sane says. Enough, don't fuss, I tell him. He's always like that! He treats me like a devi.'

I remembered Dr Sane's consultation-on-the-hoof over Lola Lavina's pelvic woes, but wisely held my breath.

'They are sharing single room, you know. Khullam khullah. Such a great writer and he has to sink so low. Men are complete fools. Oh, guess what Felix Rego told me, you'll never guess this!'

'What?'

'You know where that dancer comes from? Govandi! From the slums! I tell you, these zopadpatti people ...'

'What time is his dance tonight?' I cut in ruthlessly.

'Ten o'clock. On the terrace. I am very interested in dance. Only classical.'

'Kathak?'

'All classical. You are Madrasi, only Bharat Natyam. That is also quite good. I know that also. I pick up very fast. In my college, I was most famous girl all-rounder – athletics, hockey, dancing, singing, tennis, mimicry ...'

And before my astonished eyes she pitched into a perfect imitation of Felix Rego.

I looked in on Chili before dinner. She was sitting up groggily in bed.

'I crashed,' she mumbled. 'Do you think Hilla would mind if I crashed right through till tomorrow?'

'Of course she won't. You need that sleep. Shall I fetch you something to eat?'

'No, I'm like nauseated? When I think of food.'

Lola peeped in.

'Hi, I brought you some fruit.'

'Thanks.'

Chili, woken to her duties as host, threw a couple of cushions at us and waved us to our chairs. 'Guess you know what happened to me,' she said.

I flinched. The poor kid probably thought we were ranged

outside her door avid for detail. On cue, Ramona came in. Great. That left only La Sane to complete the pyjama party.

Chili waved a hand grandly, accommodating the masses.

Ramona settled down on the carpet, cross-legged, her animus washed away by a great tidal wave of adulation.

'I was just telling them what happened,' Chili told Ramona.

'You broke up.'

'Yeah. I broke it off. I told him it was over.'

Ramona cried out, '*You* broke it off? Then why were you so upset?'

I felt ancient, bowed with the weight of thirty-three experienced years. Lola and I exchanged sisterhood looks.

Chili shrugged.

'He's married. I just found out.' She turned viciously on me. 'That's the guy who told me, okay? Your cook? That's how I found out. I hate him. After six months I find out. I can't believe it's over.'

'It is,' Lola and I said together.

Chili looked at us in surprise.

'There's always hope,' she said. As in where there's hope, there's divorce.

'Don't you believe it,' Hilla spoke from the door.

'He's got kids, so naturally.'

'And those kids will grow. They'll soon be adolescents. Can't upset them at that delicate age. Next there's the question of college. Then careers. Finally they're grown up, but now it's the wife's turn. Menopause. Cancer. A man's got to stick around. And when he's seen her through all that safely, there's old age. What kind of cad dumps a wife of seventy? And just in case you hadn't noticed, *he's* seventy too, and with a coronary or a stroke to match her arthritis. So then Chili, just how long a rope does hope give you?'

'Oh but I feel so awful,' Chili wailed.

Lola put an arm around Chili and stayed. Ramona was crying too, by this time and Hilla and I took her with us out onto the terrace where Lalli stood watching the waves.

Tomorrow's dinner had Hilla worried. But her worry was about Chili not the menu. 'The party's for Ramona,' she said. 'I do hope Chili's okay by then.'

'Chili will be as okay as she's going to be for a long long time,' Lalli said.

I hadn't expected such pessimism in my aunt. She shrugged at my disbelief.

'Does one ever get over pain? One survives. Oh yes, one survives everything. Even – unbelievable though it may seem – Mr Bajaj. Here he comes now. Hilla, let's run!'

And, shamelessly, both of them hurried away.

Ramona blew her nose and went off to get the lanterns ready for the dance.

Once more I was left alone with Mr Bajaj.

He said he had been visiting the cook.

'I hope you have no appetite,' he said. 'This famous cook is giving us for dinner – khichidi!'

'I'm sure it will be delicious,' I said.

He smiled his orca smile and slid away.

I was almost glad to see Lola. Chili, she said, had fallen asleep again. Lola seemed distracted. She was looking for Alif. He wasn't in the room. He hadn't been himself all day, she said.

I tried not to look guilty. Eavesdropping was turning out to be more uncomfortable than I thought. My secrets were beginning to oppress me. I could say nothing to reassure Lola. She wandered away, disconsolate.

I escaped to my room for a reviving spot of solitude. It was blissfully quiet. I picked up *The Thought Cyclist* and began reading. The lilt of children's laughter drifted up from the garden. Thunder sounded a distant drum, eager, expectant. All at once life held a certitude of joy. I fought the urge to hurry out and run towards the sea, not alone, not alone.

The sea was growling. Its grumble gathered anger.

The children had gone indoors.

A keen wind swelled the curtains. I hoped it wouldn't rain till after the dance. I loved the menacing quiet of an approaching storm, the lowering omen of clouds, the crackle in the air, the thinning light, the sudden contraction of the heart that foretells the incendiary moment. I longed for these, for the zari weave of lightning on a tense sky, the heartbreak of the koel's sudden cry.

A warm purple lit the west, thickening subtly. I switched off the lamp and let in the night. Soon there would be stars.

Footsteps.

Rapid, angry footsteps on the terrace.

I wasn't going to be forced to eavesdrop again. I reached for the switch and just then Alif Bey said, 'I thought I told you to leave me alone.' His voice chilled me. It held a frightening degree of hate.

'It's time for dinner.' Lola this time. 'Hilla will expect us.'

'There is no us. I thought I'd made that clear to you in the last ten minutes. You go downstairs if you want. I will do what I want.'

'Can we be civilized about this, please? Can we postpone this till we get back?'

'Get back where? Don't you understand me? You're not coming back to my home. I'll have your things sent on. It's over, Lola. Finished. I don't ever want to see you again.'

She laughed. That was worse than his voice.

She said, 'Why don't we decide that on Monday?'

She wasn't taking it in. She was drunk with the power of her basmati. And she was applying the pop-psych principle that it takes two to tantrum.

'What's wrong with you, woman?' Alif Bey roared. 'Don't you get the message?'

There was a rushing sound, a muffled scream and a thud.

My head throbbed. I wished I were dead, in outer space, anywhere but imprisoned in this room hearing if not watching a shocking moment of intimacy.

There was dead silence outside.

I waited. My dread was unbearable. I pushed open the door as noiselessly as I could.

The terrace was empty.

I crept back to my room, switched on the light and sat there stiff in a straight-backed chair, waiting for God knows what.

8

I went down to dinner at nine-thirty, hoping everyone would have finished eating. It was to be a buffet, and a quick one. But no, they were all there. To my embarrassment, so was Lola. She was dressed in a slinky black blouse with matching trousers, spangled with some coruscant kind of bead. She had done something snaky with eyeshadow and coloured her lips a vivid coral to match the silky gloss of the scarf tossed with panache over one shoulder. Gone were the mojdis. She wore sequinned strappy shoes with silver heels, Rs 450 on Linking Road. Her earrings were remarkable, black and yellow wire sculptures, tiny Alexander Calder mobiles.

Alif Bey was there too, growing more drunk by the minute.

Lola fluttered her fingers at me and turned brightly to listen to Mr Bajaj who was inspecting her cleavage and saying nothing at all.

Everybody milled around a steaming cauldron at one end of the room. I caught a glimpse of Felix through a blue swirl of smoke, stirring the cauldron like a weird sister.

The khichidi Mr Bajaj had predicted turned out to be mahabhog, a spicy smelt of rice, daal, pumpkin, potato, cauliflower, topped with large flaps of aubergine fritters. Chunky, hot, sweet, searing the mouth with the frisson of clove and bayleaf and the heat of ginger. It was delectable.

The room swam with heat. Tarok entered staggering beneath the weight of another cauldron that held a smaller vessel in a nest of ice. The counterpoint: curds and rice, each grain yielding in a creamy cumulus. Deceptively bland, till match heads of mustard lit sulphur flares on the tongue. Keen with asafoetida, racy with ginger, cool with a salty twist of curry leaf. Perfect.

Tarok served the meal the traditional way, in leaf platters – their moulded shape a small concession to modernity.

'Where were you? I was beginning to worry,' he frowned as he passed me my cornucopia. 'This is the kind of meal I love. No washing up!'

I made some answer, but he wasn't listening. He was staring at Lola and Mr Bajaj. 'Is she a friend of yours?' he asked casually.

'Yes.'

I would have hesitated yesterday.

'He's not a nice man. Perhaps you should tell her that.'

'She's between a rock and a hard place,' I said.

Alif Bey had interrupted them. He tried to drag Lola away. Hilla moved in quickly, to save the situation. I watched them walk away.

Ujwala Sane undulated up to Mr Bajaj.

Tarok drew in his breath sharply. He was still watching Mr Bajaj.

'Why did Chili say you were the messenger?' I blurted before I could stop myself.

'Chili said that? Strange! I was the messenger in her case. You know, I was the guy who brought the bad news. I told her the boyfriend was a married man.'

'Ouch! Still it's a strange way of putting it.'

'Let's hope it's not an augury. You know what happens to messengers.'

I laughed, but uneasily.

Once more I found myself with Mr Bajaj. I wondered vaguely

if he was pursuing me, and with what possible intent. Not a nice man, Tarok had said – how did he know?

'I was a close friend of Jimmy Driver,' Mr Bajaj began ponderously. 'His widow is my responsibility.'

That had my hackles rising. Not that he noticed.

'And now I find her in this giddy whirl of cooks and dancers! We're promised a gourmet cook and what do we get? Khichidi! Now we're promised Shiv Tandav in jazz. Can you tell me what to expect? I thought jazz was music, now it turns out to be dance.

'Mrs Sane!' he called out, 'Please tell us what is this tandav in jazz!'

Ujwala Sane, steaming leaf platter in hand, shrugged unwisely. Some mahabhog splattered a fat shiny thigh. She was dressed recklessly in black tights and an adherent pink blouse, and trailed a fringed silver stole. Mr Bajaj repeated his request and Ujwala shrugged again, streaking the stole this time.

'It is not possible,' she said equably. 'Shiv Tandav is only possible in Kathak.'

'There, you see! I asked Ujwala because she's an authority on dance,' Mr Bajaj beamed. 'You should talk to Hilla, Ujwala. Explain this point to her. Shiv Tandav, as you say, is Kathak, not jazz.'

'What I am saying ...'

Ujwala Sane's voice rose an octave. The hum of conversation retreated respectfully. She had got herself an audience.

'What I am saying is, how can a man called Rafiq Khan know about Shiv Tandav? He is Muslim, no? How he can understand? Meaning of Shiv Tandav is very deep. Hilla is very wrong to make him do Shiv Tandav when he is only dancing Michael Jackson. It is insult to Hindus.'

I laughed.

The sound of my laughter shocked me. It was contemptuous, derisive, mocking. It was loud. It shocked me, but it relieved the others whose faces had turned tense at Ujwala's outburst. People smiled and turned away. Mr Bajaj fled, deserting his authority on dance. Dr Sane looked murder at his wife. Alif Bey, apoplectic but wordless, poured himself another drink.

'What is so funny?' Ujwala asked me. 'I have been brought up very different from you. I am from good family. Very well known, very respectable, very orthodox. In my mother's house without bath we cannot step into the kitchen. Till today that is maintained.'

'So you won't be watching the dance?'

She shrugged moodily and drifted away for a refill.

'Dear Ujwala,' Hilla muttered in my ear. 'I'm waiting to see her face when Rafiq appears in a deerskin thong.'

At ten we trooped upstairs. Our voices died as we neared the terrace. The air had an edge to it, a chill that bit past the sullen swell of the impending storm. It was pitch dark, the moon lost in a wadding of thick cloud. The sea roared like a chained beast.

The terrace was lit with lanterns staggered across a clothesline. Four others were stationed on the floor as footlights.

Ramona, as mistress of ceremonies, led us gravely to our seats. The chairs were set well within the shelter of the roof's overhang, leaving the vast paved area as stage. My chair was set comfortably against Hilla's emergency weather-proofing, a pile of folded tarpaulin. The orange flicker of the lanterns fumed feebly against the smoky dark and I wondered how visible Rafiq's tandav would be.

Ramona stepped past the footlights and requested our kind attention, the ladies and gentlemen clapped and cheered and the show was on. She stammered a few hesitant words put together from Rafiq's explanation of the dance and left us completely mystified.

Ujwala Sane laughed.

Everybody clapped determinedly and Ramona escaped into darkness.

A low drumbeat in the distance. A hesitant footstep. Another. Then another. Each step defined by a muted carillon of bells. Not the jewelled notes of a dancer's anklets, but a muffled chime, low pitched, reverberant.

The drum changed pace. Higher now, sharper in short staccato bursts, always cut off at crescendo. The footsteps echoed it. Faster, faster.

And then with a swift explosion of taps and chimes, Rafiq blazed before us.

One moment there was nothing but the black night, featureless, heavy, inanimate. The next, a pillar of fire whirled up from the emptiness.

Rafiq rose from the spiral staircase in a fast pirouette, a red-gold blur growing in brightness as he entered the circle of light.

The children cried out, startled.

The glittering figure slowed, ceased its giddying whirl and became utterly still, giving us time to take in that stillness, that silence.

Rafiq's stance, immobile as a rock, threw into relief his magnificent torso. He wore – not, as Hilla predicted, a deerskin thong – but a body suit of gold tissue shot with red. In its flaming mesh his muscles seemed to flow as they clenched and rippled in a tense containment of force.

The heroic tilt of his shoulders had pushed his head into deepest shadow. He presented the startling illusion of a man beheaded. As we watched, his chest swelled and his ribs ceased their motion. Beneath their generous arch the cavern of his belly grew deeper and began to shake. It was a seismic lurch, saltatory, igniting muscle after muscle in his still frame. The pillars of his legs tautened as he rose on his toes, stance unaltered, breath still held, animated only by the convulsion within his flaming carapace. Higher, higher, till he seemed to levitate half absorbed by the dark as he rippled and flowed and pulsed without motion.

A faint susurrus grew around him, gaining in voices, in loudness till it sounded like the rattle of a million leaves. He was a tree shaken by the storm within. (I noticed then his ghungroo was not the usual broad belt of bells but a much more modest affair).

The sound peaked. Headless, he flamed into the night.

It was volcanic, it was spectacular and just as it seemed as if his straining shoulders would burst their glossy skin, his arms knifed the air in great arcs of fire as his hands too disappeared into the dark. At that instant the glad clatter of the dumroo clamoured its announcement:

Look, here I am! I have arrived!

Rafiq began a pirouette so fast and so dizzying that he was no more than a blur that flashed in and out of the weak pools of light. Just as abruptly he stopped, incredibly poised as Nataraja, elegant, fluid, contained in the precise geometry of a Chola bronze.

Was Rafiq dancing out a memory? The ancient universal memory of the body's speech? His face was a mask. His limbs, his trunk, his sinuous back, these were sentient, these were his expression.

Predictably, the music he had chosen was a song popular in Bharata Natyam recitals. Tall, airy, gracile, the notes of Vasanta rose expansively. I was utterly bewitched by the ease with which the panache of the raagam appropriated the antic pace of jazz. The heroic attitudes of the style gave the *sholl* a new caprice, and I found myself taken up by the nuance of each word as I followed the dance:

> *He danced in the halls of gold*
> *with great sophistication*
> *He danced the meaning of joy*
> *In memory, in antiquity*
> *in the far north, in Kailas,*
> *He promised the wise*
> *He promised this dance*
> *He did not fail them*

He came here to Tillai
In the spring, in the reign of Jupiter
In the morning light
He danced the meaning of joy …

Yes, it was memory he danced, the exuberance of a remembered instant of joy. His wild hair was a cataract. In a tremor of glitter, Ganga sprayed the air. His shoulders made a snake: from fingertip to fingertip his widespread span became a sinuous writhe. His neck rose like a cobra's and the slow circle of his head described the spread of the snake's hood.

Then everything – river, moon, snake – everything was hurled apart in a balletic leap that seemed to span the galaxy.

Now he was back, feet firmly on the ground as the music segued into a slower, graver beat, sinking in timbre, resonant with menace. He gathered himself once more into a tense pillar of energy. From utter board-like rigidity he turned abruptly resilient, going from one statuesque attitude to the next. It was like watching the more challenging yogic asanas done very fast. It was frightening, challenging the bounds of flexibility. He bristled with aggression. With each rigid geometric stance, he grew in menace.

The music became unnecessary, and of its own accord, stopped, upstaged by thunder. Lightning tore across the sky. We cowered against the wall. The lanterns went out except one that cast fantastic shadows, swinging wildly in the wind, striping the rain like a tiger.

The moon had broken past the clouds and a strange leaden light prevailed, goosepimpled with glittering rain.

He danced as if the raindrops were rapiers. He flinched, he slid, he parried. There was no dearth of sound now. The sea, the wet trees, the incessant rain, these were the elements of the dance. He was a shadow among other shadows caught up and tossed by the storm.

The rain thinned. The dance slowed till it matched the nagging drip of the clouds. Heavily, dragging like slush, like mud, the dance came to a halt.

With the sigh that is the supreme tribute to art, we came to life. There was some uncertain applause. We turned to each other, embarrassed, relieved to find our neighbours unchanged after the nakedness of the past hour. We pulled on our masks and disguises, getting our smiles stuck, our buttons mixed.

Ramona stepped forward with a long white object which she threw around Rafiq's neck. For one mad moment I thought it was a garland, but it was only a towel. Rafiq stepped across the footlights and looked at us brilliantly. His eyes sought out the cook.

'Now I eat,' he announced happily.

I had planned to go down to the kitchen and help Tarok clear up after his late supper, but as I stumbled indoors, I quite forgot about it. Everybody milled around the staircase. Rafiq had disappeared. A confused buzz of conversation broke out. Mainly, it was the weather they spoke about. It was almost as though the dance was a subject they had conspired to avoid. Lalli had walked on ahead. I could imagine her irritation at their inanities.

I felt bludgeoned. I had walked past my room before I noticed. Extricating myself from that snarl of comment and laughter, I returned to the corridor.

The tandav had left me in a curious state, too charged for either company or sleep. The muted lighting of the corridor was soothing. The empty passage, curtained now with gauzy rain, was a safe and private place to be. I stumbled in a pradakshina of the house, leery of those ghastly Buddhas that loomed up every now and then. I lingered, trying to listen to the murmurous sea, trying to look past the storm of unfurled thoughts that swirled like dust devils in my head.

I usually pace when disturbed and I paced now, till my legs ached. I wondered dimly where the rest had got to. At least a few of them should have passed me by now, intent on sleep or solitude, but nobody came. They were probably in the dining room, nibbling sandwiches. Incredible, the amount of food they could put away.

I must have been walking a good half hour when voices erupted.

Alif Bey thundering, roaring, raging up the stairs. He seemed to be dragging something behind him.

To my absolute horror, it was Lola.

She whimpered as she broke free and flung herself against the wall. They were soon locked in a violent struggle, black marionettes in a shadow play of hate. He was shouting all the while, vile words mixed with animal sounds.

'You and your cheap shoes!'

There was a stunned silence from the rest of the house.

He said it again, tauntingly. She hurled herself at him and hammered his head with her shoes, the silver heels flashed as she struck him repeatedly till he fell away from her with a howl of rage. He stumbled past me, incoherent with fury.

I wondered if I ought to go to Lola, but decided it would only embarrass her. I went silently to my room.

The night hung heavy and oppressive. The room was hazy with heat for it had turned still all of a sudden. I threw open the door to the terrace. That eased me a little. I sat at the window, with not even the wind for company.

At length I grew tired and fell into bed.

I woke startled, certain I was being watched.

It was the moon, a leaden presence at the window. The sea's grumble had quickened to an augury. Everything seemed to beat with the rhythm of the tandav. The torque of moonlight swept its beacon across the wheeling clouds. The agitated sea leapt and towered. All the air seemed gathered up by the caprice of the invisible dancer and his hidden feet.

The day behind me lost its meaning, meaningless too, the hours ahead.

Then everything scattered, everything stilled with a woman's laugh.

A lascivious laugh, teasing, intimate.

It was answered, as it has been since the beginning of Time, by earnest male murmuring.

Two people walked across the terrace with quick light steps.

It had stopped raining.

They stopped. They were very close to my door. The door had shut to, banged by the wind. It might just as well swing open again.

She laughed again, this time, imperiously.

It was Lola.

She said: 'No.'

The man's voice rose and fell, placatory, exculpatory, caressing. The words subsumed in emotion.

Again Lola said, 'No.' Sharply, with a ring of authority.

The man laughed.

Their voices murmured back and forth as they retreated from the door. A cough, quickly suppressed. Lola's probably. And then, silence.

I was in a turmoil of guilt. Tomorrow I would tell Hilla I'd take any room but this one, even the kitchen would do. Particularly, the kitchen. I was just sick of living in this laundry where none of the linen being aired was even mine.

Now why would Alif Bey and Lola want to steal into my ambit for a bit of verbal foreplay? They were a tiresome couple, really! After coming close to murdering each other on the stairs an hour ago, listen to them now! Enough sex to keep the planet twirling.

Somehow the interlude eased my dread. Things returned to their banal perspective. But I couldn't sleep.

It was a little past two o'clock. I went back to the window and curled up in its deep cool sill, watching the sea. I must have dozed off then, because my watch said half past when I woke stiff and aching, still in my foetal crouch on the sill.

I might have been dreaming yet, for as I stared out at the murky night, a dark figure detached itself from the shadows and crossed the moonlit drive. Before I could wonder who it was, it was gone.

I needed sleep. As I crawled into bed, I heard footsteps again – slow heavy footsteps – crossing the terrace making a purposive stride towards my door. I held my breath. The footsteps stopped just outside the door. Someone nudged the door open. I cowered, trembling. Then the door was pulled to, gently, but effectively.

The feet moved away. The intruder was gone.

I burrowed deep in the bedclothes and lay wide awake till dawn.

At first light, as I expected she would, Lalli came out on the terrace to watch the sea. I joined her silently and stayed till I felt at peace again. I don't know how, but she always manages to do that for me.

I discovered this quite by accident one evening some months ago. I was still getting my messy life sorted out. I was out of work, love, money and, I was growing grimly certain, out of skill as well. Nothing I wrote read well.

I was – well, you get the picture.

I blundered about the house restlessly. Lalli, as usual at that hour, was reading on the beige sofa. I don't know what made me sit down. She never looked up once from her book. She never said a word. But after a while the storm quietened within me. Heck, there were still a lot of things left to live for.

This morning I didn't tell her about my nocturnal adventure – or rather, Lola's and Alif Bey's. Lalli would have looked mildly censorious. She might even have thought me prurient. She's a stickler for privacy when it comes to relationships. So I shut up.

At home we would each be nursing a mug of hot coffee at this hour. It was too early to expect the cook. My head ached, and also, unaccountably, my heart.

In the pale wash of morning, the terrace seemed an unlikely stage for a tandav. Perhaps I had imagined it all, the flickering lights, the fierce elemental dance. Surely the disquiet I felt, the angry dissatisfaction that prickled like a rash, surely that was all the fall-out of a long complicated nightmare.

'They'll be a rough lot this morning,' Lalli said. 'Rafiq's tandav may have unleashed more than he bargained for.'

9

It was a disgruntled bunch that met for breakfast. The rain had stopped, but there was nothing cheery about the weather, with clouds hanging low like sodden grey flannel. Hilla was in a tizzy because it was Tulsabai's day to clean and do the washing and her son had phoned to say she was down with a fever.

The domestic arrangements at Ardeshir Villa were something of a mystery so far. The place seemed to clean itself. Now I learned Tulsabai, Framroze's treasure, had cleaned the house on Thursday and given Hilla's guests forty-eight hours to wreck the place before she moved in again. Hilla said she lived near Malad station, about five miles away. That seemed the standard distance for all Framroze's human contacts, an actual measure of his arm's length. The only companion he'd tolerated was the sea.

Now that Tulsa had signed in sick, Hilla had the mad plan of packing us off on a picnic while she scrubbed and scoured to get the place in gear for Ramona's dinner. I shouted her down. The house was sparkling, we hadn't done that much damage yet. The dining room could easily be spruced up by evening. Only then did I think of the mountain of dishes that must have piled up in the kitchen sink after last night. Hilla laughed at my fears.

'Tarok cooks with one hand, cleans up with the other.'

'My virtues grow every minute,' Tarok said modestly, putting down my royal blue mug. 'Try this. Brazilian Blue Mountain. Hilla, we have a crisis.'

Hilla threw up her hands in protest, 'Not Sanebai again!'

But it was. Ujwala Sane had announced that she was not in the mood for crepes. Worse, she had shouted that out from her window, prefacing it with, 'Aik re kartya!' Forgetting that the average footpathia has a vast vocabulary of insult. More, she had pursued his vanishing back and hollered down the stairwell for idlidosasambar.

'I told her, very politely, there was no such dish. I'm sorry, Hilla, if she can't respect a dish enough to know its name, she doesn't deserve to eat it. Besides, I can't conjure the batter in an hour. I don't do instant *anything*.'

I remembered then it was the 'breakfast of your choice' morning, and requests had been handed in yesterday (mine, imaginatively, was 'anything'). Tarok and Hilla walked off to the kitchen to conspire.

The dining room was gloomy this morning. The sconced lights, switched on to relieve the murky morning, gave the place a throb of desolation. It felt like the waiting room of a large railway station. Or perhaps it was just my growing discomfort that I recognized with surprise as homesickness.

I wanted out. I wanted to be back, not in the house where I'd spent thirty of my years, but at 44 Utkrusha, now unequivocally home.

I shook off my megrims by amusing myself with the spectacle of Dr Sane at meat.

'I asked for English breakfast,' he said between mouthfuls. 'And everything, everything is absolutely correct.'

Felix, who looked pale and shuddery this morning, walked up and bravely inspected the remnants of the feast.

'Tarok missed out the kedgeree,' he said. Felix was not eating. He was not a breakfast person, he said. On his good days he had orange juice. Today, clearly, was not.

We strolled to the table by the window. I remembered my first breakfast in Ardeshir Villa. Everything had been different yesterday. Felix seemed in a kind of trance over Dr Sane's breakfast: 'Four eggs, two rashers, two grilled tomatoes, porridge, a stack of buttered toast, marmalade, coffee and do you realize it's just half past eight!'

'Think of the inside of his stomach,' I said with intent cruelty.

Felix turned mauve and fled. Framroze, with great forethought, had installed bathrooms close at hand.

Felix returned, wearing a look that told me he'd never trust me again.

'I shall put you in my next book,' he promised with venom.

'*Bloodstains at Breakfast* ?'

Of course he fell for that. He turned it over in his mind.

'I like that. I might use it. I can never tell till the last moment of course, but hey, thanks!' He grinned, his humour restored. 'Where's Chili?'

'Still asleep.'

I'd knocked on her door lightly, unwilling to wake her. Half past eight is an ungodly hour when you haven't slept in a week.

Ramona came in looking for Hilla. She made desperate signals at me. I abandoned Felix and went over.

'I need a laxative,' she whispered. 'Oh God oh God what do I do if there isn't one in the house.'

She seemed to be in acute anguish, wringing and twisting her hands. Her eyes had a hunted look.

'I have to go at least six times and without a laxative I can only go once,' she groaned.

I wondered if I should trust my ears. I asked, 'Why must you go six times?'

'Oh!' she was enraged at my stupidity. 'What kind of shape will I be in a sari if I don't go six times!'

Apparently, she was planning to wear a sari for tonight's revels and everybody, but everybody had to swallow a laxative before they could dare wear a sari, didn't I know that?

There was no point refuting her. I lacked credibility, at thirty-three having crossed the point of no return.

'Luckily we can't wear jeans to college or we'd all OD on laxatives,' she said.

'Can't wear jeans? Why not?'

She shrugged, 'Navel police. *Weird.*'

Totally.

She drifted away on her quest.

There was no sign of Lola, but across the room, Alif Bey glowered over a whisky sour, his choice of breakfast.

Rafiq came in wheeling a trolley. He parked at my table and gravely began to unload his breakfast. There were bowls of fruit. Cereal. A glass of some murky fluid and another of milk.

'Fitness breakfast,' he explained. 'Ghas-poos.'

Finally, with a look of hope, he placed a covered dish in the centre.

'When Tarok asked me what breakfast, I said fitness to be on the safe side. You know all Breach Candy is having imported poha and becoming beautiful and healthy from two three cardboard boxes only. Then this Tarok does not leave me. But are you liking poha, he is asking, you are liking ghas-poos? What can I say? So he makes for me one keema paratha. This is the fault of this cook I tell you. He will squeeze you like a nimbu. And then he will tell the world about you, sweet or sour or bitter. That is not so bad. But he will tell *you*. That is dangerous.'

'Dangerous?'

'Word is wrong, maybe? Khatarnak.'

'No, dangerous is right, but why do you say that?'

'Because do not tickle sleeping dog. This is one English kahawat that is one hundred per cent correct.'

He fell on the fruit with dutiful vigour and had just begun on the paratha when Lalli joined us. She put down her plate with an exasperated gasp.

'How can I eat this! I asked for fruit, and see what he's given me. This is not breakfast, it's an installation.'

I saw what she meant. The jewelled creation on her plate couldn't possibly be consumed.

'Fruit bird,' said Rafiq. It was a Bird of Paradise, actually, but it sounded better his way.

'What's your paratha like Rafiq?' Lalli asked plaintively.

'Home-made. But see that cook's adaa. I also ask for fruit. I get papaya pieces in steel cup. Govandi style. You are getting fruit bird.'

'I am getting fruit bird because this is footpathia style. Where do you think he learnt this? Bali?'

Bali would have seemed a safe bet to me, but Lalli's words brought back a memory of the pavement fruit carts lining the city's commercial district at lunchtime. Pineapple, melon, papaya became abstract sculptures, Cubist still lifes. Sure, the fruit bird was totally footpathia.

'What is this green fruit with black dots? For you he has grown special fruit,' Rafiq persisted

Lalli broke off a kiwi wing and slid it onto Rafiq's plate. He grinned, happy as a kid.

Mr Bajaj glided past with a distant smile. He was carrying a glass of vivid green juice in one hand and a plate piled with what looked like grated carrot.

'One more fitness freak,' I told Rafiq.

'Who is this Bajaj?' Rafiq demanded. 'He comes to my room at night and makes proposition like I am some chaiwalla chokra. "I want to make this place disco," he says "You do disco every night, everything latest. Two-year contract." Then he says this is what Dr Hilla wants to do.'

Rafiq pushed away his plate, his eyes filling.

'I don't think that's Hilla's idea at all,' I said.

An entirely unqualified guess.

'I know it cannnot be,' Rafiq said. His mouth still trembled, his fists were clenched.

Lalli said, 'Don't try to understand it.'

'But...,' his hands rose in incomprehension. 'He watches Shiv Tandav and first reaction he has is make disco? You tell me how you felt after watching my dance. Was there not storm inside you? Is it not still inside you? You cannot help it, I cannot help it. It is the tandav, not you or me. But – to want to make disco! Even Peddar Road got more sense. Latest steps they also want, I'm not saying no. Teach me quick, they say, two-three filmy steps so that I am safe for partics. First I used to tell them, that is not dance, you cannot learn dance for the sake of parties, learn it right, I will teach you. I used to tell them that. Then after some time I also said okay, you want salsa, I give you filmy salsa, you want Michael Jackson, I give you Thriller. Question of sinful stomach. But till I met Mr Bajaj, I am not knowing *how* sinful.'

He moodily pushed away his paratha and began dismembering Lalli's fruit bird.

'I saw Uday Shankar dance the Shiv Tandav,' Lalli remarked. 'Of course I was only twelve then, but I remember it as if it were yesterday...'

Rafiq abandoned the remnants of the bird and covered both Lalli's hands with one of his. 'Tell me.'

I was definitely de trop.

I looked around for Lola, but there was no sign of her. Alif Bey still sulked in his corner. He was now drinking coffee and clearly disliking it.

Mrs Sane appeared, Felix in tow. I avoided her gaze and left to look in on Chili. Her door was locked. She certainly had a lot of sleep to catch up on. Ramona and the kids were practising in the studio. Rafiq had given them their parts, Ramona told me last evening. She was to be a raindrop.

I was still unsettled by the night's events. I wanted to be alone. I ran up the stairs to Framroze's eyrie.

The small circular room had its bay windows tightly closed, but sunlight fell like a benison on the blue and ivory tiles. The telescope didn't tempt me this morning. I opened the windows and let the wind take me. The sea raged, breaking in high spumes of foam. I turned away.

The thought of my interrupted hour last evening took me to the east window. Beneath me a filigree of branches, thin twigs jewelled with raindrops, hid the yard. The grassy declivity we had strolled down yesterday was flung like a cape of emerald satin over the shoulder of the hill. There was our little tiled dais. My little pool gleamed like a mirror in the sun. No, it didn't gleam – it flashed, a scintilla of brightness in the still film of water. Funny, that!

I shut the windows and left the eyrie.

I walked down that grassy slope to the site of our ill-fated tea party and stood once more at the edge of the pool.

The water lily, its neck snapped, floated limply. Something else bloomed in its place. Something that caught the sun and flashed its semaphore. It looked like a twig, sticking up just at the scummy surface of the pool.

It was not a twig. It was the heel of a silver, glitter-encrusted sandal.

It was Lola's shoe.

The memory of her hitting Alif Bey with those shoes returned with a chill. It was exactly the kind of malice I expected of him. To sneak off with those shoes when she was asleep and dump them in the pool. How he would gloat over her dismay when she found them missing! I could only spot this one, but I was certain the other shoe was here too, stuck deep in the muddy ooze.

Close encounters of the third kind with quarrels have made me extremely chary of relationships. Somehow the equation 'that's life' doesn't work for me. I can't batten down my horror or disgust. I've walked away from rows all my life. They're too messy. And here, on what was growing less like a fun weekend every minute, I seemed to have jumped into the thick of the mother of all rows. I walked away moodily, thinking a stroll along the beach might cheer me.

Just my luck, whom do I run into at the gate, but the perp in person.

Alif Bey was even more crumpled and bleary than he seemed at breakfast. All those whisky sours seemed to be catching up, for the man was in some sort of a funk – jittery and sweaty. Any sympathy his appearance may have provoked was rapidly dispelled by his question.

'Have you seen Lola? I can't find her anywhere.'

Too furious to reply, I shook my head and would have walked past, but he stopped me with a gesture.

'Please wait. I know I made a terrible scene last night – you were in the corridor, you saw us, everybody heard us, it was awful. I had too much to drink. It was unpardonable. I'm a nuisance and an embarrassment. But I wish you'd overlook that for just a moment and tell me if Lola spoke with you this morning? I passed out last night after that awful scene. When I woke this morning, she was gone. Nobody seems to have seen her today, so I suppose she was so angry, she left. Just walked out, leaving all her things, she hasn't even taken her bag. It's a trait of hers, to walk out. You seemed to be friends. I thought she might have said something.'

'She may have spoken with Hilla,' I said, much against my will.

'No. Nobody seems to know anything. I think she walked out in a fury. She's done that before.'

'You could call her.'

'She doesn't have a cellphone. She's – she's living with me now. That's the worst of it. I have the house keys, she won't be able to get in. I have no idea where she'd go.'

'You could try a friend's place, maybe? Later?'

His face crumpled with misery. Still, he was getting no sympathy from me.

'I'm sure she'll call Hilla later to explain.'

It was the best I could offer. He nodded and staggered off towards the beach.

Oh well. If the last twenty-four hours were anything to go by, she would be back in his kitchen cooking basmati by Monday morning.

Life brightened up almost immediately after I parted from Alif Bey. I bumped into Tarok. He dodged carefully, getting the large wicker basket he carried out of my way.

'Can't afford to tip it over,' he smiled. The basket reeked of the sea. He undid the catch and raised the lid for me to peek.

I did – and ducked hastily from a waving arsenal of claws. Lobsters!

'Six of 'em! A Corsican delicacy for tomorrow.'

'Where will you put them till tomorrow? In Mrs Sane's room?'

We laughed at the picture.

'Better not, she'd eat them whole,' Tarok said sobering. 'I pity those kids, they're real martyrs.'

'So's the husband.'

'Not him. Never him.'

Tarok's voice had turned stern.

'Wait till you hear my story.'

We carried the basket between us towards the house. Ardeshir Villa drowsed in a pleasant haze of rain-spattered sunshine.

'Tell me about the Corsican delicacy,' I said. I really didn't want to know. I just wanted to hear the sound of his voice.

Then the door opened and everybody burst out. Rafiq carried stumps, Darshan a cricket bat that was almost as tall as him. We watched them set up a game on the drive, Felix and Darshan batting. Lalli bowled, a slow ball, turning nicely, deflected by Darshan for a single. Just then Chili made her entrance.

There was immediate chaos.

Considering she was dressed in very terse shorts and a tie-on polka dotted blouse, the disturbance was not what I would call excessive. The shorts were of denim, not just distressed, but *in extremis*. Darshan gallantly gave her his bat. Felix developed a fatuous grin. Dr Sane offered Chili his faux sombrero and she accepted it with a mock bow that made Ujwala bark viciously at Arpita. Ujwala Sane then flounced out, a thing I had never seen done outside a book. Ramona hung back shyly and looked away. But Rafiq's response was the strangest of all. He turned dusky red and stared. Chili looked up, fluttered her fingers at him. He turned away abruptly.

While I was taking all this in, Tarok must have been watching me, for when I turned, there was a twinkle in his eye. He gave me a quick hug, over before I felt it. He grabbed the basket and we raced round the house to the kitchen, laughing.

My luck being what it is, I ran full tilt into Mr Bajaj who had materialized from the bushes. I regained my balance by grabbing a handy branch. I apologized. He handsomely said it was all his fault. We stood there grinning like idiots. It was all very embarrassing.

'What's over there?' I blurted, pointing at the bushes he'd erupted from.

He smiled, 'Short cut to the garage. I'm in a hurry, I forgot my car keys. I promised Hilla I'd pick up the flowers from the station.'

'Flowers?'

'For tonight's dinner. It is to be very grand, I hear. The florist is sending the flowers by train. I'm going to be late.'

'Oh, so that's where he kept the Rolls,' I said.

I hadn't spotted the garage earlier, and the absence of houseroom for the Rolls had mystified me.

'Yes. There are two garages, not one.'

'Oh, I'm sorry I'm holding you up,' I apologized. He nodded

and set off at a run towards the house. I was still pottering about when he returned, out of breath.

'Where is everybody?' he snapped. 'The phone has been ringing a long while, nobody around to pick it up. Finally, I had to. It was Lola Lavina – I was surprised! I thought she was still here with us, but no, apparently she had to leave early this morning because of a domestic crisis. Why didn't you let me know, I said, my Pajero is here only for such emergencies. No, no, she said, she hadn't wanted to bother anybody so early. She wanted to speak with Hilla, but I couldn't find her. Please tell Hilla she phoned.'

And away he sped. A few moments later I heard the roar of his humongous car.

I didn't blame Lola for making up that story. It was the best she could do to save face. I fought the impulse to let Alif Bey fester in his guilt a little longer, but then, what the heck.

The game of cricket had broken up. Ujwala Sane had grown a migraine and gone upstairs to nurse it. Her husband was in the kitchen with the cook. Rafiq, Ramona and the kids were back to pounding the parquet.

Chili and Lalli were in earnest conclave. I joined Hilla and Felix and delivered Lola's message. Hilla nodded grimly.

'I might have done the same in her place. It's so unfair. He should be the one to leave after that shameful exhibition last night.'

'Oh he's walking by himself on the beach,' Felix said. 'He'll get a new chapter out of it, I bet. With such a stormy love life, where does he find the time to write!'

He sounded envious.

'It's going to get a lot stormier if he has that lobster Tarok is planning for tomorrow,' I said.

'Ah yes, lobster.' Felix was relieved to be off shaky ground. 'A fricassee he said. Actually, I don't agree. That lobster will be a mayo.'

With that mysterious fiat, he took himself off.

'I feel awful about Lola,' I told Hilla. 'I wasn't particularly nice to her.'

'Rubbish. I suppose she told you that lurid tale about the lawyer? What utter nonsense, the whole story.'

Taken aback, I protested, 'Why, Hilla, I thought you were all for her!'

'Of course I am! In principle. But all that masala, waking up in a different room every time, oh come on! I've heard that story several times over and it's grown remarkably, I can tell you that. Of course she's a very courageous woman and deserves our respect. Don't tell Lalli I said that about Lola's stories. Lalli has a very high regard for her.'

'Oh no, she thinks Lola's tedious!'

'Sure. Who doesn't. But she does think very highly of Lola.'

Chili and Lalli joined us. Chili gave a cry of disappointment when she heard Lola had left.

'She came to my room to chat late last night after the dance. The dance was something, huh? She said it was, like amazing. She was all flushed and excited. Lola knows about this thing.' Chili gave a nod of intelligence in Lalli's direction. 'This thing I want to talk about? She said like maybe I should wait because she was going to check out the scene. So that's what I had to hear from her this morning. You know because I really think I'd better tell you, but only after I've spoken with Lola. Oh I hope she's back in time for the party!'

'I doubt it,' Hilla said

'Oh that's impossible! She's got to be here. She even wanted to borrow a T-shirt for the party.'

'A *T-shirt*?'

'Sure. I know it's formal and all that, but she said like hey what can't you do with a glitter pen. So I'm all for it, you know.'

'What are you wearing tonight Chili?' Lalli asked.

Chili brightened, 'Oh, would you like to see it?'

Of course we would. We trooped upstairs after her.

She took a swathe of silk from the cupboard and with a complete lack of self-consciousness, stripped off her blouse and shorts and pulled on the dress.

Hilla whistled.

My heart sank. It was all up for poor little Ramona. The moment Chili sashayed in wearing this confection, nobody would spare Ramona a glance.

Lalli said, 'Rami Kashou.'

At first I thought that was an aborted sneeze, but evidently not as Chili squealed in pleasure.

'How did you know! I got it in LA and only because I did a shoot there. I could never afford it!'

The scoop-necked blouse of ivory silk fell in sculpted folds over a fitted skirt of magnolia that seemed oiled on to her. It fanned out in tiny pleats when she moved.

Lalli looked almost as pleased as Chili. I had discovered during the Tie and Die affair, what a fashion junkie my aunt was. When she's in the mood she can talk Suzie Menkes off her Prada feet.

You wouldn't guess, would you? I mean, look at her life: sari, jeans, salwar kameez. But her mind – that's pure Versace.

Chili also showed us the T-shirt Lola had optioned. It was black with VAGINA WARRIOR blazoned in fluorescent pink.

'My friend did the play, you know, the *Monologues*?' Chili paused delicately. 'I promised her I'd wear the T-shirt and all, but somehow …'

'Just as well,' said Hilla.

So we went down to lunch.

A slate had been strung up on the dining room door. Rice Plate is Ready, it said. Today's lunch, Hilla said with a hint of apology, was Bombay Special.

Looped around the vast length of the dining table was a sprawling railway track. I don't know if Tarok's topography was accurate, but the stations along both Western and Harbour Lines were. I've never been very sure about the Central Line.

Each station had a dish from its local cuisine. Kandivli got me khandvi and Dombivli avial. For starters I had sol kadi from Mahim and for dessert lagan nu custard from Churchgate which is as close as the line got to Colaba. It was great fun. The children – for whom Tarok had planned the meal – squealed and whooped, but we adults were not far behind. Everybody milled around sampling and exclaiming.

To make my happiness complete, Tarok ate with me. I would have delighted in the food if we hadn't been so busy delighting in each other.

Neither Mr Bajaj nor Alif Bey had returned. I think that took some tension off the meal. Mr Bajaj would have sneered and Alif Bey would have drunk himself into a stupor.

After lunch, Hilla, Lalli and I got down to work, getting things organized for the dinner. Mrs Sane developed one of her sudden migraines. Chili said she was awfully good with cleaning, so between the two of us we had the room sparkling while Lalli and Hilla fussed over china and silver. Tarok looked in once at about four o'clock to warn us that he would be busy from then on and if we wanted tea, now was the time to ask for it.

We were drinking Family Mixture Number Eleven when Rafiq arrived to fix the chandelier. He almost ran when he saw Chili, but recovered his nerve and did a neat job of hoisting the huge central chandelier.

Venetian, Hilla said. Framroze had three of them carefully packed and labelled, all of Murano glass. This one, a veritable snowdrift of flowers, was Canaletto. The architect, clearly a woman of sense, hadn't permitted Hilla to sell it. But she had sold the other two. 'Too dramatic for my tastes,' Hilla said. 'One was a dark bronze. That was Othello and the other, naturally, Desdemona. You should've seen that one, all half-blown roses, half woken, I should say. When I put them next to each other, it was enough to break my heart.'

I felt a stab of pain for Framroze, and unaccountably angry towards Hilla. Who was to say Framroze had lived unmoved within the throb of so much beauty? Hilla handled all his treasures with a grim contempt that was very close to vengeance. She had reason enough. Of Framroze's greed there was little trace left, but his ache for beauty was palpable in the chill stone of the house, in the clench of its shuttered heart. I realized the empty shell I'd seen in August was what Framroze had wanted its inheritors to see. Its true life had long been squirelled away. These stored fragments were mere props in the lost epic of his solitude.

Chili helped Rafiq in tense silence.

Rafiq told Hilla as he was leaving, 'I've asked Ramona to get some rest. She is very nervous.'

'It's the sari,' Hilla explained. 'She's scared she'll trip.'

'She told me. Glide, I told her, glide like a swan. All ladies glide in sari. Very simple. Like this.'

And he glided gracefully to the door.

We laughed. Chili looked after him bemused.

'Would you believe I actually *know* this guy? We used to meet at the bus stop when we were in school. Every single day from fifth standard to tenth. Now he doesn't recognize me.'

'Really? It seemed to me that he knew you very well,' Lalli said.

'He's just shy,' Hilla added.

She was wrong. Any fool could see that Rafiq was fatally smitten.

Chili shook her head miserably.

'It's all those stories about me that get around. All that old stuff. I wish Lola would come back. I can't tell you anything till she says it's okay. I kinda promised.'

'Take your time,' Lalli said. 'I'm around.'

But Chili's happy mood was gone. It was as though the encounter with Rafiq had jolted her back into the reality of her misery. In a while she said maybe she ought to get some rest, but could Ramona use some help later with make-up and stuff? She was good at that kind of thing.

'That would be wonderful,' Hilla said, relieved. 'I can't imagine why she's in such a state of nerves. It isn't as if there are boys to worry over! Can you imagine kids in her class swallow laxatives to show off a sexy waistline in a sari?'

Chili laughed.

'That's an old trick. It's worse these days because you have to show your navel in everything you wear!'

Soon after Chili left for one more of her compulsive naps, we heard Mr Bajaj's truck approach. Alif Bey was with him. Apparently, he had stopped Mr Bajaj on the beach road and hitched a ride. Everything seemed to have conspired to delay Mr Bajaj, but eventually when they got to the station, the flowers hadn't arrived. The florist was at Dadar, and after several phone calls he admitted he was short-staffed and the earliest he could deliver was at five o'clock. They had decided to wait right there, growing hungrier every minute, instead of making a second trip. Finally, at four o'clock they had succumbed to vada pao.

Mr Bajaj must have blown a blood vessel when he discovered Alif Bey was not going anywhere, he just wanted a ride. I suspected, from Mr Bajaj's truculence, Alif Bey had talked (or wept) all the way and back. I began to feel sorry for Mr Bajaj. Alif Bey was still in the van, waiting for help to unload the flowers, so could we please oblige. Mr Bajaj said he wanted to put the car in the garage and then shower and rest and get some peace and quiet. It had been a hell of a day.

'I seem to upset everybody,' Alif Bey said. Nobody refuted that. I was about to tell him about Lola's phone call, when I thought

Mr Bajaj must have at some point, if only to break the tedium of Alif Bey's monologue. But he hadn't. Hilla mentioned it now, and Alif Bey looked absurdly relieved.

'That's all sorted out then,' he said, giving me a hearty handshake as if we had just signed a political detente.

'The man is mad,' Hilla said when we were finally rid of him. I couldn't agree more. I was tired and irritated, and after being scratched by the small jungle Hilla had imported, in sore need of a shower.

We had one more visitor that afternoon.

A tempo sputtered uphill bringing Hilla's mother's portrait from the framer's. Hilla had the picture put in the library and was in there for a while. Later, I found she had put it face to the wall, as though the moment had been too much for her to take.

10

At eight, excited and resplendent, we gathered in the vestibule. Banks of flowers led the way to the dining room. The long table was draped with snowy linen edged with exquisite lace. Hilla said Tarok was miffed over using Framroze's table linen for tonight. He had thought it would be more in keeping with tomorrow's elaborate Continental lunch. For tonight he had chosen an armful of weaves, one from each part of the country, appropriate to the period of the dish. But Hilla had insisted on Framroze's stuff: it just made more sense to her. Sensibly, Tarok hadn't cluttered the table with flowers and candles. There was a centrepiece, again vintage Framroze. A long silver tray with a mirror that held a central urn (just right for ancestral ashes) and two subsidiary cornucopias. All three held a plenitude of fruit.

We were thirteen (not counting Tarok) but the table was set for fifteen. There were place cards, except for the two set at the head and foot of the table. While getting the room ready, I had shuddered at the cutlery Tarok had massed on a small table.

'That's for tomorrow,' he explained. 'The classic table setting with separate forks and knives for fish and salad and pasta. Idiotic! Tonight I want us to eat with our fingers like civilized people, but Hilla must have silver! So I've agreed to one knife, one fork, one spoon per head. No more.'

I sympathized with Tarok. I hate it too, when the table looks like a surgical trolley.

The chandelier shed an opalescent radiance and there were candles set among ferns and flowers to rescue the far corners from gloom.

A tremor of misgiving had quite corrupted my thrill when Hilla, in inviting us, had specified *Dress: formal*.

When it comes to dressing for a party, I take my cue from Vidal Sassoon. It's *lava y pronto* for me. One day, come the Manolo Blahnik phase, my face will be a palette for Revlon, but till then, it's plain skin. For tonight I'd packed my amethyst crepe with a silky skein of silver for border. The blouse was just a blouse. A dab of *Paris*, and I was done.

Lalli, as always, was elegant. She wore the bronze silk, with my burnt orange dupatta making a statement round her neck. Hilla was in a sari, draped in the Parsi fashion, fastened with a large, rather ugly cameo brooch. The rich crimson silk gave her an air of magnificence.

Ujwala Sane appeared in a webby black chiffon sari and a black and silver bustier with spaghetti straps. Between sari and blouse rolled miles of milky flab. In her belly button she had, incredibly, stuck a diamante bindi. The men revived immediately. Alif Bey stopped scanning the room for a drink. Felix Rego marched up bravely and took charge of her, sparkly navel and all. And Mr Bajaj, with disarming frankness, examined her every inch.

Rafiq and Tarok were both missing. Alif Bey won my vote for sartorial excess. He had formalized his basic couture of kurta-pyjama in permanently creased cotton by adding a bright Tibetan scarf, obviously Lola's. Felix had ruffles on his shirt, and a black velvet waistcoat. Dr Sane suffered in a safari suit two sizes too small for him. Mr Bajaj wore a charcoal suit that was very nearly Armani.

So there we were, all dressed up, waiting for the star of the show. And here she came now, down the grand staircase, Ramona transformed.

Oh yes, she glided. Quite easily, too, in an exquisite sea green silk sari with an antique embroidered border I could have killed for. The sari was pinned at her left shoulder with a sunburst of diamonds and aquamarine. Her hair, coiffed elegantly in a froth of curls, was held up with a crescent of aquamarines to match her necklace and bracelet. Clearly, Hilla hadn't sold *all* the jewels. With her new importance, Ramona had gained a sweet gravity very different from her usual madcap grace. She was skilfully made up, Chili had worked marvels. I was glad Ramona got her two minutes of admiration before Chili knocked 'em dead.

And then, you know, Chili didn't!

She was there all along, trailing behind Ramona with the kids. To begin with she wasn't wearing the Rami Kashou thing but a green salwar kameez. The famous hair had been disciplined into a French pleat. Even the eyes and the dimples failed to dazzle. As she hung back, searching our faces anxiously, she looked pale and drawn. She looked, in a word, exactly like the girl Rafiq had known at the bus stop.

He seemed to think so too. For as he entered with Tarok, he stopped short as he set sight on her and brightened visibly. Tarok, behind him, looked around his shoulder and mimed a wolf-whistle at me.

And so we gathered, excited, happy, chattering at the prospect of glutting on three thousand years of subcontinental greed.

At either end of the table, Tarok had placed flowers on the plate liners. Hilla made a small speech welcoming us to Ardeshir Villa, restored at last to its rightful owners, her parents Ardeshir and Nargis Vakil. In a few unemotional words, she recounted their lives of deprivation and misery.

'They are present today in spirit, as the young couple I never knew, joyous and full of hope. I want this house to be like the home they would have wanted, resounding with laughter, enjoyment and good company. You, my friends, have some idea of the plans I have for this place. I have not yet made my decision. Yesterday we watched Rafiq's magnificent tandav and tomorrow the cook will meet Felix Rego's challenge by serving a formidable seven-course lunch. But tonight, in honour of my niece Ramona who turns eighteen next week, Tarok Ghosh presents his Millennial Banquet. Ladies and gentlemen, I give you – Tarok Ghosh!'

Everybody clapped and cheered. Darshan thumped the table and had to be stopped. Tarok swept the room with that 'seeing' look. Quite without reason my heart gave a lurch. What if the Millennial Banquet bombed?

I mean, there's something called a neurotic goal, let's face it. Three thousand years of Indian gluttony, for godssake! That's roughly 3,285,000 square miles of food. Why couldn't he be content with the usual roghan josh, paneer matar, two-flavours-of ice cream?

I knew why.

I think it was at that precise moment, just before he began to speak, that I realized what should have been clear to me from the start. Tarok had no place in my careful constructs of romance and fantasy. He was never going to be my luxury, my indulgence, my dare. He was daily wear. I needed him like water, like air.

And turning, he read the thought in my eyes.

Somebody coughed.

Tarok smiled.

'Three thousand years of Indian cuisine cannot be talked about. But it can be savoured. Bon appetit!'

He poised a tray of aperitifs in the air as he said, 'Oh by the way, anybody who thinks my history isn't on par with my cooking can see me in the kitchen afterwards. We can wrestle the point. Loser does the washing up!'

The aperitifs were pomegranate nectar and rice wine, both labelled Indus Valley, 2500 BC. Alif Bey was served punch (Calcutta, 1638).

With them Tarok served small tender chunks of bitter-gourd stuffed with tangy mango and fenugreek (from Chandragupta Maurya's Patliputra, 305 BC). 'You forgot to put chilli in this,' Ujwala Sane announced. 'Red chilli is a must. Without red chilli, stuffed karela cannot be made.'

'We were out of red chillis in 300 BC,' Tarok said

'Why? Ancestors are always using chilli. It is ancient Indian condiment. In pujas also. To remove nazar. It is tradition.'

'But not alas, history. I will not argue the point, madam, as that will leave you doing the washing-up.'

Tarok held aloft a covered dish.

'The Greeks, ladies and gentlemen, visited us in 327 BC. I don't have a dish in their honour because the menu's too crowded. But I couldn't entirely ignore them. And so I introduce you to what the Greeks considered a high art – deipnosophy!'

'If you invite us to dinner, please let us eat,' Mr Bajaj said. 'Food first. Art afterwards.'

Unperturbed, Tarok continued: 'The art of dinner table conversation, deipnosophy, isn't necessarily a Greek skill. Good food is enhanced by wit, warmth and generosity. And knowing that, I have prepared a surprise for each of you. As you each uncover your surprise, you'll find it has a special meaning for you. Taste it first, and tell us what it means to you! So, as the appetizers do their good work, we shall make this hour truly convivial. You will find the portions small, mere nibbles, so that your appetite isn't blunted for the main course. Let's start with our gracious hostess. Hilla, this is for you.'

Hilla uncovered her dish. On it was a single khakhra with a glistening red chunk of mango pickle. She shut her eyes as she tasted it, as if to seal in the taste or the memory. Then she smiled brilliantly through her sudden tears.

'Although Tarok labels this – atrociously – as Sanjan 8 AD, this is my mother's famous gor-keri. The exact taste, the same racy sting to it, the same sweetness. Year after year when my mother made this pickle, we were never allowed to help. The recipe was too subtle, she said, we'd never get it right. My mother didn't need to do this for a living after we kids were grown up and earning, but of course we couldn't stop her. One summer, she was ill. I found her worn out with anxiety about her customers. They were expecting a year's supply of gor-keri and here she was too ill to move. The next day when I visited her, I found this gangly teenager measuring and sifting and mixing in her kitchen, following her instructions for gor-keri. Naturally, I wanted to throttle the kid! "Let him be," Mamma said. "The boy knows how to do it."

'After that, we got used to seeing this kid around. We were a little jealous. But once we tasted the pickle, there was no further argument.

'The scent brings back the feel of my mother's hands. I can feel them now, rough, calloused with work, patting my cheek as if I were a little girl again. Get the bottle, Tarok, let everybody have a taste.'

He had it ready, of course. After it had done the round, Felix and Dr Sane had a guessing match over the ingredients, and Tarok refereed.

Both lost.

Hilla said, 'My mother's portrait was delivered too late for us to hang it here today. I've put it in the library. But I'd like it on the wall here. Tomorrow I don't want Tarok distracted – so could I appeal to you strong men to do that job for me?'

'I will be personally responsible,' Mr Bajaj announced. 'Give me hammer, nails and twine.'

'There's a nail in place already,' Tarok smiled. 'The cord and scissors are always kept on the pantry shelf, so it's all yours.'

Alif Bey's surprise came next, in a small silver cup. He stirred it and looked up with a laugh.

'An abecedarian offering! Alphabet soup! People have been trying to get this story out of me for years now. Where did you hear it?'

Tarok shrugged off the question.

Alif Bey, his peevish ill-humour quite banished, emptied his cup rapidly before beginning his story.

'Labelled Simla, 1890 – how Kiplingesque of you, Mr Ghosh! I label it Poona, 1950, though! It takes me back to my horrid childhood. I had a British nanny, a regular battleaxe. She didn't believe in giving Indian children Indian food. Heated our blood, she said. So day after day I swallowed bland slithery stuff. I never dared ask what it was. On Saturdays we had alphabet soup. It was the only dish I could bear to eat. I was about nine then, and I used to write stories in a secret book. This nanny was always the villain. The hero, of course, was me, but I gave him a different name. Alpha Bet. It had pictures of the nanny, horrible pictures with a beard and other embarrassments. She found the book and I was charged forthwith. My defence was simple. I didn't write it, I said. I pointed to the title on the book's cover *The Adventures of Alpha Bet* by Alpha Bet Himself. After that it became a habit. I could never own up to anything I'd written. So when it came to my first book, the pseudonym was an easy choice: Alif Bey.

'But I must say, Tarok, if Nanny had served your brand of alphabet soup I might never have written at all! And Felix, this is not a story I want to read on Page 3. I command you to forget it immediately!'

But Felix by this time, was entranced by his own surprise. It was a single fig, placed on a bed of what looked like frothy pink snow. Felix flushed with pleasure as he tore the fig across and ate it, delicately spooning the snow afterwards.

'Tarok has labelled this as Cream of Figs, Raziya Sultana, AD1236. The cream is – was – delicious, but the fig was meant for me. Or rather the leaf that should have come with the fruit. Tarok, thank you. *The Missing Fig Leaf* was my first story in print. It got a Silver Bloodstain, you know. Gave my work a terrific boost.'

'What exactly is a silver bloodstain?' Lalli stepped delicately into the awed silence.

'Oh. It's an award. A prize. For detective fiction.'

'Never heard of it,' Mr Bajaj said. He turned to me, 'Have you?'

'Oh yes,' I lied, out of sheer spite.

'And what was the story about?' Lalli persisted with dangerous naivete.

'About a famous statue. It's called the David. It's by Michael Angelo. It's in Florence, Italy.'

'And?'

Lalli was relentless.

'The fig leaf goes missing!'

I glanced cautiously at Tarok. He was shaking with suppressed mirth.

'What are you talking Felix, the David has no fig leaf! It's the first thing you notice, and you don't have to go to Florence to do that!' Hilla said.

But Felix was unfazed.

'Exactly. It goes missing right in the middle of a high security political meeting. The book's set during the Cold War.'

'I'm sure it's terribly exciting,' Lalli said soothingly.

'Indians are not using fig leaves,' Ujwala Sane declared.

'That's why it's missing,' Alif Bey said. He was enjoying this immensely.

She took no notice of him.

'Curry leaves, dhaniya, pudina we are using. Methi also. But not fig leaves. I have not seen single Indian with a fig leaf.'

'Neither have I madam,' Tarok said with perfect gravity. 'Now may I present your surprise?'

She eagerly uncovered the dish and gave a little scream of pleasure.

'Bombay duck with green chutney! My favourite! How did you know?'

'It's from Mahikavati, circa 1260. Or should I say – Silvassa 1988?'

Ujwala Sane stared at him, her large face collapsing in ashen folds.

'I can't eat this, it's too salty. Take it away!'

And she gave the dish a petulant push, upsetting a glass of water.

Tarok made no attempt to mop up. He had disappeared into the kitchen and now returned with an omelette he placed before Rafiq.

'French food,' they said together and laughed at some private joke.

'Pondicherry, 1750.' Rafiq read the slip that Tarok had placed on his plate.

'I don't know why Pondicherry. But I know why omlet. I was in France one full year, all that time only French people's food. Very nice people. Very bad food. My stomach is aching all the time for daal chawal. Then one day suddenly beautiful girl living downstairs gives me omlet-pau. So you learn Indian food, I tell her, this is very nice. I am thinking maybe this one also knows keema paratha, daal chawal. This is French food, she says. Excuse me, I say, not to argue, omlet getting cold, but come to Govandi and you get double omlet bun maska chai in Star of India Cafe from morning six a.m. to night midnight and you are saying this is not Indian? French, she says and takes away the omlet, talking very fast French, saying I have insulted her food.

'Now Tarok tells me tomorrow is French food. "Bas karo," I told him. "Make me one omlet-pau and I will eat in studio." Then he upsets me. I thought he was my friend. Now I find out he is the same as that French girl. He also says omlet-pau is French. But this time I hope the omlet does not go away.'

When we had done laughing Chili asked, 'What happened to the girl?'

'What girl? Who girl?' Rafiq's eyes sparkled wickedly.

'That beautiful French girl.'

'Nobody like that. No beautiful girls in France.'

Ramona got a chocolate truffle that Tarok blamed on the Dutch (Coromandel, 1790). That brought up the story of a schoolgirl prank on April 1.

Chili got a solitary potato chip that Tarok said was Portuguese (Goa, 1700).

Chili laughed and said last year when she was fat she used to carry a single chip in a lunch box on shoots, and everybody thought that was way out.

'Now I've got more sense,' she declared. 'My eleven o'clock vitamin pill does the trick. Tarok that's what you should have given me! A vitamin pill. One capsule at eleven a.m. and I'm charged for the day! That's one thing I never fail to do, come what may.'

'I'll argue over that capsule later Chili,' Hilla called out. 'But you'll have to prove to me that you've got more sense now by eating a hearty dinner.'

Then it was Dr Sane's turn. Tarok brought his dish steaming to the table.

'Shorshe maach. Fish in mustard sauce, Siraj-ud-Daulah's kitchen, 1756.'

Dr Sane sampled it.

'Is this all you made?' he asked piteously.

Tarok smiled.

'There's plenty for everyone. It's on the main menu. But what do you think of it?'

'Superb!'

'Thank you. I value your opinion. As you know the soul of the dish, its heartbeat so to say, is the sting of mustard in the sauce. Nothing but the finest mustard oil will do. And Dr Sane, ladies and gentlemen, is a connoisseur of mustard oil. He is famous as one of the foremost authorities on the subject. By merely glancing at a sample of oil he can deduce its purity. In tribute to his skills I have used, alas merely the best oil I could find. I wish, Dr Sane, I could have used that very grade of oil on which I once heard you pass judgement.'

Dr Sane had set out to weakly protest during this long speech, but gave up very soon. He merely blinked stupidly at us.

'Wouldn't you like to tell us something about your experience, Dr Sane?' Tarok paused delicately.

'No, no, nothing! Thank you very much!' Dr Sane said feebly.

'Mad,' Ujwala said. 'We are never using mustard oil.'

'As you wish. But Arpita and Darshan will not get away so easy. Here you are, then!'

'Yuck! Boiled eggs!' wailed Darshan. 'I hate boiled eggs!'

They did look disappointing – two plain eggs sitting in fat white crockery cups.

'Take it away!' Ujwala snarled. 'You don't have to eat it, Darshan.'

'Oh I'm going to eat it,' Darshan the Brave said. 'It's my Special. Thanks, Tarok Uncle.'

Arpita watched as he cracked the top of his egg.

Darshan's face broke into a grin. 'You fooled me! It's ice cream! Arpita, break yours fast, it'll melt!'

Hers was chocolate and his was strawberry.

'It's not ordinary ice cream is it, Tarok?' Darshan appealed.

'It's not even ice cream. It's a bombe.'

'A bomb! Cool!'

The kids were enchanted.

Tarok, as expected, cited this as French, Chandernagore, 1710.

'No story, Arpita?' Felix asked. But their delight was story enough. It took away the unpleasant edge of their mother's malice.

Not quite, though.

'Too bad Lola could not stay for this dinner, Hilla,' Ujwala Sane raised her voice. 'I am sure she would have given us some chatpata story, really spicy. Or maybe she left because she was afraid her story would come out?'

Unexpectedly, Chili said, 'Lola has nothing to hide, unlike some people at this table.'

Tarok put a calming hand on her shoulder and bent down to whisper something in her ear. She smiled uneasily and nodded.

'And now for Mr Bajaj. A dish straight out of Chengiz Khan's urt. The Mongols were connoisseurs of horse flesh. They not only rode their horses, but ate them with relish. Steak tartare, Mr Bajaj, is as ancient as Chengiz Khan. But for you, I chose something more recent. Between 1630 and 1632, the country was in the grip of a famine. Historians tell of sudden feasts following days of starvation. Many of these feasts were impromptu affairs, cooked off highways frequented by unsuspecting travellers. This recipe is from that time.'

Tarok's presentation of steak tartare would have seemed a tad fussy to the Mongol hordes. The neat pat of red meat was crowned with a raw egg on the half shell, and fenced around with small piles of diced and grated vegetables.

Mr Bajaj didn't turn a hair at Tarok's grisly introduction. He laughed and practically *breathed* in that steak.

'The story!' Felix prompted.

'Too many racing stories to choose from,' Mr Bajaj protested. 'After dinner, perhaps.'

I was distracted then, by Tarok placing a plate before me. It held just one murukk.

'Inspired by Kannagi's anklet,' Tarok said. 'Silappadikaram, AD 8. Let's break it and see if it spills pearls.'

He broke it and took half. I laughed and ate the other.

And because Ujwala Sane's blank look told me she didn't know Kannagi's story, I chose to tell that tale.

As usual, the men were all for Kannagi and the women all looked sceptical except Ujwala Sane who said, 'The story reminds me today is Saturday. Normally I don't eat dinner on Saturday. Only fast food.'

'Pizza?' enquired Tarok. 'A burger perhaps, or pau bhaji?'

She froze him with a look.

'*Fast* food. No rice. Sabudana vada, like that.'

An appreciative murmur spurred her on.

'On Saturdays, no rice. On Thursdays no chillis. On Monday and Tuesday no sweet or salt. Wednesdays and Thursdays, full diet.'

'And what are all these fasts for, Ujwala?' Hilla asked.

'For my husband.'

Dr Sane protested loudly at this, but she quelled him remorselessly.

'No, he is not allowing, but still I fast, so that in my next birth also I am married to him only.'

Ramona giggled and choked on her glass of water.

Tarok said, 'While Ramona recovers, I take a moment to prepare the last, and to me, the most important surprise of the evening.'

He returned with a silver plate which he placed ceremonially before Lalli. A spectrum of badam leaves was fanned across it, red, gold and bright green. Nestled in the centre was a glistening pat of halwa, crowned incredibly with a small gold coin. I was seated across the table from Lalli, and the luxury of aroma almost made me swoon. A silky waft of ghee, a subtle current of saffron and then the abrupt slide into a deep plenitude of almonds, smooth, voluptuous, very nearly narcotic. I inhaled deeply. Tarok paused in the act of offering Lalli a small silver spoon on a salver to acknowledge the compliment with a grave bow.

Lalli took a spoonful of halwa and shut her eyes.

'Incredible!'

'From the court of Harihara I, Vijayanagar, 1336. But I should say more correctly – in memory of a certain encounter in 1976.'

'But that had nothing to do with almonds!' Lalli protested.

'True, but I found out about you through the Crawford Market case.'

Lalli laughed.

'That was before your time, Felix, or you would have grabbed that title for a book! You know what the Hindi papers called it – *Badami badnaami!*'

'And while everybody has a taste of the halwa, please tell us about 1976.'

Lalli paused.

'Are you sure?' she asked Tarok.

'Of course.'

'Very well, then, 1976 it is. One rainy afternoon in Arthur Road Jail waiting to question a suspect, I was distracted by a brawl. When I walked in there was this skinny fifteen-year-old punching a big tough guy, and what's more, he knocked him down before my surprised eyes. I was impressed by the kid's determination, though his fighting technique left much to be desired.

'The man on the floor was an old quarry of ours, a habitual offender, booked for assault. He had been terrorizing an old man picked up for vagrancy when the kid intervened. I didn't know then what the boy was in jail for, but I found out he was one of a bunch of Bangladeshi lads who worked as polishers for a jeweller in Kalbadevi. The jeweller reported a robbery, a bag of gold coins was missing – and these boys were arrested as natural culprits. That enraged me. I looked into the matter. It was an insurance fraud, as I suspected. The boys were innocent.

'Five years later a young man came to meet me. He was working with a caterer in Matunga. He said he had something to give me. It was this coin. I recognized it before I recognized the young man. The coin came from that jeweller's horde. And this was the kid I had met in jail. I could not accept the coin then, Tarok, but I do so now, with pride. Thank you, Tarok.'

'So!' Ujwala Sane sang out her triumph. 'He completely fooled you, eh? All along he was the thief.'

'What nonsense you talk, Ujwala,' her husband said uncomfortably.

'Nonsense? Very good sense I think. More sense than this lady has here. He had the coin with him. That's proof! Hilla, count your spoons, your cook is a clever thief! '

'Really, Ujwala,' Lalli sighed. 'You have a very strange mind. That young man hoarded I don't know how many months of salary to buy this coin off that rascally jeweller.'

'Four months, to be precise. By then I had graduated from washing dishes to chopping and grinding.'

'So you see, Ujwala, it is impossible to set a value on this coin. One can only treasure it.'

'Tell us about the badami badnaami,' Felix ventured bravely into the dangerous silence.

'Oh Felix, you know I never discuss murder! This was a small epidemic of cyanide poisoning. The victims, all unconnected, had one trait in common. They were all health food freaks. I won't go into details, but the trail led me to almonds.'

'Really? You can get poisoned by almonds? Almonds have cyanide in them?' Chili asked.

'Nonsense,' Ujwala said with satisfaction. 'Listen to me Chili, if you are looking for foolproof cyanide, better use rat poison next time. You will have happy and successful suicide. Hilla has very good rat poison, for big rats, land rats, bandicoots, so should be enough for a little girl like you. You will find it in a red plastic mug on the top shelf of the cupboard beneath the stairs. Ask Hilla. Am I right, Hilla? Isn't that cyanide?'

'Rat poison's never a cyanide compound,' her husband said incautiously. 'It's usually an anticoagulant, like warfarin.'

'No, Ujwala is right,' Hilla said, surprising me. 'I was telling her about how dangerous it was to keep it lying around. It's sodium cyanide granules. When the drive was being built, lots of burrows were opened up and the place was overrun by rats. I almost dumped the house and ran. The pest control fellows did a wonderful job. They dissolved the granules and pumped the liquid into the burrows. They insisted I keep the rest in the house in case we have a second attack.'

'So Chili, don't waste any more time,' Ujwala Sane trilled richly at her own joke. 'Take a dose of cyanide instead of your eleven o'clock vitamin pill and feel the difference!'

There were a few half-hearted laughs.

Chili smiled with strained politeness and turned with gratitude to Rafiq who was amusing Arpita and Darshan by balancing a lemon on a twirling knife.

Ujwala Sane had grabbed the coin from Lalli.

'It's not even half tola,' she said with contempt.

Rafiq leaned across the table, took a badam leaf from Lalli's plate, parcelled the coin in it and returned it gravely to Lalli.

'Better you hide it,' he said. 'Simply by looking at it this lady has made it lighter. Already it is half tola. If she keeps it any longer, it may turn into brass!'

Tarok led the laughter, but my own feelings were not so easily sublimated. He sensed that and moved around to my side of the table, stationing himself behind my chair as he introduced the main menu.

'And now, ladies and gentlemen, let the feast begin!'

Menu

Aperitifs

POMEGRANATE NECTAR: Harappa 2500 BCE
Pomegranate juice sweetened with champak honey.

RICE WINE: Harappa 2500 BCE
A sweet wine, with a bouquet reminescent of hot steamed rice.

PUNCH: Calcutta, 1638
From Albert de Mendeslo's recipe for 'palepuntz'

Bitters

KARVELLAMRUTAM: Pataliputra, 305 BCE
Karela stuffed with mango and methi.

Starters

RESHAM KABAB: Awadh, 1765
Kabab of chicken mince

KHAMAN DHOKLA: Kathiawar, 1560
Leavened channa dal, steamed and garnished.

BOMBAY DUCK: Mahikavati, 1265
Crisped bombil fish

AMMINI KOZHAKATTAI: Tirunelveli, 1465
Tiny dumplings served on a bed of spicy dal.

MADDUR VADAI: Mysore, 1800
A crisp, flat racy vadai

MAKHMALI SHORBA: Delhi, 1645
Mutton broth with pine-nuts and walnuts

ANASI PAZHA RASAM: Madras, 1850
Pineapple Rasam

SOL KADI: South Konkan, 1660
Coconut milk with kokum

➤ *Relish* ➤

PEACH CHAAT: Delhi, 1857
Peaches teased with spice

PULI INJI: Palakkad, 1780
Ginger, sweet and sour.

KACHUMBER: Bombay, 1900
Cucumber salad

BOONDI RAITA: Varanasi, 1700
Crisp boondi in dahi.

➤ *Main Course* ➤

Rice

Steamed Rice
Food of the gods

NAVRATTAN PILAU: Fatehpur Sikri, 1590
Rice bejewelled with fruit and vegetables.

TANDLACHI ROTI: Savantwadi, 1560
Rice flour roti

BISI BELE HULIYANNA: Mysore, 1700
Spicy meld of rice, dal, vegetables

Wheat

HALEEM: Golconda, 1676
Spicy meld of wheat, lamb and barley

ALU PARATHA: Amritsar, 1628
Flaky paratha stuffed with spiced potato

GODUMAI RAVA PONGAL: Coimbattur, 1800
Fragrant meld of bulgar wheat and moong daal

Meat

SALI NE JARDALOO MA GOS: Navsari, 1800
Mutton flavoured with apricot and garnished with potato straws

NARGISI KOFTA: Awadh, 1765
Kofta of minced mutton and hard-boiled egg

TABAK MAAZ: Kashmir, 1622
Ribs

Bird

MURGH MUSSALLAM: Delhi, 1632
Chicken stuffed whole

AGRA BATTAKH PASANDA: Agra, 1628
Duck with cream sauce

PURA KICHILI PAZHAM MILAGU VARAVAL: Nagapattinam, 1776
Pigeon with orange sauce.

Fish

SHORSHE MAACH: Calcutta, 1756
Fish in mustard sauce

FISH RECHEADO: Goa, 1560
Stuffed pomfret

SHEVANDA MOILEE: Kozhikode, 1510
Lobster in coconut sauce

Vegetables

KADAMBAM: Madurai, 800 BCE
Medley of sauteed vegetables

ALU POSTO: Calcutta, 1900
Potato flavoured with poppyseed

SARSON KA SAAG: Punjab, 1800
Mustard greens

Vegetable Palette

Daal

OSAMO: Baroda, 1800
Sweet and sour toovar daal

RAJMA: Ludhiana, 1947
Spicy beans

THAYIR VADAI: Madras, 1900
Urad dal vadai in seasoned curd sauce.

⊷ *Mithai* ⊷

Sweets are old as Time, constantly innovated
and transcend all regional boundaries.

Rice

Vel Avil
Rice flakes with jaggery and cardamom

Wheat (whole)

Halwa

Maida

Mallika Pasandi
Choux pastry filled with cream and almonds

Coconut
Narkel naru
Crisp coconut candy

Fruit / Root
Gajjar halwa
Carrot, cooked in cream and ghee

Elai adai
Steamed rice dumplings with a filling of jackfruit

Sitaphal ice cream
Custard apple, cream, sugar. No additives.

Besan
Pateesa, Mysore pak, Mohan thaal

Nuts
Kaju katli: Cashew
Badam halwa: Almonds
Chikki: Ground nuts

Milk
Rossogolla, Aflatoon, Paal poli

⇥ Chef's Special ⇤

Main Dish
Rui maacher kaliya served with Shokti Ghor chaal
Dhaka, 6th September, 1971
Curry of rui fish served with steamed rice,

Dessert
Ishrat ul firdaus, Cheesecake

12

Tarok's menu didn't follow the usual pattern. Instead, he had grouped the dishes according to content. The ornate Edwardian script was the only concession to artifice: for the rest, the explanations were concise and brutal. I did not, for instance, find pasanda described as filet mignon, or kachumber as salsa.

'Soup must be served first,' Ujwala Sane said loudly. She had eaten the Bombay Duck after all – Tarok had discreetly placed a second dish within her reach. Now she was digging into the small pots of pickle, sniffing spoonfuls and dropping them back disdainfully, untasted. 'You should have given us soup before kebab.'

Mr Bajaj, who had taken out silver-framed spectacles to scrutinize the menu, said with disbelief, 'There is no soup!'

Tarok smiled. 'Soup is an invention of indisciplined nations. Its purpose is to buy respect for the cook. To moderate unseemly gobbling and bolting. To silence the stomach so that the tongue might taste. With our historic discipline of starvation and want, we Indians know how to respect food. We don't need soup.'

'I disagree,' Felix said, 'We do have soups, traditional soups. What about shorba? Rasam?'

'Have you seen how they're served at home, Felix? Never as soups. Shorba is enjoyed as gravy. Yakhni as a nourishing broth.

Rasam is served between courses to reawaken the palate and recharge appetite. Flavour is everything. In texture it is delicate, even ephemeral. Serving shorba or rasam as a soup is a restaurant convention. It has no domestic precedent. But you'll have both shorba and rasam tonight.'

(The shorba was a silky meld with walnuts and pinenuts, very subtle. The rasam, served in expertly made leaf donnai, was garnished with a fine dice of pineapple that spun a sugary skein within its fiery heart.)

'I thought pickles and chutneys had the job of getting your tastebuds to concentrate,' Hilla said. 'And I notice you have miniscule amounts of those on the table. Why? Usually there are dozens to choose from.'

'Only if the cook lacks conviction. Personally, I'm offended when anybody asks for condiments at my table!' Tarok said. Ujwala Sane stared at him and upturned a pot of pickle on her plate.

Tarok served her resham kebab almost immediately. Predictably, she didn't touch the pickle. The khaman dhokla lacked the choky rasp of Eno's fruitsalts, inevitable in these days of instant cuisine. Maddur vadai, remembered as a platform delight on some childhood railway journey, was crisper than the station version.

'You must indulge me a little further,' Tarok said as he brought in the rice dishes. 'Beneath the menu each of you will find an envelope with your name on it. Please wait till the end of the meal to open it. It contains a prediction. Quite unlike a fortune cookie, this is my guess at the dishes each of you preferred.'

'That is too much,' Rafiq protested, 'how can you guess? I haven't heard of half the dishes on this, even I don't know what I'll like.'

'Ah, but I do,' Tarok said. Smug, wasn't he.

'Plain rice. Where's the history in that?' Mr Bajaj asked with some disdain.

'Really,' murmured Alif Bey. 'There's more history in a grain of rice than in all the battlefields in the country!'

'For each of us, history begins with memory,' Tarok said. His voice had turned tense and angry. 'Each little surprise I prepared for you told its history through what it triggered in your memory. You, Mr Bajaj, had steak tartare because of the label you wear in my memory …'

'Race horses, horse flesh,' Felix said sagely.

'Perhaps,' Tarok shrugged. 'Rice is where my memory begins. When I was planning this meal, I chose each dish from a family cookbook. I was almost through when I realized that unless I included the only home-cooked meal I remember, this meal would not be complete. I give you my taste of home, the last Sunday lunch I enjoyed with my family in Dhaka. Rui macher kaliya with Shokti Ghor chaal.'

It was simple and delicious, but it carried the taste of tears.

'Your navrattan pulao belongs in a jeweller's window,' Hilla said, 'Really Tarok, it's too pretty to eat.'

'Navrattan pulao is not a domestic dish,' Tarok confessed.

'It is only vegetable pulao,' Ujwala Sane shrugged, 'nothing great. And tandlachi roti we are getting in village. Too bland.'

'Try the bisi bele,' her husband suggested.

There were three rice dishes with three of wheat as complement. Ujwala Sane declared bisi bele and haleem were the same dish.

'The flavours are different,' Chili argued.

Mrs Sane was not taking that from a mere kid. 'What you know?' she said. 'You ever been in kitchen, miss?'

Everybody started talking suddenly.

Tarok brought in colourful bowls of vegetables. 'Flavour is a chancy thing,' he remarked. 'When we talk about masala, we confess to total sensory confusion. Masala is a word I abhor. Incidentally, it has no place in the lexicon of cooking. I'd like you to sample these vegetables. Each dish is cooked with one distinctive flavouring. The spice stays two paces behind the flavour of the vegetable itself. Felix, you first.'

There was cabbage with a hint of cumin, cauliflower with fennel. Potatoes nutty with sesame. Apple with ginger. Brinjal with ajwain. Green moong with cinnamon and urad with clove. Onions with, well, just onions. 'Only sugar,' Tarok smiled as I was puzzling that out. He took the bowls away from me with determination.

After a while everybody fell silent. Tarok's face cleared. He helped Darshan with his fish and slipped a puranpoli into Arpita's plate when her mother wasn't looking.

'Everything's wonderful Tarok, but we must have some place left for dessert,' Hilla protested. 'What are you giving us?'

'In Switzerland we are having Tiramisu,' Ujwala said, 'after that no other dessert for me. There are no Indian desserts.'

'I beg to differ,' Tarok said, 'and so, I hope, will all of you a few minutes from now when I bring in the dessert trolley.'

'Oh, a trolley full of dessert,' Darshan jumped.

'More puranpoli,' Ujwala scoffed

But there was more than that. 'I've chosen sweets that best convey the richness and subtlety of their ingredients. Again, I have avoided sweets with flavouring.'

'You haven't flavoured the ghee in the cooking either,' Felix frowned. 'You can't have Mughlai cuisine without flavouring the ghee with cardamom.'

'True. That's because the Mughal cooks were not skilled in making ghee. They never could, and still can't get the water out completely in the process. That leaves a rancid tang in the asli ghee sold by halwais. Without the cardamom their ghee has no character. To know the aroma of real ghee, try their three besan sweets: each is different and yet each is the same, an amalgam of besan, sugar and ghee. Pateesa, mohan thal and mysore pak.'

~ 150 ~

Of the three, mohan thal is kindest on the cook's abilities. Pateesa is seldom attempted except by the most experienced. Even with discerning confectioners, a brute chunk of brick often passes for mysore pak. All three golden cubes Tarok put on my plate melted in the mouth.

'This is too soft to be a balushahi,' Felix frowned as he bit into what looked like a ball of pale gold fluff.

'It's had a gender change. This is Mallika Pasandi,' Tarok grinned.

'Definitely,' Dr Sane agreed. 'Inside is pure mawa.' Ujwala made a rude noise.

While we were all marvelling and exclaiming, Tarok brought in the piece-de-resistance. 'My own invention,' he said, echoing the White Knight. 'Cheesecake is called the most voluptuous of all sweets. But I call this Ishrat-ul-firdaus, the pleasures of paradise. Tell me if you agree.'

I did. So did everybody else except Mrs Sane and her kids who wanted something sweeter. Felix and Rafiq pounded the table in applause. Tarok flushed and bowed and slid another slice into my plate. It *was* cheesecake, but with complications, as Hilla said. It had a tender fringe of vermicelli over a topping of thick unsweetened cream subtly stained with saffron. The cake was luscious and moist and the biscuit base crunchy with walnut.

Eventually, even Dr Sane finished and we tore open our envelopes. There were cries of surprise and outrage. We read our lists aloud, dismayed to have so much of our tastes revealed. My list read: peach chaat, assorted vegetables, ammini kozhakattai, nargisi kofta, tandlachi roti, pateesa, Ishrat-ul-firdaus. It was uncanny.

Ramona and the kids mobbed Tarok, and we gave him a standing ovation. He acknowledged that with a wave and fled to the kitchen.

Rafiq and I cleared while Tarok ate his usual spartan dinner of rice and vegetables. Rafiq jived his way between the dining table and the sink, whistling all the while. He twirled on tiptoe, balancing plates. He picked up lemons from the fridge and juggled them expertly as he tap-danced.

Tarok watched him with amusement.

'So no pretty girls in France, eh?'

'Not even one!'

'And all Indian girls are pretty?'

'No, no. Only one. Only one beautiful girl in mera Bharat mahan. Okay, maybe two. Definitely two.'

And before I knew it, I was whirled in a tango across the kitchen.

'Watch Tarok getting ready for big fight with me afterwards,' he whispered as he leaned over me, swung me around and all but hurled me from him as he ran out of the kitchen.

It was exhilarating, even if it wasn't Rafiq I wanted to tango with. Tarok, dinner abandoned, caught me just as Rafiq let me go. If had been giddy from the dance, I was giddier still in the next five minutes. As kisses go, ours was an aperitif, light, tender, yet racy with promise. But as he drew back, his eyes were troubled.

'Why did you do that?' I blurted.

He flinched as though I'd slapped him. I had to clarify then.

'I meant what you did at dinner. Why did you bait them like that?'

'*Bait* them?'

'Oh didn't you? The mustard oil connoisseur didn't know where to look.'

'Ah, that.'

'Yes that. And you baited Alif Bey too, but he took it in good humour, and Felix too, though he's too dumb to understand.'

'And you? I baited you too?'

'Yes, you did! You baited every one of us.'

'Did you mind?'

'Of course I didn't! But I might have, if I'd had something to hide.'

'My point, exactly.'

'So people shouldn't have secrets?'

'Not shameful ones.'

'But why winkle them out?'

Rafiq asked from the door, 'Fighting already? You need umpire?'

'She says people should not have secrets. She thinks people's secrets are their own business,' Tarok said.

Rafiq shrugged.

'Sometimes. Sometimes not. Depends on happy or unhappy. If I am sad about French girl's omlet, it must be secret. No hurt, no secret. You, Tarok, want to find painful secret.'

Tarok made a face.

'Life's such a minefield. It helps to know when the ground's going to explode.'

That was lousy logic.

'How does somebody else's secret hurt you?' I demanded.

'I don't know. I just like the truth to be plain. I don't want to know people's secrets. I just want them to know that I'm not taken in by their pretences.'

'Like if you're a cook, call yourself a cook, not a chef?'

'Exactly.'

We glared at each other, sworn enemies.

Clearly, I'd crossed a line.

In the aftermath of a kiss, the landscape's an Impressionist blur. Evidently, it wasn't, for him. Lines were still clearly visible. My heart sank an inch or so, but I kept on bloodymindedly. I was too far gone to stop now.

My words were all wrong. I wanted to say he'd been dazzling and deeply troubling. I blinked at him miserably, not knowing what to say.

His face cleared. He touched my cheek, and all my misery went out of me.

Rafiq the umpire said, 'Tarok does not like to be made fool. I agree. I also do not like to be made fool. But difference between us is, when someone makes me fool, I wait. Time comes when I also make him fool. Bas, it is finished, we are equal. But you, Tarok, when somebody is making fool, you are hitting dindora. Actually, it is not even necessary they are making fool of you. You are against each and every ullu.'

'Then what's your advice?' Tarok demanded with more curiosity than truculence.

Rafiq threw up his hands helplessly.

'What I can say? What I am doing with tandav, you are doing with dinner – but not, I hope, inside stomach. We are artists. In Paris I am learning this: the purpose of art is to disturb. To make thorns in the heart. What then the heart does is not our concern. Enough for us if it can feel the thorn.' He turned thoughtful. 'You know, I am feeling very bad for that Lola lady. Such a life, first that husband, then that lawyer, now this drunk. And nobody, nobody, is her friend. But still she feels the thorns in her heart, and is not frightened of other people's laughing. I am thinking that is courage. What was her surprise, Tarok? Maybe you did not make?'

'Oh I made one, all right. I thought she might just return for dinner. Here.'

He took from the fridge an artfully carved cucumber.

'I was planning to serve it with a mint dressing. I saw her interviewed on TV once. The anchor asked what her message to suffering women was, and she said, "Keep your cool. No matter what, keep your cool."'

I thought of that while clearing the flowers from the dining room later. We had decided to put them out in the verandah where the fresh air might keep them better overnight. When I was moving a particularly plumy fern, something bright caught my eye. It was

Lola's Alexander Calder earring. It had probably dropped off during the scuffle she had with Alif Bey last night, and had been swept up by a trailing branch of fern when the pots were placed here. Chili wasn't such a dab hand at cleaning if she hadn't spotted that earring!

Lola would miss it. There was something pitiful about the way she'd jettisoned her vanities as if to unburden herself for flight.

Tarok came in to help and I showed him the earring. He frowned and put it back gently on the fern where it swung forlornly like a forgotten Christmas ornament.

Very soon the kitchen became a crowded place. Hilla and Dr Sane, and even, fleetingly, Mr Bajaj, on his way, apparently, to the bathroom. Lalli, being energetically badgered by Felix. Alif Bey looking thirstily for a drink. Everybody was loud and congratulatory. There wasn't the remotest shade of reproach. Over their exclaiming heads, Tarok met my eye with an ironic twinkle.

I couldn't understand it. I couldn't understand it at all.

I did what I usually do when baffled. I walked away.

As I walked into the darkened vestibule, I almost ran into Chili. She was standing with her back to the wall, absolutely still. I was reminded of a prairie dog, every hair alert, intent on what the air carried in its waft. She held up a hand either in greeting or avoidance. I mirrored the gesture and walked past.

I was too restless to read. I sat at the desk and began writing. This isn't a tranquillizing exercise. We scribomaniacs don't ever write away our demons. We merely transfer them to a different plane.

I got down to my moneyspinner, and was soon bogged down with the miseries of Lulu who seemed to be having a goofier week than usual.

And then, somewhere down the page, I found Lulu's anxieties were being answered in Tarok's voice.

'... I just don't know what to do!' wailed Lulu, her customary cant every one hundred words or so.

~ 155 ~

'Get a good night's sleep,' said Tarok.

Of course he wasn't saying that to Lulu.

The darn door was ajar again and I was back to eavesdropping.

Then, in a neat reversal of roles, Tarok spoke the words made famous by every simpering ingenue in the book.

'This is so sudden,' he said. 'You must give me more time.'

I felt as foolish as Lulu.

His voice was low, pleading. 'Please.'

'Promise me you won't let me down.' This was Chili. 'I've been let down once and I'm not going to take it a second time.'

'I promise.'

'Promise forever and ever.'

'I won't ever let you down.'

'Why can't we tell everybody right now?' she demanded. 'Why can't we yell it from the rooftops? Is it something to be ashamed of?'

'I beg of you, Chili, please give me time.'

Oh, he wasn't impatient at all. Not one spark of friction between them. Obviously, there were no lines Chili couldn't cross.

'But why can't we tell Hilla now? Only Hilla. Please. Please please please.'

'No. I don't want to cause more hurt than I actually have to. I need time.'

'Okay, okay. Just asking. Have it your way. Okay.'

They were silent.

Did he kiss her?

I didn't know.

I had to know.

I didn't want to know.

My heart buzzed between my ears like a heavy duty electric saw, my mouth burned.

Before I realized I had pushed open the door and stepped out on the terrace.

Chili was gone.

Tarok stood at the balustrade, staring at the sea. He did not turn around.

But somewhere in the deep shadows of the eaves, I heard breaths that matched mine. Light, quick, tense.

Whatever had transpired between Chili and Tarok, there was someone besides me who cared.

13

After a night which felt like Dali's Raphaelesque *Exploding Head*, I fell asleep at dawn. It was way past eight when I woke to a cacophony that sounded like Khar fish market at noon. It was, in fact, a one-woman production.

By the time I'd showered and dressed, the ranting had subsided to a grumble. I dragged myself downstairs and ran full tilt into Hilla who was sitting on the landing, face buried in her hands.

'Hilla! What's the matter?'

'Didn't you hear? La Sane wants me to fire the cook. Either he goes or she does.'

'Nobody's going anywhere today,' Lalli called from the head of the stairs. 'We're marooned – or hadn't you noticed?'

I hadn't, actually. Surprisingly, neither had Hilla. The rain hadn't let up since last night. Its thunderous downpour was a mere patter though, against the more ominous rumble of the sea. Steady as a heartbeat, it pounded the air as if some gigantic invisible beast stood crouched over us. The oculus, so bright an ornament on the wall, now glinted malevolent as a glass eye. All that I could see from the window was a thick grey curtain of water, and the cataract from the waterspout on the roof.

We ran to the verandah for a view of the sea. Presently the rain thinned and we could see further. The sea advanced on us like a moving wall of cement, heavy, impenetrable. It had engulfed the rocks completely. The beach road was now submarine territory. The lower reaches of the road up the hillock were barely visible as the sea lashed and drew back in a froth of frustration, baffled by the steep rise of the hillock. Ardeshir Villa was afloat, washed up on Ararat with its hold full of complaining animals, none of them comfortably two-ey two-ey.

To the east, the village was completely cut off. There was water as far as the eye could see, a great big dim cracking mirror of water.

Even as we watched, the curtain of water drew thicker and closer, till all we could see was a blurry haze.

'We have food, running water, electricity, enough tantrums to keep us amused till help arrives,' Hilla shrugged.

Lalli said, 'The phone must be dead by now. Who has a cellphone? Besides Mr Bajaj?'

Nobody, apparently. Hilla had left hers behind. Neither Lalli nor I owned one, and the Sanes, Hilla said, hadn't brought theirs. Everybody seemed to have looked at this weekend as a total getaway. That left Chili, Rafiq, Tarok and Felix. I knew neither Tarok nor Rafiq had one. Chili had thrown hers from the autorickshaw on the way here to keep from calling her ex. Felix might have one built into his body parts, he looked the sort. Alif Bey was probably unaware of the invention.

Lalli nodded at my inventory.

'Then we're truly cut off from civilization, and we shall get as brutish as we please.'

Which seemed, really, a strange thing to say.

The shouting began again, with Ujwala Sane's voice rising in hysterical fury. Before we could duck, she had descended on us.

'So what are you going to do Hilla? Will the cook leave or must we?'

'The weather doesn't permit anybody to leave this morning. You couldn't even swim your way back into town. It's too dangerous. What is the problem, Ujwala? Surely we can find some solution.'

'It's that bloody cook. He knocks on my door when I'm fast asleep, barges in before I can get up, bangs down a tray, pours some stuff over a plate and sets a match to it! "It's half past eight precisely," he says. "Madam, your crepes are served!" Can you believe it?'

I could, though my surge of glee was abruptly flattened by the memory of last night's events. But she wasn't done yet.

'Why wake me up in the middle of the night? I asked, and you know he back-answered me! "I have to get breakfast ready. I can't keep everybody waiting for the sake of your whims." To talk to me like that! A cook! *Oh*.'

'Don't eat it,' Hilla soothed. 'I'll take it back to the kitchen and get you a boiled egg instead.'

'I don't want a boiled egg! I won't eat a morsel cooked by that man, I'm warning you!'

Dr Sane joined us, looking uncomfortable. He had a towel knotted around his generous paunch and half his face was covered with lurid lime green froth.

'Why don't you let me shave in peace?' he grumbled at his wife. 'Fuss, fuss all the time. I've eaten the stuff, it was growing cold anyway.'

'Come along downstairs, we'll find some hot coffee,' I offered.

But Ujwala shook that off impatiently and stormed back into the room, shutting the door on her husband. It was difficult not to smile.

Hilla, the practical one, advised him to get in through the children's room and said she'd send up a tray later. He went in looking grim.

'What am I going to do with the lot of them?' Hilla wailed. 'There's Alif Bey in the room next to mine, groaning with a hangover. I can't step out into the corridor without being ambushed by Mr Bajaj and his documents. Dr Sane will begin his act as soon as his wife has a lucid interval. And God knows what tamasha she will think up next. And the cook …'

She pointed an accusing finger at me.

'*Your* cook, is in a fine state of nerves because Felix Rego's asked him to change the menu for lunch.'

'Felix can't do that!'

'It's a challenge or some such nonsense. These men behave like ten-year-olds. *Now* what?'

Ramona came tearing round the corner looking like ten furies.

'I slapped him!' she announced, a saint proclaiming martyrdom.

'Hurrah. All of them need slapping. Which one was this?'

'Alif Bey.'

'Good-oh. I can boot him out into the rain. Hands off my niece and all that.'

'Oh no, Hilla Aunty!' Ramona was horrified. 'It wasn't like that at all. He's crying.'

'What!'

'Yeah. His heart is broken. It's really very sad, but when he put his arms round my neck and started sobbing, I threw him off. When he did it again, I slapped him hard.'

'He's drunk,' Hilla said in disgust. 'Honestly, it must be easier running a zoo!'

'Dr Hilla! One moment please!'

Mr Bajaj loomed large and silver, brandishing a sheaf of papers. Hilla gave a small scream and shamelessly decamped.

Lalli advanced bravely on Mr Bajaj.

'Hilla has a crisis in the kitchen. Have you had your tea? I noticed you don't drink coffee. I'm sure we could all do with a hot breakfast in weather like this!'

And with that calm persuasiveness I have so often envied, she led Mr Bajaj away.

I turned to sneak upstairs to Framroze's eyrie when Felix's door burst open and out he popped.

'What a woman! I heard it all. La Sane I mean,' he clarified hastily. 'Passionate, volcanic.'

'Erumpent.'

'Huh? You sure? Must look it up. *Eros Erumpent,* sounds great, actually. Thanks!'

'Any time. What's this I hear about changing the menu at the eleventh hour?'

'Ah, I forgot you were championing his cause.'

'I'm doing nothing of the sort. By the way, how come there was no oxalic acid spilt last night?'

'I was too busy taking in history to notice.'

'You must have got copy out of that.'

'You bet. And from Rafiq's dance the other night. The storm. Elemental forces churning. One blood red pane of glass skewered by a jagged fork of lightning. Silhouette or chimera? Next morning – a drying bloodstain.'

'So you've given up on Lalli?'

'Not at all! Was she really in the police?'

'I believe so.'

'Personally, I think it's a great idea. Social workers for sex offenders and dowry deaths and all. Leaves the cops free to concentrate on crime. Oh good morning Doctor! What a downpour we're having!'

Dr Sane, spruced for the day, announced, 'My wife has a migraine. She suffers terribly. I've asked her to lie down till lunch time.'

I left Felix to murmur his sympathy and ducked back into my room where I found Ramona holding my cadmium capris admiringly against herself in the mirror. Today she wore a yellow bandeau that pushed her frizzy hair into an auburn cascade.

'Try them on,' I suggested.

'Oh can I?' she peeled off her jeans joyfully and stepped into the capris. They were perfect on her. I gave her the shirt too, and she carefully transferred the silver butterfly from her discarded blouse.

'Oh what about you?' she wailed, stricken. 'What will you wear?'

'Ujwala Sane's diamond belly button.'

Ramona giggled.

'I bet she's going to turn up for Rafiq's class in leotards. Arpita says she's got tiger-skin leotards.'

'How appropriate.'

'You're really down this morning, aren't you?'

'Everybody seems to be!'

'Poor Alif Bey. He smells awful.'

'He's a great writer,' I said.

I seemed to be saying it all the time.

'He kept saying he had nothing to live for. He won't do anything foolish, will he? I mean kill himself or something.'

'We can't stop him if he wants to. But let's hope he puts it off till he gets home instead of messing up Hilla's life.'

'Oh you're just pretending. Bet you'd howl if something happened to him. We had an essay of his in the eleventh, it was deadly yaar. Couldn't make out what the guy was talking about. I just gave up half way.'

'Come on, let's get some coffee.'

'I've had mine. Tarok's thrown a fit, Aunty told you? Felix has demanded mayonnaise, loads of it. It wasn't on the menu, and now there's no time, so Tarok's in a flap getting the rest of the cooking done so that he can beat eggs in peace over ice, he told me. What a life for a man!'

'What do you want him to do? Go out and kill a bear for breakfast?'

'Breakfast is hoppers and stew and eggs florentine with pineapple jam. He asked me to specially mention the hoppers to you. What's hoppers?'

'Come on, I'll show you!'

We raced downstairs, heartened.

Chili drifted in looking pale. She pulled up a chair at our table and yawned.

'So how's the princess this morning?' she teased.

'Thanks, Chili. You'll never guess I was almost hysterical over that sari,' Ramona gushed. 'I'd probably have given up if you hadn't helped.'

Chili made a funny face at her.

'Why are you so glum?' she demanded of me.

I didn't think it showed. Abjectly, I blamed the weather.

Chili nodded.

'Yeah. I'm a sun person too. You know one time in London I didn't see the sun for a whole week. I was so sick I thought I'd die. But then the doctor said it was SAD. You're telling me, I said, I know I'm sad and that isn't normal. But apparently I had a disease called SAD. You get it if you don't see the sun.'

Both of them scrutinized me as if I were terminal.

It was impossible to dislike Chili. I did resent her, though. It was Tarok I loathed.

'Today's the great lunch challenge isn't it? The seven course one? Gosh we really do live to eat! I bet I've put on ten kilos this weekend.'

Ramona's loyal protests were cut short by Rafiq's voice, 'Chalo, get some exercise, ladies! Ramona, bring your friends!'

Ramona cleared her plate hurriedly. I begged off, but Chili said she'd have a go at body movement, as Ramona called it.

'But only half an hour, okay? I must catch up with my sleep or I'll be ruined tomorrow. I simply have to get to my room by eleven, pop my vitamin and catch a couple of hours before lunch or my skin will be like mud tomorrow.'

I felt unreasonably lonely after they left. I fought the urge to knock on the kitchen door. Tarok had reportedly blown a fuse over the mayonnaise and the last thing he needed now was a confrontation.

And what, really, could I confront him *with*?

How, eventually, does one gauge a relationship? If through words, then we must prepare to be betrayed every time.

I had a more cheering thought. Perhaps the lobsters had all crawled out of the basket by now and were making tracks towards the Sane boudoir. About now we should hear a scream ....

'Hey, there you are. I've been looking everywhere for you. I haven't seen you at all this morning. What's up?'

His face, blurry through the steam rising from my royal blue mug that he carried, was the most welcome sight in the world.

And then I remembered, and my smile sagged and his eyes clouded. My rage subsided and left in its wake harsh black laughter like shards of broken glass.

'What were you thinking?'

'That the lobsters might have got to La Sane by now.'

'Alas, I popped them in the freezer but ten minutes ago.'

'They're off the menu then? What about the mayonnaise?'

'Rego will get what he wants. Lobster mayonnaise, though what's so great about that, I can't imagine. Popping it in the freezer for twenty minutes is the kindest quietus for a lobster, but Felix deserves something more painful. However, that was not what you were thinking.'

'No, it wasn't. But that's not important.'

'Your eyes tell me it is.'

'After lunch, then. After the lobster mayonnaise.'

'Not for you. For you especially, I'm serving my Corsican delicacy.'

'Which is?'

'Sheer heaven. Lobster with its lobsterishness enhanced by a delicately flavoured cream, served in a nest of angel hair.'

And, covering my hands with his, for an instant, he was gone.

14

I finished my coffee and resolved to keep from analysis and surmise till after lunch. Tarok did not look burdened with any kind of secret, either painful or joyous. More likely, being a complete professional, he had put his promise to Chili clean out of his mind till he was done with the lunch.

It was stupid of me, really, to look beyond the weekend.

There, it was almost done now.

I would play it cool till tomorrow morning and then we would be gone and I need never see him again. I would be back in my neat ordered existence at Utkrusha, erupting as Lulu once a week and for the rest of the time there were books to write, awful gloomy stuff guaranteed to drive readers to instant suicide.

Naturally, then, I went into the library.

I had been waiting to do that since I arrived here, but till this morning I had never been satisfactorily alone. I cannot, simply cannot, stand human company at a bookshelf. Framroze's library was the one room Hilla's architect had left untouched. It was large and on a fine day it would be airy and sunlit. Tall windows with deep cushioned seats overlooked the drive. This morning a watery swirl was all one could see through the panes. There was a ghostly gleam in the air, and for a moment I was tempted to lose myself in the womby armchair, content to sink deeper still in my particular morass of despair.

I switched on the lights eventually and the place sprang into life. Books regarded me from every wall, the dull gilt of their worn bindings catching fire in the warm blaze of the lamps. The lamps were from Framroze's time too, their wide porcelain shades making gold pools on the linoleum floor.

The next hour was bliss. Eventually, I carried my book to the window seat, avoiding the armchair. I was mildly irritated at having picked up Browning. I found the line I was looking for, but that returned me to the uneasy present. I really would have to deal with it after the Corscian delicacy – for which I no longer had any appetite.

A cough roused me. Alif Bey.

'I've been meaning to have a word with you. I read your book last night.'

Alif Bey had recovered poise and was prepared now to play Nestor.

'You're in great danger of becoming a clever writer. Clever in the pejorative sense, of course.'

Pejorative. Like acquiesce, not a word you hear spoken. I cast about for a suitable exit line.

'Your mind is not curious enough. You are too trusting. You will never be a good writer unless you learn to suspect. You must take nothing at face value. You need a mind like our cook's.'

'Does he have a suspicious mind?'

'If you must ask, I must conclude you were completely oblivious of the game he played last night.'

'He baited us.'

'Oh no, no! That's too mild a term. He played us. He menaced us. He tortured us. He drove us within an inch of murder.'

'Surely, that's too extreme!'

'Is it? You must ask your aunt some time.'

I shrugged. I did not want to discuss the cook.

'A mind like Tarok's is invaluable. I wish I had a mind like that! So. What are you writing these days?'

'*Lulu's LogBook*,' I said promptly, intent on shocking him.

He laughed. 'Good heavens! That yours? I love it! It's fabulous!'

Now I was taken aback. I. couldn't imagine him enjoying an idiot like Lulu. But apparently, he did, as he kept on about her for a while.

I would have enjoyed it too, but I couldn't help thinking all the while of Lola's shoe. That act of malice simply didn't fit with this guy, but that just showed, didn't it?

Could I have suspected at ten o'clock last night that well before twelve Tarok would be promising Chili the sweet forever?

You never can tell.

Alif Bey brought up Lola's name very soon.

'Take Lola, for instance. She has a good story. She has a great story. But she doesn't know how to tell it. Her manuscript reads like a municipal report. Incidentally, that's how we met. She's been trying to write her autobiography. Finally this week she got the damn thing done. It's no good. I told her so. You can imagine how that went down.'

I held my peace and gave myself an A for tact.

'Mind you, I don't blame her for wanting to write her life. There's money in it. Besides, she doesn't have to imagine it all. I envy her that. You and I, who live dull uninteresting lives, must invent dangerous ones to write decently.'

'Felix certainly does.'

'You don't call that writing, surely. The man just yammers on. I hear he's driven the cook demented this morning.'

I refused to be drawn into that.

'Now that we've talked my book to death,' I said firmly. 'Tell me about *The Thought Cyclist*.'

He paused, a hand over his brow. There was nothing theatrical about the gesture. It was simply hopeless.

'There is no Thought Cyclist,' he muttered. 'The whole thing is a sham. The Thought Cyclist never was.'

I did not know what to say.

'It's too late at my age to discover you've built your life upon a myth, too late.'

He rose to leave.

'I have a terrible headache,' he said, descending to the mundane. 'There's no coffee to be had, the cook has locked himself in the kitchen.'

'He must have left some out in the pantry. He usually does.'

He shuffled off, his faith in ministering angels forever routed. Where were the splendid creatures that peopled his books? Women with arms like bolsters, breasts like Dunlop pillows, hearts like kitchens in perpetual lunchtime? Where indeed were the snows of yesteryear?

My fragile peace was shattered.

It was not yet half past eleven. I had a couple of hours to kill before I faced Tarok again.

I browsed fitfully. At the back of the room was a big picture propped with its face to the wall, probably the portrait Hilla spoke about last night. I raised it off the wall with difficulty, and took a peep. I was startled to find Ramona staring at me out of that ornate frame. If this was Hilla's mother, the resemblance was uncanny. The woman in the portrait was very young, scarcely older than Ramona. The artist had been subtly flattering, using sunny pastels to heighten the freshness of youth. She did not in the least resemble the tragic figure of Hilla's girlhood. But this was how Hilla wished to remember her.

'Do you know if there's any coffee left?'

Ujwala Sane this time, looking martyred, her purple salwar kameez very much the stuff of tragedy. 'The kitchen's locked. The cook won't open the door. What's he doing inside?'

The cook's spokesperson, ce'st moi.

'There's coffee in the pantry. The cook mustn't be disturbed. He has a lot of eggs to beat.'

'Mad! Total screw loose. I never got my mushrooms on toast.'

'Did you like Rafiq's dance?' I asked wildly, determined to lose the cook.

'Horrible! I only like classical!'

'The children are going to put up a show tomorrow. They're very excited about it!'

'Huh. Rain Dance, pain dance. So clumsy, that Arpita, no charm, no grace, nothing! Nobody can believe she is my daughter.'

Luckily, I was saved a reply by her husband.

'What are you doing here?' he demanded curtly. 'Go and lie down till lunchtime. Do you want a full-blown attack?'

'I wanted coffee,' she said in a small voice, like a scolded child.

'I will bring you coffee later. You can get two hours sleep before lunch. Come, now.' They left.

This time, I did nothing to avoid the womby armchair. I sank into its luxurious cushions, enjoying the silence.

Sounds knocked on the outside of my shell. The sough of the sea, the harsh rattle of rain. Rafiq's voice calling the beat. Something heavy being moved. Feet up and down the corridor.

I wondered what Lalli was up to. There was something I had to tell …

I must have dozed off.

When I woke, stupid and ravenous, my watch said it was nearly two o'clock.

I scrambled out of the chair guiltily and wandered out.

15

They were all gathered in the hall. The living room, I should more properly say. But a hall it was, with its high ornate ceiling, its deep bay windows and many gracious spaces opened up and cherished by the intelligent decorator. The furniture was mostly Framroze's rococo, but there were one or two pieces less insistently phony. The more fragile and precious antiques were in tamper-proof display. There were no occasional tables to bark my shins on, the carpet did not sneak up and rub against my ankles and the pictures, faded photographs of Bombay Harbour, did not invite comment. It was a room to be comfortable in, and everybody was certainly being comfortable in it.

Alif Bey was asleep on the chaise longue. Dr Sane was sitting by himself at a small table, frowning over a sheaf of documents. Hilla, Lalli and Felix were in animated discussion. Chili was probably still napping in her room. Rafiq and his troupe were not here either, and Ujwala was presumably still raging with migraine.

Felix called out, 'Look what we got! Something better than oxalic acid. Get the picture – Lalli in purple silk …'

'Ivory temples, half-moon eyes.'

'I'm glad you remember,' he approved. 'Purple silk. No better make that blue. Got it? Deep secret midnight blue. Around her neck, sapphires. Two tears of flaming blue drip from her cowrie ears.

'She gazes across the table, remembering. Then she swiftly unhooks an earring, leans over and drops it in his glass. "Drink to me," she murmurs languourously.'

Lalli looked demure.

'What's in the glass?' I demanded.

'Curacao. Also blue. He drinks it. It's not a sapphire at all – it's pure copper sulphate. Before he knows it – dead.'

'The Cleopatra act.'

'Yeah. It was in our chemistry book in school. A pearl wasn't it? I've got it. Copper sulphate is lethal, man, simply lethal.'

'But will it dissolve in curacao?' I asked.

Felix brushed that off with contempt.

'Hilla, you will have the pleasure of seeing your mother at lunch,' said Mr Bajaj, startling us all. He dazzled, fragrant and pristine in crisp white. His wet hair, slicked back from his blocky forehead, had an aluminium gleam. He explained that he had hung the portrait on the dining room wall, and now needed Hilla to approve the angle. It was hot dusty work, he said, and he was glad to refresh himself with a shower just in time for lunch.

'You got back quicker than me,' he smiled toothily at Dr Sane who had helped him with the picture. 'Did you return the cord to Tarok?'

'No, the kitchen was still locked, so I left it in the pantry when I went there for coffee,' Dr Sane said.

Apparently all of them had tried to break into Tarok's domain, and none of them had yet succeeded.

'Still, your cook is a man of his word, Hilla,' Mr Bajaj laughed. 'Your guests had forgotten their promise, but sharp at eleven-fifteen I meet the cook in the corridor, carrying a coil of nylon cord and scissors, on the way to the dining room. 'Hilla would like that portrait there when we go in to lunch,' he tells me. You go and beat those eggs, I told him. This you leave to me.'

Ramona's resemblance to the portrait was now commented upon and Felix loudly regretted not having included her in his copper sulphate disaster. It came as a surprise when the clock struck two.

'I'd better go and find Rafiq and the kids,' Felix offered. 'This is not a lunch we can afford to be late for.' Dr Sane too, went in search of his migrainous wife.

To my surprise, Tarok did not appear.

We were all, except Chili and Mrs Sane, assembled in the hall by two-fifteen. The table was not yet set. At two-thirty, Hilla broke the cardinal rule that the cook must on no account be disturbed. She returned, looking irritated. The kitchen was still locked and there was no response to her knocks.

'Leave him alone,' Rafiq advised. 'All artists are sometimes nervous. Mr Rego is waiting with paper and pencil, so Tarok wants a little breathing space. Wait a little. More appetite.'

Ramona, eager to relate her morning venture into body-movement, drew me urgently aside.

It was well past three when Lalli appeared at the door – I had not even seen her leave the room.

She did not enter. She stood there silently till we noticed her. Words froze. A chill dread possessed me at the sight of her stillness.

I knew before she had spoken.

I waited in unbearable torment to hear the words.

The cook was in the kitchen. The back of his head had been beaten in and he was very dead.

16

From this point on, I must tutor my narrative. My own turmoil is no part of the story. I think I blacked out when Lalli made that announcement. The next thing I remember was Hilla's comforting largeness enclosing me, as though I had shattered and must be gathered whole again.

I returned slowly to a room full of strangers staring emptily at the woman at the door.

Who was she? Why was she addressing me?

She said: 'You are going to feel like this for a long time from now on. Unreal. As if it's a nightmare, and you'll wake up eventually. Listen carefully. This is real. This is now. Tarok Ghosh is dead.'

She turned to the others.

I remembered her now. She was my aunt. She was family. She ought to be holding me, she ought to be hurting for me. But she was standing remote and intent on something quite different. I couldn't see what that was. Not yet.

She looked taller than usual. Her eyes had a feverish brightness that nobody could mistake for tears.

'Please stay in this room till I return. That may be half an hour or more. I am taking charge of the situation and expect each of you to cooperate at every step. We are isolated till the weather lets up. Phones are not working. We still have power, but it may quit on us any time. Please stay together. Mrs Sane and Chili are in their rooms. I will get them to join you here. Nobody is to leave here till I return. Stay calm, please.'

With that, she shut the door behind her.

The children, whimpering, clung to their father who looked helplessly around the room.

Mr Bajaj said, 'If Tarok Ghosh is dead, I would like to see for myself. I don't take orders from old women.'

'This old woman, as you unfairly call her, has seen more murders than you ever heard of,' Alif Bey said from his corner. 'Be advised, Mr Bajaj, the police commissioner takes orders from her when it comes to homicide.'

'The commissioner is a personal friend. I will call him immediately.'

A cellphone leapt in his hand. He made an impatient sound – obviously, it was as useless as the land line.

'Let's wait peacefully till Lalli returns. She can pick out the murderer, and the rest of us can go home,' Alif Bey said.

'Pick out the murderer!' Mr Bajaj exploded. 'Are you suggesting one of us is a murderer?'

'What do you think she meant when she asked us to stay together?' Felix snapped. 'Shut up, man.'

Mr Bajaj, surprisingly, shut up. Arpita and Darshan had crept up to me. Their terror was wordless. Their small bodies were chill and trembling. I put my arms around them and held them close. Ramona clutched wildly at Hilla.

Rafiq and Felix were in conclave.

Felix said: 'Hilla, there will be a lot of difficult things to do. Rafiq and I will take care of that. What about Tarok's family?'

'He had nobody,' I said.

Nobody but me.

'He has us,' Rafiq said roughly. 'We are his people.'

'And one of us killed him,' Hilla said. 'In my house. He was my guest. Somebody hurt him and destroyed him.'

I envied her. She could weep. I knew I would have to wait a very long time for tears.

Felix came over to me.

'Is it true, what Alif Bey said about Lalli?'

'Of course. She's retired now, but the police still call her. She does this for a living now. Murderers, thieves, embezzlers, kidnappers. I meet one every week.'

'What a fool she must think me. Do you think she'll let me in on this one?'

'We're all in it, aren't we?' I retorted with some bitterness. Tarok was already a memory. What remained was the body. Tarok wouldn't have enjoyed the thought of Felix revelling in his bloodstains.

'You might even get a book out of it,' I said nastily. '*Carrion Cook.*'

'Hey, that's a great title.'

Really, it took so very little to make him happy.

My mind was racing all the while, trying to remember the last time I saw Tarok. I could remember nothing. I couldn't remember his face. At that thought, the abyss yawned.

Lalli returned sooner than expected. She sent me to call Chili and Mrs Sane.

'Bring them back with you.'

I hated leaving the living room. I crossed the vestibule hurriedly, trying to keep from thinking of what lay beyond. I ran up the stairs and banged on Mrs Sane's door. It opened on the fifth knock. Her room was darkened by a thick shawl pinned across the window. She was in what writers politely call dishabille – in her case a brownish Mother Hubbard. That purple dupatta was wound like a turban on her migrainous head. It had a large damp patch where it covered one eye and gave her a faintly piratical air.

'What do you want?' she asked with exasperation. 'I sent a message with Devdutt. I don't want lunch. I have a terrible migraine. I've been lying down with a cold compress.' She winced as she pressed the damp patch on the turban.

'There's been an accident.'

I don't know what made me say that. Unless it was murder by accident which sounded like a Felix Rego title.

She waited for me to go on.

There was something strange about that, but I couldn't pin it down.

'Everybody has been asked to gather in the living room.'

'Who asked?'

'Lalli.'

'What she wants now?'

'She wants us to gather in the living room so that we can decide how to handle the crisis.'

'Why for she is giving orders? What crisis? Someone is sick, Dr Sane is available. Some other crisis, call police. My cousin is ACP.'

'Lalli is the police. She's investigating the crime.'

'What crime?'

'Tarok Ghosh has been killed.'

There was a moment of silence. Then Ujwala Sane laughed.

'That is not a crime. That is good riddance.'

I kept up a dogged silence. It was rapidly becoming clear I had to spend the next few hours forgetting Tarok. I had to be here, now. Seeing, hearing, touching. I had to connect with the present.

If Ujwala Sane had expected her laugh to get a rise out of me, she was disappointed.

Still laughing, she said brightly, 'You're feeling bad, no? Never mind. You'll get over it. Okay, baba, tell your aunty I will come.'

'I'm supposed to take you and Chili downstairs.'

'I can't come like this! Go call Chili and I'll change meanwhile.'

I took her advice, but Chili was fast asleep after her disturbed night. With that huge sleep deficit of the past week, this was only to be expected. I gave up hammering on her door and returned to Ujwala. She had changed into a white salwar kameez. The purple dupatta was now around her neck.

As we approached the living room, she pushed past me and strode in dramatically, tearing the two children off Hilla and smothering them with kisses.

'Devdutt, we must leave now. AT ONCE. I will not allow my children to remain for one minute more under this roof. Not even ONE MINUTE. Sorry Hilla, you are good-hearted but this is too much for us to take. We are respectable people, from good family and we are not used to such things. Please don't tell me now that I did not warn you. I knew it would turn out like this. The moment I set my eyes on that cook I knew he was roadside trash and now he has proved it.'

I was awed by her stupidity. It was magnificent, operatic, utterly irrefutable.

Alif Bey gave a high sharp giggle which he quickly converted into a cough. Dr Sane threw the room a pleading look as he reasoned with his wife in low menacing tones.

'Chili is still fast asleep,' I told Lalli.

She nodded absently, her eyes raking the room.

They stopped talking and looked at her. During my absence, Mr Bajaj must have made his point and got his answer. He was sulking in a corner now. There was very little anarchy in the air.

'The body is now ready to be shifted,' Lalli said. 'Rafiq and Felix, I will need your help.'

She looked questioningly at me.

'I must see him,' I said. She nodded.

The three of us followed her to the kitchen. When Lalli unbolted the door, Felix hurried in after her. Rafiq stepped back to let me enter.

Tarok was slumped over the workbench in the centre of the kitchen. He had fallen forward, still seated on the rough wooden stool he had liked so much. His face was turned away from the door, and I was glad of that. It gave me a little time to prepare. One arm hung limp by his side. The other was sprawled across the bench, fist clenching a fork, its tines webbed with congealing yolk. The back of his head glistened purple, thick hair matted with blood. A welter of blood had dyed his collar a dense crimson. Above it, the dark skin of his neck had an angry sheen. His face, contorted in a grimace of intense pain, lay in a congealing pool of blood and egg yolk. The bench was slick with water. My feet touched a block of ice. I retreated hastily, but not before it had slid a little further on the floor. The floor was spattered with yolk. I spotted the upturned steel bowl beneath the sink. It must have bounced off the bench when he fell, rolled right across the kitchen floor before coming to rest beneath the sink.

Lalli took no notice of me. She gave instructions to Felix and Rafiq in undertones and then she turned on her heel and marched me out of the kitchen. We went down the corridor to the library. Lalli shut the door and sat me down in Framroze's womby chair. She drew up a chair next to me and was silent.

Lalli's silence has often comforted me, but never before had I felt its power to energize. It did not comfort me in the least now. It made my anguish keener and infused me with strength.

'I need your help,' Lalli said eventually. 'Savio's not here. Hilla is too shattered. Rafiq may have more problems ahead. Felix is useless. I need your help.'

'Of course.'

'Make notes.' She nodded at the stack of paper waiting on the desk.

'Is it one of us?'

'Definitely.'

'Will you get him?'

'Or her. Yes.'

'But – don't you need equipment? Forensic stuff?'

Lalli sighed.

'Yes, yes. I do. I will do a formal examination a little later, and gather evidence, but I have no idea how long we're going to be stuck here. I must have answers soon, I simply can't wait for lab reports. We'll have to go back to the crime scene now for a check. Frankly, nitty-gritty apart, all the equipment you need to solve a murder is between your ears.'

But I was impatient for detail. I simply needed to know.

'When exactly did he die?'

'Around twelve o'clock, I'd say. About three hours before I discovered the body.'

'How can you tell?'

'Body temperature. In still air, for a man of his size, I'd say about three hours. Hilla has a neat first aid box, I found a thermometer. Heat loss is around 1.5 degrees per hour after death, but he was lying face down in a pool of icy water, so I had to factor that in. Couldn't be later, because of the eggs.'

'What about the eggs?'

We were interrupted by Felix. He came in with a tray bearing steaming cups of coffee (instant, at first whiff) and sandwiches. I flinched.

'You have a job to do!' Lalli said coldly plonking a cup in front of me. The coffee scalded my tongue, but I was grateful for it.

'Felix, what's a Baked Alaska?' Lalli asked.

A flash of intelligence leapt in his eyes.

'So that's what he did!'

'What?'

'That's what he used the whites for. I upset his cart by demanding lobster mayonnaise at the eleventh hour. He exploded, you must have heard that. It's an accepted part of the challenge that there must be no waste. He'd need about fifteen yolks for the mayo. That would leave fifteen whites – so he decided on a meringue for Baked Alaska.'

'Which is?'

'Egg whites and sugar, basically. He'd originally planned a different dessert, but the basics were the same, sponge cake and ice cream, so the switch would not have been bad. Baked Alaska is just layers of cake and ice cream covered with a meringue and baked just before serving.'

'Thank you, Felix. Is Rafiq done?'

'Yes. Ready when you are.'

Lalli put a gentle hand on my head and drew me close for a second. 'Stay here and make a note of Baked Alaska,' she said.

17

I knew what they were about to do. They were going to shift Tarok's body. I had heard Savio say how critical it was to be around when the body was shifted. There was always something they'd find. Or hoped to find. It all sounded very vague. I hated the thought. Tarok had never been one to rely on hope.

I expected cameras, a glittery array of steel and cellophane, busy fingers picking, garnering, dabbing, printing. Vacuum cleaners. Infrared cameras. High-tech stuff straight out of prime-time television. Tarok was going to be cheated out of all that.

Rafiq and Felix would have prepared a cold chamber. Probably Tarok's own room adjacent to the kitchen, with the AC turned on high. And all that ice waiting in the freezer. Thank God for electricity. They would lay him on a flat surface, rig up strong lighting. Perhaps they had managed a camera, though I didn't remember anybody taking pictures that weekend, not even of Ramona in all her glory.

Lalli would cut away the bloodstained clothes and begin a detailed examination.

The worst of it was that I kept thinking of him, from whatever dimension he now occupied, looking on with an ironic twinkle. I could hear the dry humour in his voice, see that knowing look with which he met my eye. I realized he would always stay for me beyond grief, a touchstone for truth and irony.

I crumpled then, baffled by my loss. But very soon, anger hardened me.

I was angry at myself, for the peeve that soured me all morning. I was angry at my anger towards Tarok that still hurt unreasonably.

I would talk frankly with Chili. I would show her no resentment. I would not blame her for importuning Tarok.

I made these resolutions as I began writing down the conversation I had overheard between them last night.

When Lalli returned, she hurried me to the kitchen, so I left my notes on top of the ream unweighted. Time enough to think over that later.

As I entered, I remembered my first morning here and felt sick with pain. I remembered how the sunlight slid between us as we sat drinking coffee in this large airy room delightfully lit by the east facing French window. I imagined Tarok sitting at the bench. He would have had his back to anyone coming in from the storeroom. (There's no door between the kitchen and the storeroom, just a cutout in the wall between. The kitchen counter runs along two walls. The serving hatch to the pantry is placed over the counter, the one to the dining room is closer to the range.)

When Lalli had gone in search of Tarok at three o'clock, the kitchen door was locked on the inside. Adjacent to it, at the end of the corridor, is the storeroom door. This was bolted on the outside. The kitchen window was shut tight against the rain. The serving hatch that opened into the dining room was shut and bolted on the inside. The serving hatch that opened into the pantry was shut, but not bolted.

If the murderer had entered through the main door, then Tarok had let him in. Extremely unlikely, as he had been so particular in keeping us all at bay. The DO NOT DISTURB sign, still dangling there, reminded me how edgy he could get.

The only way the murderer could have entered was through the storeroom door. This door, I now remembered, was never bolted on the outside. In fact I had seen Tarok bolt it on the inside as he locked up for the night.

Had he left it open then? Unlikely. The door stood at the edge of the corridor, angled towards the side of the house. The spiral staircase ended almost at its threshold. It was unprotected by the eaves. The rain beat in. Leaving the door open would have the storeroom flooded in no time. Tarok would never have done that.

'Well?' Lalli asked. We were still standing at the kitchen door.

'There's no way the murderer could have entered the kitchen unless Tarok let him in. He would have locked both the kitchen and the storeroom doors on the inside.'

'And would Tarok have let anybody in?'

'No, I don't think so.'

'I don't think so either. Then it's a sealed room murder isn't it?'

'You sound almost pleased about it.'

She smiled.

'Sealed rooms always please me, because it's such fun unsealing them.'

I frowned.

'The murderer couldn't possibly have squeezed in through the serving hatch.'

'Only if he were in a Felix Rego mystery.'

'So how did he get in?'

'If you'll go into the storeroom and bolt the door, I'll show you.'

I didn't like doing it, but I did it just the same.

I bolted the door from inside, using the latch at the top of the door.

Before the minute was out, Lalli's hand appeared at the ventilator. It was a swivel window. She opened it easily, slid her hand in and undid the latch which fell noiselessly as if it had been oiled. I pushed open the door and ran out. She was nowhere to be seen.

'Up here!'

There she was, on the spiral staircase, drenched to the skin. By leaning over its abrupt curve, a woman of Lalli's height could easily reach the ventilator. The rest was easy. It was so obvious I could have kicked myself.

'You see what a lot of damage a label can do,' Lalli murmured. 'Tarok knew that. He hated labels. He would have hated the thought of a sealed room. Come on, let's enter with the murderer.'

18

As we entered the storeroom together, I felt, for the first time, the chill of violent death. Till that moment I had confronted loss. Even when I had viewed Tarok's body, it was despair I felt, the sinking bafflement of grief. Now, standing in that empty room, the fearsome act of murder and the terrible compulsion that had spurred it throbbed in the humid air. There was hate and anger and revulsion in that room. I imagined them all, I felt them all.

'What do you see?' Lalli asked.

I saw the room now like a stage when the players have left. From these scattered props I would now have to reconstruct the play.

The storeroom had a freezer, and the crate on which I'd seen the kids sitting that afternoon, eating ice cream. Was it only two days ago? A lifetime had passed since. Next to the crate was a large zinc tub with a block of ice, still in its sawdust-encrusted sacking. Satellite boulders of ice sat around it. A metallic gleam caught my eye. On the floor was a small ice pick.

'The weapon?'

Lalli shook her head.

'Doesn't match the wound.'

I could see nothing else.

'What else did the murderer see?'

'Two hours ago? He saw Tarok.'

The doorway to the kitchen was to my right. Straight in my line of vision was Tarok's bench. He was sitting there, beating those darned eggs when the murderer saw him. He would have had his back to the intruder. Did he look up, turn around and greet him?

'No. He didn't see the murderer.' Uncanny, but that's Lalli for you. 'Unless *you* murdered him.'

'What!'

'Sorry if that hurt, but I meant it logically. Tarok was edgy. He wouldn't have gone back to beating eggs knowing he had company. He would have walked the intruder to the door and shut it firmly on him. But if *you* were the intruder – he would have kept on beating eggs while talking to you, he wouldn't have minded turning his back on you. He felt safe with you.'

'Safe?'

'Yes. Didn't you spot that? A man who has lived like Tarok never lets down his guard unless he feels really safe with somebody. He let his guard down only with you. You could have walked up to him making as much noise as you liked, kept him talking and hit him on the head. He trusted you completely. Unfortunately, that's not how the murderer did it.'

'No?'

'No. He, or she, stood to a little left of you, hesitating. I think he stood there fuming, not really certain what he wanted to do. Then he caught sight of the weapon. He picked it up, advanced on tiptoe, struck a right-handed blow from above.'

'Wait on. You're guessing. How do you know, for instance, that he hesitated, or that he stood there fuming? That's surmise.'

'Granted. His emotional state is surmise. But here's physical evidence to show he stood here hesitating. Look.'

On the cream tiles were muddy marks, I could faintly discern a footprint, blurring into another misshapen print.

'Large feet. Size nine, I'd say. Lots of women have large feet. Print's too smeary to say much about the sole, but there are ridges there. Vinyl sole most likely, but then most monsoon footwear has that. Notice the smearing. That's the sort of print you leave when you shift your weight from foot to foot. There's a lot of it too, so I'd say he was here for a few minutes, he was agitated. Then he advanced on tiptoe.'

'On tiptoe?'

'Sure. Two of those marks ahead of you certainly suggest that. And then he struck.'

I followed her into the kitchen. The bench and the floor hadn't been cleaned up yet. The block of ice had shrunk to a small weepy boulder.

'The weapon was smooth, blunt, rounded. It impacted with considerable force – enough to break the skin and temporarily stun him.'

'Temporarily! It *killed* him!'

'Not true. Of course I can only be absolutely sure after the autopsy, but there's no fracture of the parietal bone beneath the wound. He had a concussion. I doubt if the force was enough to cause a closed brain injury. He bled a bit.'

'A bit!'

'I know it looked like a lot, but a scalp wound of that sort usually bleeds torrentially. There's this small bit on the table and then his collar was soaked, that's about it. He should have bled more. He would have bled more if …'

She stopped and dived suddenly, reaching under the bench. When she straightened up, her eyes were glittering. She had something concealed behind her back.

'He would have bled more if …' I prompted.

'If he hadn't been murdered soon after that!'

She dangled a piece of rope before me.

'With this! '

I gasped.

I recognized the rope. It was a piece from the coil of nylon cord used to hang that portrait.

'Soon after he slumped on the table stunned from that head injury, almost within a few minutes, Tarok was strangled with this piece of nylon cord,' Lalli spoke slowly. 'I realized when I examined the body that he had been strangled with a narrow ligature. The mark suggested a twisted cord. Rather like this one. I'll have to match this with the mark.'

'I don't understand. Why strangle him *after* hitting him? Why not strangle him in the first place?'

That brought the mad vision of the murderer, stopwatch in hand, bending over Tarok after hitting him. If he wasn't dead within the stipulated time, switch to Plan B.

'You didn't know he was strangled when you first told us he was dead, did you?'

'Of course I did. I only saw the ligature mark when I cut away his clothes. But there were other signs. You really don't want to hear the details.'

'Yes I do.'

I wanted to see the enemy. I had to.

'Congestion of the face: his face was more than dusky. Small bleeds in the skin, from the nasal cavity. Pinpoint haemorrhages, petechie. All of these suggested strangulation. Also I knew he'd been strangled soon after that first injury because the wound had bled so little ...'

'Don't you need a doctor for this kind of thing?' I demanded. 'A medical examiner or something?'

Lalli smiled. 'You need a degree? I have an MD in forensics. Good enough for you?'

All this while Lalli had been prowling around the kitchen opening fridge, oven, microwave, peering into the covered pots and dishes on the counter. She kept squinting at a scrap of paper. I realized it was the menu. She took a bowlful of white froth from the fridge to show me. It was the meringue mixture, she said. She hovered over the glittering array Tarok had assembled ready to be transported to the dining table. The sparkling crystal, glass and crockery, the polished silver and snowy drift of lacy napery lent a ghastly note of luxury to the room of death.

'He'd just begun beating the eggs when he was attacked. Look, some of the yolks are still whole. Look at the oil.'

There was a small glass jug of oil on the bench. Still standing, miraculously. It was almost full. He probably hadn't started adding it as yet.

'When I entered, the spilt yolk had almost completely congealed. Yolk takes about an hour in still air to form a skin. It should have been spilt about three hours ago to get as tough as it had. That's roughly the time of assault. Fits with the time of death by body temperature. So you see it all adds up.'

'It still doesn't answer my question. Why kill a man twice?'

'I think the murderer only struck once. Swiftly, surely. He was garrotted expertly. The murderer has done this before.'

'But …'

'Oh the head injury's a different matter all together. We're dealing with two different minds here. One impulsive, violent but easily frightened. The other – cold, opportunistic, arrogant.'

I wasn't listening.

A cold wave of fear prickled at the edges of my mind.

It rushed into me till I was an icy pillar of dread. I stared at Lalli too frightened to speak.

What had I done?

My petty peeve had kept me from telling Lalli something I ought to have mentioned hours ago.

Her words clashed like cymbals inside my skull, shattering my bones with their clangour.

I think the murderer only struck once. Swiftly, surely. Tarok was garroted expertly. The murderer has done this before.

I let her lead me to a chair in the storeroom. I swallowed the water she brought me. I opened my mouth to speak, but the words wouldn't come. Then I remembered the notes I'd made. Lalli could read those. I sprang up, and dragging her with me, rushed to the library.

The ream of paper stared at me white and blank. The notes I'd made were gone ...

Words poured out of me then, all the terror that had locked my throat the last ten minutes broke free. Lalli didn't wait for me to finish. She was racing up the stairs, with me thundering after her.

She banged on Chili's door just once. Then she turned to me.

'Get Rafiq.'

I ran back to the living room. He looked up as I entered. I didn't have to say a word. He was past me and running up the stairs.

How did he know where to go?

Lalli was still labouring at Chili's door. She drew back wordlessly as Rafiq approached. He took one look at the heavy double panelled teak and didn't waste any time throwing his weight against it. He got a chair, climbed up, peeled off his T-shirt, bundled his fist in it and smashed in the fanlight. Then he let in an arm and opened the latch.

Lalli motioned us back and entered the room alone. At my side Rafiq uttered a low howl of despair. It was the animal cry of grief, ancient, all revealing. I didn't have to look past Lalli to learn the truth.

Chili lay asprawl on the bed, the bedclothes a wild tangle, her hair fanned in a black web across the pillows. Her face, suffused and contorted beyond recognition, was smeared with bloodstained froth. There was blood on her lips, making a thin tarry trickle down her chin. Her open eyes were glazed and dull.

Strangely, my first feeling was one of outrage that death had marred her so. Of her elfin grace, her vibrant charm, not the faintest trace remained.

Lalli's first thought, surprisingly, was of Rafiq. She retreated to where he stood sagging against the wall, staring wildly at the bed. He turned a questioning look at Lalli.

She nodded grimly. 'I'll get him.'

I had never seen her so angry. *Get him*? Did she know who the killer was? Had the killer struck here as well? Or was this suicide?

Somewhere I felt a stab of envy. Chili had scored over me again. Tarok's murder hadn't brought out this fury in Lalli. He wasn't as important to her ...

I was wrong.

She said, 'He has killed twice already. He will kill again.'

Her assurance irritated me. How could she presume so much?

'Go back to the library. Make notes. Write down everything. Every word, every gesture you remember about Chili. Everything she told you. Nothing is too trivial. Write it down. You too, Rafiq. Do that. Now. I have work here that's better done alone. Don't tell the others yet.'

I had to drag Rafiq away. I pushed him into a chair in the library and told him about the missing notes. I told him what was in them – fearfully, but I told him.

'You think someone read what you wrote and went upstairs and killed her?'

'No. I don't know much about these things, but it looks as if she's been dead a long time.'

He shook his head in amazement.

'This morning she was so beautiful, so bright. I asked her if she wanted a part in the Rain Dance. She clapped her hands like a child, "Oh what can I be?" So full of happiness.'

He broke into harsh sobs. Everybody seemed able to cry but me.

He shook with grief, looking up now and then with empty eyes. There was nothing I could say to him. There was nothing he could say to me. We were each, in our separate griefs, entirely alone.

Lalli came in. She looked *old*.

'Chili has been dead for more than six hours. It's past six o'clock now. She probably died before noon. Did either of you see her this morning?'

Rafiq related what he had told me earlier in a calm heavy voice.

'And what part did you give her in the dance?'

Lalli's question shocked me. In these circumstances, it sounded frivolous, almost prurient.

'Bijlee. She was lightning, so suddenly, so brightly, dangerously …'

His voice grew sullen and inward. He dropped his English like a soiled shirt, and said in Urdu, 'Like lightning she blinded me. Like lightning she betrayed me.'

Lalli ignored that.

She turned to me. I went over what I remembered of this morning. Unfortunately I remembered my own feelings during that encounter better than the words that passed between us. I did not speak of that now.

'I remember she said she could dance only for half an hour. Then she had to catch up on sleep or her skin would be bad for tomorrow's shoot. "I'll pop my vitamin and catch a couple of hours sleep before lunch," she said.'

'She did pop that vitamin,' Lalli said grimly. 'Died within minutes of swallowing it. What kind of breakfast did she have?'

I tried to remember. She had been nursing a cup of coffee, nothing else. I didn't remember her finishing that either.

'Ah,' said Lalli, as though I'd made a discovery.

'But how can that be?' Rafiq blurted. 'First day she swallowed six, nothing happened.'

'Those were vitamins. This was poison. Chili's vitamins weren't pills, they were capsules. It's easy to tamper with a capsule. Empty it and refill it with whatever else.' She paused, searching our faces. 'Rafiq, I want you to sit guard outside Chili's room. I've latched the door. Nobody should get in till I return. Please stay with her.'

He was gone before she could finish.

'Poison!' I erupted angrily. 'You talk as if people walked around carrying poison in their pockets! What poison anyway? Don't tell me it's that old chestnut, the rare Oriental poison unknown to modern science. That bluff may be enough to stall Rafiq, but it's not good enough for me.'

'It's no bluff. No Oriental poison. Sodium cyanide granules. Hilla's rat poison. The same that Ujwala kindly offered Chili last night.'

'Good heavens! You think Chili took that?'

'*Took* that with suicidal intent? No. All the capsules in the bottle are doctored with cyanide. If she did it herself, she'd only fill one or perhaps two, or if she's really desperate to succeed, four or five. Not thirty-odd capsules. That's what I was doing all this time, emptying out the capsules in the bottle. The stuff is the same as that in the rat poison packet – looks the same, at any rate. And there's no mistake about the cause of death. Cyanide poisoning. You could smell it.'

I couldn't take it in. It seemed theatrical, incredible.

'I thought cyanide went out with the Borgias,' I said.

'That was Nero, not Lucrezia. Cherry laurel water. He carried it around. The Borgias used arsenic. Cyanide's as modern as it gets. Iraq used it in '98 against Iran. Of course, by then the Europeans and the Americans had forgotten all about Zyklon B. Still, it's unusual to find it in the house. The conversation at dinner last night, Ujwala Sane's silly comments, all practically put the weapon in the murderer's hands. I never discuss murder. Never.'

She was trembling with fury.

'Do you think Ujwala Sane did it?'

'If she did, her bragadoccio's unparalleled in the history of crime. No, she is a dangerous woman, but stupid. Of course, all the murderers I've known have been stupid people.'

She paced angrily, and then threw herself down on the window seat. Her voice was choked with tears, but they were tears of fury, not sorrow.

'We have to tell Hilla. This is going to devastate her. I'll bring Hilla in here and tell her. But after that I must return to Chili's room. You stay with Hilla. Keep her together.'

If Rafiq had been shaken by Chili's death, Hilla's reaction was no less intense. After the initial dismay, she insisted on going up to Chili's room at once. Rafiq and I waited outside while the two of them stood over the dead girl.

A frightening deja vu oppressed me. Just two days ago I had waited at this spot, at this very hour, listening to a woman sobbing. On that evening too, Chili had swallowed vitamin pills in an operatic gesture of despair. This was the dark side of that comedy. Chili's vitamins had gone from fatuous to fatal. Death, so elusive when courted with tears, now possessed her dry-eyed.

Next to me, Rafiq breathed stertorously. From time to time he made impatient movements as if he would burst his skin.

At length Lalli and Hilla came out. They took Rafiq with them down the corridor. They walked past me wordlessly, leaving me to break the news.

19

I tried to make it sound pragmatic, I prepared a bulletin. And of course when I said them, the words came out all wrong.

Everybody looked up as I entered.

I shut the door carefully behind me and bolted it. I remember wondering why.

They looked up, reading my face before the words spilt in a garbled rush.

'Chili is dead. They broke down her door. Lalli thinks she's been poisoned.'

The silence was absolute.

Then Ujwala Sane laughed.

'Robert Bruce! I knew I would remember the name. If first you don't succeed, try, try again. Remember, Arpita, Darshan, in your history lesson? How many times that Chili girl tried. Finally I gave her good advice, I think. Try, try again. See Arpita, Darshan, just like incy-vincy spider! At last she is successful!'

'Lalli thinks Chili was murdered.'

'Lalli thinks, Lalli thinks! Who is this Lalli? From where she came? Without even surname? Just like that – Lalli? Like some deshi Tom, Dick and Harry. Why she thinks so much?' Ujwala ranted.

'It's her job to think,' Dr Sane said roughly. 'And it's your job now to shut up. Say nothing, do you hear me? Nothing. Nothing but disaster every time you open your mouth. Now shut up.'

His wife gave a wounded cry and drew herself up indignantly.

'I have put up with many things, but this is the END,' she announced.

As exits went, this one was pure V. Shantaram. But womanhood outraged never made it past the door, for I stood with my back firmly against it. She changed her mind and fainted unconvincingly on a particularly squashy sofa.

This brief diversion served only to heighten the horror of our situation.

Dr Sane said, 'Lalli will need my help. This is now a serious matter.'

As though Tarok's murder had been a passing frivolity.

'If you will wait a little longer, Dr Sane, Lalli will be here. I'm sure she'll want you to help. She's with Hilla at the moment.'

I gave myself an A for guile. My next job was to discover who had left the room around six o'clock.

A little gentle prodding produced answers. All of them had. Any of them could have stolen my notes, but it was probably Felix. It was the kind of thing people frequently did in his books. Mostly, they ate the evidence. If he'd stuck to the script, the first bout of colic should hit him any time now.

Ramona and the children crowded around me. In a small voice, Arpita said they had eaten. Felix had made sandwiches.

'I think the lunch was inside them,' Ramona said. 'We just ate them quickly before we could think about it.'

Darshan began to cry. He wept noiselessly, heartbrokenly and nothing would comfort him.

'He's upset because we ate the things Tarok gave us,' Arpita said with some scorn. 'The engine and the rose and the longest apple peel in the world. He thinks we could have kept them. Now we've got nothing.'

After a while she asked, 'Where is Chili right now?'

Nobody answered.

Mr Bajaj said, 'Where is that dancing boy? There is a new murder and I do not see him around.'

'Yes!'

Ujwala Sane rose dramatically.

'Yesterday I saw him looking at Chili. See how that man is looking at you, I told her, don't talk to him. You know what his background is. Not respectable. I warned her. Still he was looking at her like that, for so long! It was abnormal.'

Alif Bey laughed. 'All of us looked at Chili like that. It was perfectly normal.'

Ujwala was prevented from reacting to this as Hilla and Lalli came in just then. Hilla slumped in a chair distractedly.

Lalli said, 'You have been told of Chili's death. She died around noon today, soon after she went to her room for a nap. She was poisoned. The vitamin capsules she usually took every morning were filled with rat poison ...'

Ujwala gave her Cassandra wail again.

'I told you! I told everybody! I knew! Moment I heard, I knew!'

Lalli took no notice of her.

'What are we going to do now?' Alif Bey asked, with a hopeless wave at the window where the rain still thrashed furiously.

'You mean, who's next?' Felix put in.

'No more murders,' Ujwala said. 'It is now finished. That Chili girl murdered the cook, then killed herself. They were having affair. It is finished.'

She spoke brightly, and with great conviction, nodding her head in agreement with herself. Everybody stared in disbelief.

'No. That is not true. Chili did not kill Tarok,' Lalli said. 'My examination shows she died more than six hours ago, probably before Tarok. I do not think the cause of these murders is a soured love affair. It is a matter that involves us all. I see you have had something to eat. Good. You are not to leave this room for the night. You may not go to your rooms upstairs. Please use the bathroom on this floor. We have no way of summoning help till this weather lets up. I will now take your statements in the library.'

'How long will that take?' Alif Bey asked. 'Can't it wait till morning?'

'No. I begin now and will hear each of you by turn.'

She stalked out before they could question that.

A flurry of indignation swept the room. Hilla raised a tired hand to quell it. She spoke to them with what I can only term great forbearance and concluded her appeal for cooperation by bursting into tears. Naturally, everybody behaved well after that.

I joined Lalli in the library.

It was nearly nine o'clock. Everything seemed unreal.

Lalli pushed the stack of paper at me. There was a fresh mug of coffee. I gulped it down greedily.

'Felix is getting us something to eat. He wanted to sit in on this. I refused.'

'Is he a suspect then?'

'Yes. So are you. You had motive, opportunity. The weapon was easily found. I need to check your alibi. I had opportunity, no alibi, weapon, but no motive. In the next few hours we'll meet someone who had motive, opportunity, weapon and no alibi – but didn't commit these murders. Nothing works to rule when it comes to murder.'

'How do you find out then?'

'That depends on the murderer. On the pressure he feels. On his loneliness. On his desperation.'

'Loneliness?'

I've read stacks of detective stories, but never heard of this one before.

'Most murderers I've known have killed from loneliness or desperation. Dread of loneliness, dread of abandonment. Desperation because there don't seem to be any other options. But there always are other options. People do stupid things when they grow desperate. Murder is an act of great stupidity.'

'Lonelines, desperation – these are emotions I'd sooner grant the victim …'

'That too. Then there's the dialogue, you see, before the actual deed. That's important to notice.'

'You mean they talked with each other? Murderer and victim?'

'Not in words. No. Words are really a very superficial way of communicating thought. There are deeper, more urgent ways.'

I shook my head. Her words made no sense to me.

But then, nothing did, any more.

I could only think of the conversation I had overheard last night. Try as I would I could not recollect the touch of his hands.

'Time enough for all that later,' Lalli sighed. 'There's work to be done. Have you told anybody about what you overheard?'

'Only Rafiq.'

'From now on, don't talk. Just listen. We'll start with Alif Bey.'

That would have been the logical moment for me to relate *all* the furtive conversations I had overheard. Somehow I didn't.

20

Alif Bey came in with a purposeful stride, very different from his usual dispirited shuffle. His eye was keen, his chin pugnacious, his manner brisk.

'I want you to know that I consider myself completely responsible for the death of Tarok Ghosh,' he said.

Then he seated himself with considerable aplomb and stared challengingly at Lalli.

'Did you murder him?' she asked – conversationally, as one asks about the weather.

'Not in actual physical fact, no. But I colluded with the circumstances that brought about his death.'

'You conspired to kill him?'

'Not directly. I colluded with the idea of a house party, an unnatural situation where people of opposing temperament must maintain a polite propinquity. It is a situation that would be intolerable to a laboratory rat. I also colluded with the idea of this extended gastronomic orgy. That makes me responsible for his nausea at the spectacle of a practically insatiable human greed. I was part of the vast machinery that compelled his death.'

'Tarok was not killed by a heart attack or a stroke. He was murdered.'

'The method is irrelevant. The man was destined by the very predicament of his existence to meet an untimely death.'

'In that I agree with you,' Lalli said, baffling me.

'And if he was murdered, I was part of the ethos of that murder.'

'That too I accept.'

'Good. Then there's nothing more to say.'

He didn't exactly hold out his wrists to be handcuffed, but almost.

'Just a few details to clarify,' Lalli murmured.

He waved her on expansively. He leaned back in the chair. I noticed he didn't loll in it as usual. The man was wary as a cat.

'How well did you know Tarok Ghosh?'

'I met him for the first time this weekend.'

'Tell me, I'm curious, what did you think of him?'

Alif Bey glanced at me, then quickly looked away.

'He was a marvellous cook, of course. A true artist. That apart – restless, curious, intelligent. Could be dangerous. As I said, a true artist.'

'Dangerous?'

'He was a meddler, wasn't he? He riled a lot of people at dinner last night.'

'Did he rile you?'

'He might have, had I been in a different sort of mood. Normally, I don't care to have my privacy assaulted.'

'You seemed to enjoy it last night.'

'I liked the man. I regret his death with more than just politeness. I liked him. I like very few people. And even fewer like me.'

'When did you last see him today?'

'Today? I didn't see him at all. There was some sort of fracas in the morning. Mrs Sane, I believe. I did look for him around eleven. I had a splitting headache. I thought some coffee might help. But the kitchen door was shut with an ostentatious *Do Not Disturb* sign.

That was just before I met your niece here, in the library. After that I went into the living room to watch the animals. I was still there when you brought news of his murder.'

'Do you have frequent headaches?'

'Only when I've been drinking. I haven't touched a drop since Lola left. I guess you know about that.'

'You had a row.'

'A bad one. She walked out when I was still asleep. Walked out without a word, leaving all her stuff behind for me to cart back. Not that I'm going to do that. I shall leave it all here. That woman thinks every man is her beast of burden.'

'Not too enthusiastic about making up, are you?'

'That's none of your business. But since you ask, no. I'm not a squeamish man, but there are some things at which I draw a definite line.'

'And Lola does not?'

'Apparently.'

He was irritated now.

Lalli said, 'What about the others here? Are any of them old friends of yours?'

'None, except Hilla. Even that isn't strictly true. Jimmy Driver was my friend. We were drinking buddies at first, then friends. He wasn't the loser he's made out to be. Or maybe he was. As I am. We were both losers.'

'What about Chili? Did you know her?'

'We'd met a couple of times at parties. That's part of my other life, the one that pays my bills. Sweet kid, not yet in the lovely woman category if you know what I mean. Stooped to folly, I hear. Shameful waste of youth and beauty. Why don't the young realize they don't need to prove themselves? They don't have to suffer. It is enough that they are young. That itself is paradise.'

Any more of this blather and I would have made a hole through the ceiling. I couldn't switch off either as I was taking notes.

'Good to see shorthand skills still alive,' Alif Bey said. 'Computers have taken all the joy out of writing, haven't they?'

When the door had closed on him, I confronted my aunt.

'How could you stand for all that hot air? For godssake Lalli, the man is a total fraud.'

'Really? I thought he was a great writer.'

'Go on mock me, but it's the truth. He's full of lies.'

'Funny, I spotted only one. Tell me the rest.'

I took a deep breath and launched into the complicated history of my eavesdropping career. Lalli whistled as I related the Sane bit.

'Good heavens, she's *Mohini*? Who would have believed it! How idiotic the man must feel about it all now.'

'That's not all. The Lola bit is yet to come.'

So I told her everything, ending with my discovery of Lola's shoe.

'That was a really malicious thing to do, to fling her shoes in the pool, knowing she was so pathetically proud of them. "You and your cheap shoes," I heard him say when they were wrangling on the stairs. Then she hammered him with those heels. I remember their eerie sparkle in the dark. And the more I think of it, I'm sure he ripped off her earrings too.'

'What, those mobiles?'

'Yep. I found one of them caught in the ferns in the dining room last night when we were cleaning up after dinner. You know, in one of those pots we put near the door.'

'What did you do about it?'

'I didn't know what to do. Tarok put it back. He was with me when I found it.'

'In the ferns?'

'It's still dangling there for all I know.'

'Anyone else see it?'

~ 204 ~

'Only Tarok. He looked puzzled. He looked puzzled much of yesterday.'

I tried not to think of the look in his eyes after our kiss.

But Lalli was not listening to me any longer. Her eyes were intent on the distance.

I finished my notes and went to call the next name on our list. Rafiq Khan.

21

'First find out who killed them. Then leave him to me.' After that matter-of-fact statement, there was little to be got out of Rafiq. At the mention of Chili's name, he lost control. He looked around wildly for escape.

Lalli calmed him by speaking in a comforting tone words that meant nothing at all. But they served to bring him back to the present.

'She killed me,' he said. 'What can I say? She destroyed me.'

To my surprise, Lalli said, 'Yes. You will have to live with that, Rafiq.'

He raised blind eyes, baffled with grief and rage. They focused on Lalli slowly with dawning horror.

'What will happen to me now?' he whispered. He spread his large hands on the table and stared at us. He expected an answer.

Lalli said, 'That will depend on what happens next, Rafiq. You know that. We can only wait and see. But till then ...'

He nodded. 'Till then you tell me what to do, I do it. First you do your job, then I do mine.'

'Can you think of anybody who might have wanted to hurt Chili?'

'Only somebody whose heart she's broken. Only somebody she destroyed. If she were here now, I would kill her for the pain she has caused me.'

Lalli seemed quite unperturbed by the terrific illogic of this.

'Rafiq, do you think Tarok was in love with Chili or she with him?'

For answer, Rafiq turned to me. I could not meet his hard questioning gaze.

Without a word, he left the room.

'Now what was all that about?' Lalli demanded.

'I told him what I overheard last night.'

'And maybe he overheard too?'

The place was lousy with eavesdroppers. And this in such wild weather. It would be worse than a public promenade on a fine summer night. Anybody in any of the seven rooms that opened on the terrace could have overheard any of these conversations. But, equally, anyone lurking in the shadows of the eaves would have heard too.

Lalli said, 'Let's have Mr Bajaj.'

Mr Bajaj too, like Alif Bey, strode in purposefully.

This was his power strut, I guessed, the swagger that intimidated boardrooms. But intimidation was very far from his mind. He gave Lalli a respectful nod, me a sympathetic look and sat down with every appearance of a man ready to be helpful.

'At dawn I set out,' he announced. 'Two dead bodies in a house with small children is intolerable. I will take my Pajero and make it to the village somehow. I will set out at dawn.'

'If there is a dawn.'

Lalli indicated the window where tall spears of rain slipped through the bright bar of electric light to lose themselves in the featureless night.

'There is always a dawn,' he said with great earnestness. 'One has to wait, but eventually dawn breaks. I have lived through many long nights, as dark as this one.'

'Dawn seems very far off now,' Lalli said. 'Unless you can help us.'

'Anything, I will do anything to end this nightmare for poor Hilla. She has suffered too much. Just tell me what I can do to help. Now ask your questions and I will answer as clearly as I can.'

'Thank you Mr Bajaj. If everybody were as cooperative as you, my job would be a lot easier. How long have you known Tarok Ghosh?'

'I'd never met him before this weekend. I was very sceptical when Hilla discussed her plan with me when I arrived. I was very disapproving. But he was a superb cook. That resham kebab! Wah-wah!'

'What about your steak tartare?'

'Ah, his joke about horse flesh! I was flattered! To have a dish specially prepared for one is a great honour. He honoured each one of us yesterday. And look how we repaid him.'

'But was steak tartare appropriate? Do you breed horses?'

'Nothing so ambitious, I'm afraid. I have a stallion, Bruno. He's won a couple of races. I had several good horses earlier, but to maintain a good stable you need more than money. You need time. I like looking after the horses myself. They respect you if you treat them well.'

'Not an easy skill to learn.'

'I've had some experience. I've ridden in a rodeo. Texas made me. Yes, you could say that, in many ways Texas made me. But I never went back once I came home again. Never. This is my home. My roots are here. Here I stay.'

'You're a businessman, Mr Bajaj. What exactly is your business?'

'A difficult question. I have so many careers! I made my money in oil, then moved on to less competitive areas. I buy sick businesses, make them work again. At the moment I deal amost exclusively with electronics.'

'You have some idea of collaborating with Hilla to turn this place into a hotel?'

'I thought so earlier. Now I'm not so sure. After these tragedies, the property will become a liability. News gets about.'

'When did you last see Tarok today?'

'I can give you a precise answer to that. Eleven-fifteen. I met him in the corridor, just outside this door. He was carrying a coil of nylon cord and a pair of scissors. "Hilla would like us to hang the picture before lunch," he said. "I have a lot of work left," he told me. "So I am going to lock myself in the kitchen now. I have put some snacks and coffee out in the pantry in case people get hungry. When you're finished with the picture, please put these things back in the pantry." Those were his words.'

'And what did you do with the cord?'

'I went into the dining room carrying it, to check where the picture should go. Then I brought the picture from the library and tried to do the job singlehandedly. But it was a bit too heavy for me. I needed help to hold it up. In fact, as I was raising it, the clock struck half past, startling me so much, I nearly dropped the picture! That's also how I know the time so precisely. So then I left the picture there and went to the living room to ask for help.'

'Who helped you?'

'Devdutt and Felix. In about ten minutes we had the job done.'

'What happened after that?'

'We stood around chatting about the picture for a while. Devdutt said he was going to make some coffee for his wife, did we want some, and both Felix and I said no. I gave him the coil of cord and the scissors to return. I had got myself dusty and tired, so I went up to my room. I felt a mild discomfort in my chest. I had a bypass last year and I have to be careful. I stretched out on the bed for about an hour. I felt better after that, I may have slept a little, I don't remember. I took a shower, changed, went downstairs with a good appetite – to find this!'

'What about Chili? Did you know her earlier?'

'Not at all. They tell me she's a top model, international, but seeing her that was difficult to believe. I saw her at dinner yesterday for the first time. I was not impressed.'

Lalli nodded encouragingly. She liked Mr Bajaj today. Perhaps, like me, she was impressed by the man's response in a crisis. A refreshing change from Alif Bey's aesthetic pose.

'The two deaths are not necessarily related are they?' he asked. 'I hear the girl made several suicide attempts recently. Disappointed in love. Girls that age are very sensitive. Boys are animals.'

'You have a daughter?'

His eyes turned opaque.

'I had a daughter. Our only child. We lost her just before her tenth birthday.'

'I'm sorry.'

'Brain fever – what do you call it? – meningitis. Any tragedy that happens to a young girl affects me deeply. She would have been nineteen this year.'

Perhaps that was why his wife reacted so nastily to her young students. I wished I could judge her more temperately.

'What about the others here, Mr Bajaj? Do you know them well?'

'Only Hilla and the Sanes. They're old friends.'

He now took over the questioning. He quizzed Lalli on procedure, what would happen once communication was restored. Should he go to Malad Police Station or directly approach his friend the commissioner?

To all of which Lalli replied with endless patience.

'I will set out at dawn,' he said, as coda to his recital.

'So how many lies did you spot this time?' Lalli asked when he had left.

'No lies, no secret conversations, no rumours. I was so prepared to hate this guy when I knew he was Lata Sandeha's husband, but he seems the most decent of the lot, Honest. Helpful.'

'Which our next suspect may not be. Call Dr Sane.'

And that's when I remembered the half-recollected dream I'd woken up from on Friday morning. Tarok and Dr Sane had been talking together on the terrace.

'It doesn't matter to me anymore. Those that mattered to me are dead. It's over. You've never seen me before ...' Tarok's voice had said.

I told Lalli what I could salvage from my foggy brain. The rest was lost in the grey acres of a dream.

22

'My wife is having a crisis,' was Dr Sane's opening statement. 'I hope this won't take too long.'

'Then I'll cut right down to the important questions. What happened when you went to the pantry to make coffee for your wife?'

'How do you know that?'

'Everybody seems to know that was where you were headed after the picture was hung. Or did you change your mind?'

'No. I did go to the pantry. I did make that coffee. I did carry it up to our room. I sat with Ujwala coaxing her to drink it, then after chatting a little, I came downstairs again.'

'What were you carrying when you entered the pantry?'

'Nothing. Oh, Bajaj asked me to put the cord and scissors back in the pantry. The kitchen door was locked, you know. Don't Disturb sign was on. So I left those things in the pantry.'

'Where did you put them?'

'On the counter. That is, not on the counter with the heater and cups.'

'On the other limb of the L.'

'That's right. It's an L-shaped counter.'

'Was the serving hatch open?'

'I didn't notice.'

'It's directly above where you left the cord and the scissors. At eye level.'

'It was closed.'

'You can remember now?'

'Yes, I remember thinking I would exchange a word with Tarok, but then I saw it was closed, and I didn't want to knock.'

'How long were you there in the pantry?'

'As long as it took for the water to boil. My wife takes her coffee black. All I had to do was spoon in some instant coffee.'

'And what were you doing while the water was boiling?'

'Nothing.'

'Dr Sane, memory is a chancy thing. It must be cued. While you were waiting for the water to boil, you investigated the two tins next to the heater.'

He looked shamefaced.

'Yes. The first one had banana chips. I may have eaten a few.'

'You didn't open the other tin?'

'Oh I did. Biscuits. I don't like biscuits.'

'Now that you can clearly remember the events, try and recollect if you heard any noise or movement.'

'No. I don't remember anything.'

Lalli changed tracks abruptly.

'Chili was killed with rat poison. We heard Ujwala talk about it last night. The murder took place along those lines.'

'You must not suspect her,' he said urgently. 'Ujwala talks like a fool sometimes, it's all class pride. Her family is very aristocratic. She feels ashamed to mix with ordinary people like us. You cannot suspect her, you cannot question her, I am her husband, I have the right to protect her, please consider we have two small innocent children.'

'Calm yourself, Doctor. I do not suspect your wife of murdering Chili. But I would like to know if she expressed any animosity towards Chili.'

'Only the hatred she feels towards all beautiful women. She has a very jealous temperament. But her heart is pure. Please believe me.'

Lalli shrugged sceptically.

'Besides, she does not have a mind like that, she cannot calculate or plan. I doubt if she even knows a capsule can be opened and emptied out.'

'What kind of mind does she have?'

'Impulsive. Quick. Rash. Followed by deep regret.'

'The kind of mind that vents its anger with a swift blow? Grabbing whatever weapon is at hand?'

Dr Sane was silent. He stared at his trembling hands.

Lalli said, 'Why was your wife so antagonistic towards the cook?'

He said again heavily, 'Class pride. In her family, a cook is a servant and a servant is a slave.'

'And do you share that opinion?'

'I'm democratic. I hope to bring up my children to think like me. But it is too early to tell. That's marriage.'

'That's marriage,' Lalli echoed with a much married sigh. 'What exactly do you have to do with mustard oil, Doctor?'

For a moment he looked taken aback. Then he steadied himself with an easy laugh.

'I'm afraid my friend exaggerated a bit last night about that. I'm no expert! Tarok felt that way because he had heard me testify in a case that involved some friends of his.'

'In 1985?'

'Eh? No, no, 1988. They were exonerated.'

'Tarok's friends were exonerated?'

'Yes, so he thought I had worked wonders. He was just being generous.'

'Do you remember their names?'

'I'm afraid not, it was such a small matter and so long ago. They were small shopkeepers, they also started off as footpathias like

Tarok. They did not do so well as him, but he kept track of his friends.'

'I don't understand, Dr Sane. How exactly did you come to be giving evidence in a case like that?'

Dr Sane laughed.

'In those days, I was also poor like them. I had a small practice in Kalbadevi, mostly labourers, small shopkeepers, poor people. I had to explain my clinical findings in court. There was no sign of poisoning or adulteration in the oil. I remember meeting Tarok then. I recognized him at once when I met him here. He remembered too. So you see, we were old friends.'

'Perhaps Mrs Sane remembered him too?'

'No, no. Ujwala knows nothing about all that. It was long before I met her.'

'You no longer practice at Kalbadevi?'

He laughed easily.

'No thank God! I have a good clientele now. Civilized people.'

'Ujwala brought you good fortune then,' Lalli smiled.

He smiled too, a rich appreciative smile that took years off his pasty face.

'I was lucky in marrying her! My family is middle class. Upper middle class. Respectable, but middle class. Her people are Bolinjkars. Sugar, you know.'

'Ujwala knew she was marrying a successful man!'

Dr Sane laughed self-deprecatingly, rubbing his neck in a boyish gesture. 'Perhaps! I had just started my practice in Opera House when my marriage was fixed. Her father thought I was an up and coming man, much better than some rich good-for-nothing as son-in-law.'

'So he had heard of your skills?'

'Ujwala was my patient, actually. Some minor trouble, but her father was impressed by the way I handled it. I suppose he saw good qualities in me, Ujwala needed a steadying influence. Definitely, my marriage helped my career. Why should I hide it?'

I gritted my teeth and waited for the inevitable phrase. And here it came, 'I am a practical man!'

Lalli was not finished with him yet. She really pitched it strong this time.

'Dr Sane, I can't help asking a man of your experience this question – after all who can be a better judge of human psychology than a physician? Who do you think is the killer?'

He didn't bat an eyelid. He leaned back in his chair with a ripe smile.

'This is a crime of envy! He has been eating dish after dish, each exceeding his wildest expectation. He is frustrated by his own inadequacy, probably sexual as well as culinary. I advise you to read his books. First the cook, then the girl, both unattainable desires.'

'You mean ...'

'Isn't it obvious? Felix Rego.'

23

I was severe with Lalli. 'I'm ashamed of you,' I said. 'He swallowed it all. And the man is so guileless, he's open about everything.'

'Is he?'

'Of course it's a bit upsetting how easily he believed in his wife's guilt. But you really can't judge him on the basis of his values. They're awful, but that doesn't make him a murderer. At least he didn't lie.'

'He didn't?'

'Not perceptibly.'

'I have to cross-check some dates with his wife, so I'll hold my thunder till after.'

'I notice you didn't say anything about Tarok being strangled – don't you think he deserved to know that?'

'Deserved to? How has he deserved anything?'

From time to time my aunt lets me know just how much of a stranger she is.

I had never before glimpsed such coldness in her. Her adamantine eyes, bright, even dazzling, were shrewd and punitive. The contempt in her voice made me shudder. Clearly, in her book, one couldn't sink any lower than Devdutt Sane.

Felix Rego entered like a conspirator.

He pulled his chair close and leaned across the table, palms down, crouched for a spring.

'We should trap her now,' he growled. 'Before she strikes again.'

Satisfied with the sensation he had produced, he leaned back leisurely. Then he began to spill, straight out of *Carrion Cook*.

Those of you who have read the book will realize that at this point of time the first three chapters weren't yet written in Felix's brain. He plunged headlong into the psychological vortex you'll find in the fourth chapter. I give it to you exactly as he spoke it, even to the italics.

'All night she had strangled the scream of her ravening, deep visceral gut-twisting ravening. She turned impatiently from the man who snored beside her, flinging off the flimsy covers, she ran into the rain.

'The rain punished. Bare acres of wet flesh whipped till blood welled up, whipped by piano wires of stinging steel glistening in the lightning. The flagellant pursues her across the terrace, bare soles slip, and she falls, the white corolla of her limbs unfurled. Lightning flares against the throbbing black leathery bulge of cloud. Thongs lash ceaselessly. Opening her eyes to the acid sting of rain, deeply, from the birthing darkness crouched within her belly, rises a primitive moan. Her spine is alight with a thousand fires.

'She raises her head blindly and through thickened lips, cracked and flecked with foam she groans his name.'

He held up a cautionary finger as Lalli began to speak.

'Wait!'

'The rain stops. The woman rises. The fever has left her. The scent of blood quivers in her nostrils. Revenge alone she must live for. All else is mirage. This, certainty.

'She pretends a migraine. They leave her there in the darkness, a smouldering ember, a firecoal. She dresses as for a ritual. Then she goes down the twisting stairs.

'She surprised him. Once more her woman-vile will not admit defeat. She cajoles, she seduces. He laughs at her. She strikes him …'

'With what?' Lalli interrupted.

'Anything, anything!' he barked. 'A blunt object.'

'What blunt object?' Lalli persisted. 'Nothing lying around in the storeroom or kitchen fits.'

'Oh. Then she brought it with her.'

'So it was premeditated.'

'Certainly.'

'In that case, Felix, I should tell you that the head injury did not kill Tarok. He was strangled with a piece of nylon cord from that coil.'

Felix whistled, 'But I didn't notice a ligature.'

Ligature. To me, the word carried its common meaning: tie, knot. But Felix used it with a specificity that made it the weapon of murder. The man of gore had done his research.

'No, the murderer removed the ligature from his victim's neck. He was swift, brutal, efficient. I won't be surprised to find that he's done this before.'

'It's an open and shut case, then.'

'Is it?'

'Of course. Dr Sane enters the pantry to make coffee for his wife – we all heard about that. Opens the serving hatch, sees wife. Wife wrings her hands, comes to hatch, says Tarok not dead yet, only zonked. Dr Sane to the rescue. Cuts piece off coil, skips next door. She lets him in. Sane completes job. Exit married couple up the spiral stairs, locking storeroom door behind them.'

'What about the coffee?' I asked. 'He did take the coffee up to her room. The cup was still there when I went to call her.'

'That's easy. He passed it in to her through the serving hatch before he left the pantry. They carried it upstairs.'

The vision of Mrs Sane fleeing the scene of crime in pelting rain, still clutching her cup of *café noir* definitely belonged in *Carrion Cook*.

'What about Chili?' Lalli asked.

'That's a doctor's murder, isn't it? Filling capsules with poison? The Sanes probably sat up all night doing that.'

'And their motive?'

'Oh I never bother about motive. Murder's a caprice. Ujwala's a real primitive, all anger and appetite.'

'Very persuasive, Felix. I'm not surprised your books read so real.'

'Thanks! That means something, coming from you!'

'I'm waiting to read what you'll write once this is over. Now tell me, when exactly did you open the serving hatch?'

'Wha-what?' Felix was stumped.

'Oh come, you didn't expect me not to notice that! I just need to know the time. Was it before or after Dr Sane went to the pantry with that coil of wire? Now don't tell me you didn't go into the pantry, because I know you did.'

'Okay, okay, cool. I did go into the pantry, okay? I did go in there on my way back from the loo. I thought I'd see what snacks Tarok had left there. It was around one- fifteen. There were two tins. One was nearly empty – banana chips, the other was biscuits. Ginger nut. I took one. I never have breakfast, so I was a bit hungry. I don't remember opening the serving hatch.'

'Why?'

'Why what?'

'Why don't you remember opening the serving hatch?'

'Because I didn't open it!'

'Or perhaps you don't remember because you have to forget it. You did open the serving hatch, Felix, and you'd rather forget what you saw through it. Felix, what did you see?'

Felix grew very still.

'From the hatch anybody with a normal field of vision can see into the centre of the kitchen. Is there anything wrong with your vision, Felix?'

Felix said, 'I did not kill Tarok Ghosh.'

'I did not ask you if you did. I merely want answers to two questions: A – What time was it when you opened the hatch? B – What did you see through the hatch?'

All his panache had deserted him.

He looked about wildly, intensely confused.

To my amazement Lalli left her chair and came and stood by him, placing a calming hand on his shoulder. It took a little while, but he relaxed eventually. Lalli did not return to her former station. She pulled up a chair next to his.

He said, 'I went into the pantry at about one-fifteen. I ate a biscuit. I opened the hatch cautiously, thinking Tarok might not notice. I didn't open the hatch all the way at first. Then as I didn't spot him, I opened it about half way. I was looking out for the basic stuff, you know? The dishes before the dressing and the garnish? An artful dressing can hide a multitude of sins. As I expected, most of the cold dishes were laid out on the counter. Yes, I could see the centre of the kitchen, but only the floor, I couldn't see the bench or Tarok from where I stood without opening the hatch further. And then I saw it.'

'It?'

'The spilt egg on the floor. I gave him a black mark for it, Lord forgive me. But I swear I didn't see anything more.'

'Very well. Of course when the news broke, you did not tell me this because it struck you that the murderer must have entered through the storeroom. Just as *you* did, didn't you?'

That took my breath away. Felix looked bludgeoned. Lalli kept up the pressure.

'When you realized that, you decided to keep what you'd seen through the hatch to yourself. But you had better talk now, Felix. What were you doing in the storeroom? When were you there?'

'It was a little after twelve – twelve-fifteen perhaps. I left the living room to go up to my room to fetch a copy of my last book for Alif Bey. I didn't go up to my room, not at once. I stole past the kitchen just out of curiosity – and then I saw the storeroom door open. I wasn't there for more than a moment. Just popped in, grabbed the bin ...'

'The what??'

'The garbage bin. He kept it near the door, you know. I dragged it around the side of the house. Took a quick look through it, put it back and left as silently as I could. I went up to my room after that. Dried my hair. I wasn't too wet and it didn't show on my black T-shirt. I got back to the living room. Nobody had even noticed I'd been away.'

'What were you looking for in the garbage?' Lalli asked.

'So many chefs use instant sauces and mixes and dressing! Continental cooking! A scandal these days. One intelligent morning in Crawford market and you can whip up a gourmet lunch by noon – all out of packets. I wasn't going to stand for that sort of thing, was I? I always examine the bin. There was nothing but honest garbage in Tarok's bin.'

It was so totally in character. Felix Rego had the morals of an alley cat.

He said, 'I didn't kill him. I liked him. Why won't you believe me?'

'Oh I believe you,' Lalli said.

He looked outraged.

'What are your ideas about Chili's death, Felix?' Lilli asked.

'If you ask me, she killed herself. I knew her ex. Heartless twerp. The kid was more heartbroken than she let on. And you know what? She knew how to fill a capsule. She told me that on the day she'd tried to kill herself with those six capsules. "The best way to kill yourself is to fill poison in one of these capsules," she told me. "It looks so pretty and you can't taste a thing." Lalli, I'm certain

Chili killed herself. And now Rafiq has got it bad. You noticed? Once we've grabbed the murderer, we'll have to look to Rafiq – or there will be one more murder!'

I noticed the 'we' with irritation. Lalli was unfazed.

'Tell me Felix, how exactly would Tarok have made that mayonnaise?'

'Well, in our kind of weather, especially if you're making a large quantity, it's better made by whisking the egg yolks on ice. A good cook never uses a blender or an electric beater. Too much heat. You can place the bowl in a trough of ice, or scoop a hole in a large block of ice and support the bowl in that, leaving both hands free. The oil must be added drop by drop, or it'll curdle, and you won't get a smooth emulsion. I use olive oil, but some chefs like to use sesame – you know, til oil? Tarok picked that. The technique is very simple. Break eggs, separate yolks, whisk with a fork till yolks break, add oil drop by drop, whisking all the while using a strong regular wristy movement till half the volume has gone in. Then you can move faster with the rest of it. That's all there is to it unless you want to add flavouring, garlic maybe, or mustard, whatever.'

Lalli had no more questions for Felix.

'You don't mind if I use the title?' he asked me.

I shook my head dumbly and he went away.

'What title?' asked Lalli.

'*Carrion Cook*. That's what he is going to call his next book.

'Good heavens. He spoke out of his book, didn't he?'

'Almost. He'll delve deeper still into his bag of moist adjectives.'

'Ugh. Anyway, we must thank the man. We now have our blunt weapon.'

'We do?'

'Yes. But let's hear Ramona first.'

24

Ramona burst in. 'I thought you'd never call me. I can't bear it any more. I have to tell. You have to get Lola. At once. She knows everything.'

'Sit still for a moment, Ramona,' Lalli said in pedagogical tones. 'Pull yourself together, please. Talk in clear complete sentences. Whatever you tell us may be of utmost import.'

If she had said very important, it wouldn't have worked. *Utmost import* had Ramona popeyed with gravitas.

'What does Lola know?' Lalli asked gently.

'She knows what Chili wanted to tell you. I know Chili never did, because that's the last thing she said to me, just before she went to her room. She said, "If only Lola were here, I could tell Lalli everything and be rid of my worry." Those exact same words. "Lola wouldn't let me tell and now Tarok says I mustn't either. Wait!" he says. "Everybody tells me to wait!" That's the last thing she said to me. Maybe it's the last thing she said to anybody!' Ramona broke down and sobbed in earnest. Lalli waited patiently till the first paroxysms had subsided. Then she asked, 'What else did Chili tell you?'

Ramona blew her nose in a ragged bit of tissue and said, 'She wasn't pregnant.'

'She told you that?'

'Not exactly. She said she never went all the way with her boyfriend, she never really trusted him, and thank God for that or she might even be pregnant. Anyway, that's what everybody out there is saying now. That she killed herself because she was pregnant. How does it matter to them anyway? Is that all they can think of? What about her life? Her whole beautiful life, years and years of it all lost now, what about that?'

And that was all really, that Ramona could say.

For the rest, she was by turn incoherent and indignant.

'I was really mean to Chili that first day,' she said. 'I thought she'd be a snob, being so rich and famous and beautiful. But you know, she wasn't like that at all. She was kind and friendly. She was a beautiful person. And she wasn't that rich either. You saw what she wore for my dinner? I mean you'd think she'd dress up for something formal, right? But no, just that frumpy salwar kameez. I can loan you something of mine, I offered, though actually I was scared she'd stretch it, we aren't really the same size. But she laughed and said it was nice to be comfortable for once. I really felt sorry for her.'

A look of pain crossed Lalli's face and I knew she was thinking of the Rami Kashou Chili had left unworn.

Ramona chattered on.

'Guess what, we're from the same college, and she knew all the gossip and everything. I was telling her how scared we were to go to the physics lab and so many had dropped out of science because of it and, what a surprise, she had been right there when it happened.'

'When what happened?'

'The urban legend. There's a ghost that turns up on Friday evenings.'

'And Chili knew about the story?'

'No! She knew the *ghost*! She was her best friend. Of course she wasn't a ghost then, she was Payal. And then she hanged herself from the pulleys in the physics lab.'

'So you call that the urban legend?'

'Yeah. The science block is supposed to be like, haunted. And on Fridays, second Friday of the month, nobody will go within a mile of it. That's when Payal hanged herself. It wasn't just suicide, okay? Lots of stories go with it. I thought Chili would know details, and actually she said she did, but she couldn't tell as Lola had told her not to. Lola knew all about it, she said. Lola's great and all that, but she's like, a little scary. I wouldn't like to cross her. But *you* can, Lalli Aunty. You can *make* her tell you now, force her. Maybe that's why Chili died.'

It sounded ridiculous, but Lalli was sweet to her, keeping her talking, telling her after all this was over tomorrow, they must do the Rain Dance to cheer up poor Hilla.

'Try and catch some sleep now,' she said. 'There must be at least one sofa that Alif Bey hasn't snored in.'

Ramona giggled. She caught Lalli in a sudden hug.

'I know you'll make things okay,' she said.

'The faith of children is a terrible responsibility,' Lalli sighed. 'I'd better look into this. I'm going to be away for a while. Stay here. Don't worry if I'm gone for some time.'

She had probably gone to check on some grisly detail. Tarok's room was air conditioned, and much to Rafiq's chagrin, the two bodies had been placed there.

It was nearly an hour before Lalli returned, showered and fresh in a white Lucknowi suit. She brought a plate of the ginger nut biscuits Felix had sampled. In her other hand she carried a plastic bag that she placed on the floor. Which reminded me...

'How did you know Felix had opened the serving hatch?' I asked. 'Biscuit crumbs?'

'No. I didn't know. I guessed.'

Her wet hair, slicked back in rectitude, gave her a severe look.

She bristled with menace. Her small hands had the steely look of talons. She turned the eyes of a stranger on me.

'Get Alif Bey.'

25

He swaggered in. His melancholy had been replaced with a sneery sort of cockiness. He took a biscuit. 'In the parlance of the call centre – how may I assist you?'

Lalli moved the biscuits away.

With great deliberation, she shook something out of the bag. It fell on the table with a muffled thud. It was a clear plastic packet. Within it, muddied, distorted, but still easily recognizable, was Lola's shoe.

Alif Bey crumpled.

'Do you recognize this?'

He smiled weakly.

'As a matter of fact, I do. It looks very much like Lola's ridiculous shoe. I thought she'd walked off in these. Her other shoes are up in our room.'

He laughed suddenly.

'Can't you just picture it? That's Lola all over. She must have sat up all night fuming, and at first light walked out. I don't blame her. I'm not a pretty sight early in the morning. Stomps off in a fury – but how far can you stomp in these ridiculous heels! She must have torn them off, chucked them over her shoulder and gone on ahead barefoot. That's her style. Where's the other one?'

'I found just this one.'

'On the beach road?'

'No. In a little pond in the back garden. That's a little off course, isn't it?'

'In a pond? Maybe a crow dropped it or a rat dragged it. Crow, more likely. Crows like flashy things.'

'I also found this.'

She placed the Alexander Calder earring on the table.

'This is hers too,' His voice had gone quiet. 'This makes me worry. She wouldn't have dropped this. She loves these earrings. She'd turn the house upside down if she lost one. She's like a kid over trinkets. Doesn't give a damn about jewellery, but trinkets she'll kill for.'

'What did you quarrel about?'

'An indiscreet question.'

'Answer me, please.'

'The usual. Things have not been going well between us. We're really not compatible.'

'Do your quarrels often get violent?'

'No. Never. I am not a violent man. I abhor violence.'

'And yet you were brutal that night.'

'I was drunk.'

'Or angry?'

'That too. I am often drunk, but I have never been violent before.'

'What were you angry about?'

'Her endless pushiness. It's always embarrassed me. Once she started the "us" and "we" act, I wanted out. I don't need this, I said. I don't need to dig this deep for gold. I don't care for the way she gets mileage out of her misfortunes.'

'You cannot tell me what instance of her pushiness angered you?'

'No. You will have to ask her that yourself.'

'And then you say, you fell asleep.'

'Passed out.'

'And you have no idea how this shoe got into the pond, or where she dropped the earring.'

To my disgust he whimpered.

'I'm frightened. I'm so very frightened.'

His terrified eyes darted to the door.

'Give me something,' he pleaded. 'Make it go away.'

'Oh for godssake!'

I had never seen Lalli so impatient before. She yanked him out of that chair and abruptly let go. He had only two choices. He could either keel over or stagger to his feet and leave. He left.

'He's lying,' I said. 'Of course he chucked the shoe in the pond. He is a malicious man. He said the most awful things to her. He can be very cruel.'

'Cruel? No, he's not a cruel man. He just can't take pressure, and she thrives on it. She finds it heady. He finds it oppressive. She won't see that, she keeps up the pressure. He explodes.'

'You'll have to talk to Lola.'

Lalli shrugged.

'I may not be able to do that. But Lola will talk to me.'

I went out into the corridor for a breather.

Like Alif Bey, I too didn't want to face the lot of them. Each had the finger of suspicion pointed at his or her neighbour. They hid their terrors beneath a froth of malice. But its itchy sting would wear off soon enough as the day began. Of that, though, there was no sign. It was past five o'clock on my watch but you couldn't have guessed that from the black cataract that roared outside. Lalli must have had a bad time on her trip to the pond.

The sea growled throatily above it all. Suddenly my legs would not hold me up any longer, I slumped on the floor, my back to the cold damp wall. Everything ceased but the rain. Everything else was a hollow, without feature, without name. There was nothing but the rain.

26

Ujwala Sane sat down unwillingly. She had the defiant snarl of a cat trapped in a basket. The turban was back round her head. It had dried badly and gave off waves of musty damp when she moved her head.

'How long are you going to keep us here?' she barked. 'This is too much! We are respectable people, such things are never heard of in our family.'

'Do behave yourself, Ujwala,' Lalli said. 'Don't try to seem sillier than you are.'

I was flabbergasted. Lalli was actually treating her *rationally*.

'Tell me about your migraine,' Lalli invited.

Ujwala Sane didn't seem surprised in the least. Like most hypochondriacs she thought it only natural that her ailment should be of vast public concern. She described the aura in some detail, and was in the throes of a full-blown attack when Lalli interrupted her.

'Yes, but what happened today? When did your attack begin? What medication did you take?'

The cook's misbehaviour had brought it on, what else? Need Lalli ask? And upset her all over again?

~ 232 ~

'Okay, skip that,' Lalli said hastily. 'But you did try to see him later in the morning. Why?'

'I wanted to give him good,' she said. 'What he thinks, I am ordinary person or kachra like this Chili, this Lola?' She turned triumphantly on me. 'In my mother's house, I don't have to lift a glass of water.'

'Do they pour it down you throat then?' I asked, but Lalli broke in. 'Any idea what time it was?'

'How do I know? It is not my business to know such things. Ask your questions quickly and let us leave.'

'Just a few more questions, then. You went up to your room at a little past eleven, according to your husband. What did you do?'

'What do you do when you have a headache? Dance? Like that zopadpatti dancer? All Hilla's fault. After all we have done for her, this is how we are repaid.'

I was aghast to see Lalli bend over and pat the purple turban murmuring, 'Yes, yes, so very upsetting for you, poor child.'

Ujwala Sane grabbed her hand and burst into tears.

'So you went upstairs to lie down. Did you fall asleep?' Lalli asked gently.

'Yes. No. I am not sure. There was a terrible pounding in my head.'

'I can see you're feeling a little better now.'

'Better? With my innocent children exposed every minute to the murderer?'

'And who do you think is the murderer?'

'I don't know. I don't know anything about things like this. I'm just a wife and a mother. My husband and my children – that's all that matters to me. I'm not clever like you, but then, you don't know what it's like to have a husband and children, do you?'

Lalli responded to this strange attack with a grave nod.

'Yes, indeed I understand what you're trying to say. With you, your husband and children take precedence over everything else.'

'Yes, that's it.' She turned the artillery on me. 'If I hadn't married I would have done many things. I hear you have written a book. Let me tell you I could have written many books, not just one.'

'You still can,' I said. It seemed terribly important to assuage that craving.

'No. Not now. All that is finished. Only my husband and children count.'

'You feel as every good mother should,' Lalli said.

'I am a good mother. I am a very good mother. Ask Hilla. So many mothers she meets day in and day out, but she has only one thing to tell me, "Ujwala I have yet to see a mother like you."'

Mrs Sane had quite a collection of equivocal compliments.

'You have a very successful marriage. Dr Sane is a very happy man.'

'He is a god,' she said simply. 'Dev-manoos, you know? Like Mother Teresa. He has spent the major part of his life working for the poor. First seva, he always says, only then mewa.'

'Oh?'

'Yes. He used to work at Kalbadevi before we were married. All low-class patients, really dirty labourers, drunk half the time and low mentality, not paying single paisa. He had a small place, like a shed. I have seen it with my own eyes. I go to Kalbadevi sometimes to sell old zari or to buy Surti undhiyo, the best in the city you get only there, you know. He used to slog day and night.'

'But he got his reward. He married you.'

'No, no, don't say that, it's unlucky. It is my good fortune that I found a husband like him. His reward came from his patients. Once he saved the life of Mirajchand Sethia himself. You have heard of them? The Sethias? Taj Oil Mills? They were very grateful to Devdutt. They bought him a small place in Opera House. It was very small, not at all like what my father gave us, but it was a beginning. All Sethia's friends started coming to Devdutt. Then one year later, in 1988, we were married.'

'Your husband told me you too were his patient, that's how you met.'

'No, no, nothing like that. Except for migraine, I am very healthy. No other disease. Today, my husband is the most famous doctor in Bombay. Ministers, film stars, and all by appointment. Sorry, Devdutt says, you may be chief minister or chief justice, but you are at total mercy of my secretary. But once they meet him, no patient will ever leave him. He is not grand like that. He is a very simple man at heart.'

'I think you are very simple at heart too, Ujwala. That's why I feel so sad that it was Dr Sane who took the murder weapon to the scene of Tarok Ghosh's death. You know, the coil of nylon cord that was used to hang Hilla's mother's portrait.'

She stared, grey eyes starting out of their shallow sockets, 'What weapon?'

'Tarok Ghosh was killed with a piece of cord from that coil. He was strangled to death. Dr Sane took it into the pantry when he went there to make coffee for you. A few minutes later, Tarok was killed. The murderer sneaked up behind him as he sat on the bench beating eggs – and quickly and expertly strangled him with that wire.'

Her face looked like a lopsided origami, translucent, paper-white, pinched into strange folds and creases.

'The cook died because he was hit on the head. That's what you told us,' she said in a distant voice.

'Sure. He was hit on the head, but that injury didn't kill him. It merely stunned him. Soon after, he was strangled with a piece of cord.'

'That is impossible!'

'Why?'

'If you are thinking my husband did it, you are wrong! He came to my room with the coffee. Then he stayed with me till lunch time.'

'That's not what he says.'

'I am telling you he could not have killed the cook. I am telling you. That is enough.'

'I found this in the wound on Tarok's head.'

Lalli put a plastic envelope on the table, slid a sheet of white paper beneath it. Snaking within that white clarity was a single purple thread. It was the unmistakable purple of Ujwala Sane's dupatta.

'Take off your dupatta, Mrs Sane. I would like to examine it.'

'No.'

'I need your dupatta.'

'I will call my brother, he will show you. He is a lawyer. I will not say one word more till I have spoken with him.'

'Please yourself. You can go now.'

'She did it,' I said.

It seemed an incredible idea.

'I didn't get what her dupatta had to do with it.'

'When you went to her room to call her, was she wearing the dupatta?'

'Yes, as a turban wound around her head. It was wet. She said it was a cold compress.'

'She was wearing a matching salwar kameez yesterday morning. When you brought her into the living room, she had changed into this white thing.'

'So? Maybe this was more comfortable.'

'Or maybe that was wet.'

'Wet?'

'It's the only feature that's definite evidence. Anybody who went up or down the spiral staircase would have been drenched. Anybody who wasn't drenched couldn't have opened the storeroom door through the ventilator.'

It seemed a chancy thing on which to judge a crime.

'Why didn't she discard the dupatta as well, then?'

'Aha. Now you're thinking. It's a bit like *The Purloined Letter*, isn't it?'

The Poe classic with the immortal line: *Where will you hide a leaf? In the forest.*

I couldn't see the parallel.

'The clothes were merely wet. She stepped out of them without a thought. The dupatta was more intimate. She hid it where nobody would look for it. She *wore* it. She may have washed off the bloodstains, but she couldn't be sure they wouldn't show. So she wore it damp as it was, as her migraine remedy. Clever, that one.'

'But ...'

'Oh, she hit him with that dupatta. Wrapped a chunk of ice from that tub in it, whirled it and let fly. It can make an extraordinarily lethal wound. Felix told us, remember, that Tarok scooped out a block of ice to rest the bowl in? Knowing him, he would have chiselled out a neat boulder with that ice pick. Remember the fruit bird? Tarok was not the kind of man who'll come away with a handful of slush when he attacks a block of ice. She picked up a handy chunk from that ice tub, just the right size to have caused that wound. Of course, she could've used the ice pick with greater ease, but it was hidden beneath the sacking. She probably didn't see it.'

'It's a funny way to hit somebody, with a piece of ice.'

'It's funny to hit somebody. It's not usual to give in to the impulse. It is an undisciplined, rather wild choice of weapon. It conveys the intense pressure she felt. She hadn't come in there to hurt him – not physically. She was baffled with fury. She had tried knocking on his door – no answer. Her husband escorts her back to their room, makes her lie down, leaves. She grows even more furious. She hardly noticed the rain, I think, as she burst into the storeroom. And there he sat, his back to her, cool as ice, beating eggs. There's something so unbearable about the fact that the object of your fury is untouched by it. She grabbed the first thing she saw, knotted her dupatta around it. For an athlete, the rest was as easy as throwing the shot-put.

'He fell at once. He bled. She was horrified, I think. She fled up the stairs, leaving the door open.'

'She still killed him,' I said stubbornly. A great weight oppressed me.

'In intent, yes. In fact, no. Tarok is stunned, wounded, bleeding. The storeroom door stands open. Enter a murderer.'

'Through the open storeroom door?'

'I think so.'

'So again this person, too, came in with no intent to murder. He saw Tarok injured, but not dead. He finished the job by going to the pantry, getting a piece of nylon, coming back into the kitchen and strangling him. That's kind of clumsy.'

'And the murderer is not a clumsy man. No, I think he came in with the intent to murder. He came in carrying the nylon cord with the intention of garrotting Tarok. It was not so much a crime of impulse as one of opportunity. A brilliant crime.'

'I thought you said murderers are stupid,' I reminded her.

'Bedazzled by their own brilliance, they do stupid things. This one planted the cord.'

'*Planted?*'

'Sure. He dropped it on purpose. To convey a certain idea which he has been subtly propagating since then.'

And ask what I would, no more was to be had from her.

There was no doubt in her mind, then. Ujwala Sane had confessed to hitting Tarok. Dr Sane had efficiently finished the job. It was depressing to think that Felix had got it first.

I remained unconvinced.

Chili's death could not have been contrived by the Sanes. It was too unnecessary.

Besides, I knew the murderer.

I felt no rage. I felt no pity. Only compassion and dread, for there but for the grace of God, went I.

Lalli had left Hilla's statement for the last. I wondered what she would do now that she thought she had the murderer.

27

'I think I'll be able to get over everything except Chili,' Hilla said miserably. 'Not that I don't care about Tarok, I do, I do, but Chili was my child! I've looked after her since she was a baby! Do you know she has no family? Her mother died of cancer when she was five. Grandmother brought her up, and very lovingly, I must say. Then last year the old lady popped it. Cancer again. Luckily by then, Chili had her foothold on the ladder, so to say. One or two international notices, a shoot in Rome, one in Paris. Clearly, she was all set to go places. It was such a relief after that dreadful fracas in college.

'And then, when the grandmother died, the kid took up with this creep on the rebound. I never liked him, you know. Too old for you, I told her, but who listens? Glad she had the sense to dump him when she found out.

'I'll tell you one thing, Lalli, despite those foolish attempts earlier, Chill never would kill herself. She was too angry with death. When her grandmother was ill, she saw a lot of others too in hospital, she would stay back to help out, taking care of them. She was a very loving child.'

Hilla's tears hadn't really stopped since we told her about Chili, and now her face stayed twisted in a bitter paroxysm of grief.

Lalli said, 'Chili didn't kill herself. Tell me about the fracas in college.'

'I think she never really recovered from that hurt. She had this close friend, some Piyush or Payal. One day this kid hanged herself in the science lab after college hours. There was a rumour that she was pregnant, but then there always is when a woman kills herself – you should hear them go on about Chili in the living room. Anyway, the matter didn't end there. The police found out this kid had been a call girl. Her family then descended on Chili, accusing her of corrupting their daughter. Chili had just got her first modelling assignment, so apparently it made her "that sort". It was extremely traumatic for Chili.'

'Did Chili talk about that matter with you recently?'

'How odd that you should ask! Actually she did, when she was getting Ramona ready. She said there was a regular traffic of girls from college to the so-called hotels in Juhu. To my horror, Ramona agreed. Apparently, they all know about it, it's an open racket in college. And then Chili said when we'd left Ramona's room "Remember Payal? The police questioned me about Payal's boyfriends. But she didn't have a boyfriend. The only person who picked her up from college occasionally was her uncle. Her parents said she didn't have an uncle. I saw him several times, and Payal said he was wonderful. They all thought I made it up, but you know what Hilla, I keep having nightmares about that uncle. And you're not going to believe this, Lola knows about him too. She said she'd tell me all about him later." I suppose it was just some silly terror of Chili's. The uncle, the bogeyman.'

'No wonder she took a shine to Lola,' I said. 'Lola has the courage to stand up and spit on people who hurt her. Sometimes I think she's right in using her past as a battering ram.'

'But only sometimes,' Hilla said. 'She and that Alif Bey – oof! Why must people have sex right in the middle of the living room?'

'They did?' asked Lalli.

'Not actually, that would have been more normal. I just hate the way they let it all hang out in public. Go home and quarrel, I say.'

'Except that this is murder.'

'What did poor Tarok and Chili have to do with these people's muddled sex lives? Look at the way they're going on, the Sanes and Alif Bey and Lola and Felix.'

'Felix?'

'All over La Sane, isn't he. Answer my question, Lalli. What did Tarok and Chili have to do with these people's lives?'

'What indeed?' mused my aunt.

Hilla took Lalli's hand in hers.

'We'll get over this. I'll sell the house. We'll put it all behind us. We'll forget all this.'

'I will make this stop, Hilla, but it will never go away.'

'You mean there may be more murders?' Hilla asked in a hollow voice.

'I will try to make this stop. If the weather continues like this, I'll be forced to get extreme.'

Hilla rose to leave.

'All Jimmy's friends. The Sanes, Bajaj, and Alif Bey as well. They were always a bad idea, Jimmy's friends. I'm finished with them now, after this. I don't owe them anything. I'm not saying they brought these troubles on me, but enough's enough.'

At the door she paused and asked Lalli, 'I may forget it, but it never goes away for you, does it?'

'Never.'

'And?'

'And what happens to me?'

'Yes, Lalli. What happens to you when you grab the murderer?'

'It's a little like when you have to sit up with a very sick baby. You think you're trying everything, but you know you're not doing a damn thing, just being there while the baby fights for life. I, too, do the same. I enter a mind so dark and lonely I am frightened. I have to make sense of that fear. It is bleak.'

'What a life you've chosen. I couldn't stand it, not for a moment.'

Lalli smiled.

'Aren't you going to arrest them? Not formally, just lock them up or something?' I asked.

'Oh I can make a citizen's arrest, so can you. But arrest whom?'

'Ujwala Sane and her husband. And maybe Alif Bey.'

'What, all three?'

'They were lovers, weren't they? Alif Bey and Ujwala Sane? A dirty weekend in Silvassa.'

'Sounds like it. And Tarok knew. She was frightened – perhaps it was more than just a dirty weekend. I don't think Alif Bey gave a damn when Tarok mentioned Silvassa.'

'Then it was Dr Sane.'

'Or any one of the others. All of them are lying. All of them have something to hide. That does not make them murderers.'

We sat silent for a while, listening to the din of wind and rain.

I was so tired, the room blurred around me.

'Make notes,' Lalli said. 'I'm going to be away for a while.'

28

Sometime during my fanged and punishing sleep, the night ended and a new day began.

It was late, at least my watch said so. Seven-thirty. Outside, the raging elements denied all time.

After the first blank moment of wakefulness, the waiting horrors rushed in and claimed me again.

Tarok and Chili were dead. Dead by violence. Struck down by an unknown hand that waited patiently in the wings till it was time to strike again. United in helplessness, we were imprisoned in this vast chill prison that grew more sinister every hour. Our cluttered lives had somehow got mixed up, and we lied and pretended in our desperate need to extricate ourselves from our neighbour's guilt. Every gesture was false, every word a lie. We were stuck in this virtual reality of malevolent intent and civil exchange.

It was a situation that would have provoked Tarok to the point of disgust. For the first time since it happened, the thought of him was not painful. I found I could converse with him, anticipate his replies. It was the *fact* of him that was so dreadful, the broken shattered shell I knew as Tarok, the thing that was not really him at all.

This morning the conversation I had overheard between him and Chili was not in the least bit threatening. Perhaps because I now understood how jittery and sad Chili had been. Chili had grown in dimension with Ramona's account. She was more real now than she had been when alive. But, I reminded myself, all we knew of her was the remote past, her fears and anxieties, nothing to do at all with the bizarre events of yesterday.

The more I thought about it, the more certain my suspicions seemed. I would have to confront the murderer. Perhaps he would opt for the honourable way out.

Meanwhile, all I wanted was sunshine, was life. The closed room felt unaccountably cold. The air was stale with guilt and evasion. My muscles, cramped in that womby chair, felt like rigor mortis. I wanted out.

I staggered towards the bathroom, and on the way stumbled once more on another secret tryst. This time I listened in without guilt.

'You've made me wait long enough,' Ujwala Sane said. 'I must get back now. What did you want? Why did you ask me to meet you?'

'I hardly know why, except that I wanted to see you. You still baffle me, Mohini.'

'Not that name. Do you understand? Never that name again. Not after what I've been through yesterday ...'

'That's what I wanted to talk to you about. Why did you do it?'

There was a heavy silence. At length she said, 'What is this, blackmail?'

Alif Bey drew in his breath sharply. 'I don't deserve that. I've nothing more to say to you, now or in the future. I beg of you, think and act with more responsibility. What are you so frightened of?'

'I'm afraid of nothing now. If you insist on coming back into my life, I will be afraid of you as I was afraid of that cook.'

'You're threatening me.'

'You can think so if you wish.'

'You have children, beautiful children. Please ...'

'They are not your children.'

'Yes, but Sane is a good fellow, you owe it to him to act more responsibly.'

'You keep quiet or I will do the same thing to you.'

'Your threats don't frighten me. Your mind frightens me. Your loneliness frightens me. Who can solace your loneliness? But I suppose you will tell me you're never lonely.'

'Of course I'm never lonely. I have my husband. I have my children. Nothing can take them away now.'

'I'll leave you to them,' Alif Bey sighed and walked away.

I waited till he was gone, then followed Ujwala Sane to the bathroom. She looked up from the sink.

'When is this nonsense going to end?' she demanded.

How does one talk to a murderer? I could not meet her eye. I would have blundered past, but she barred my way.

'Tell your aunt to have a care,' she said. 'Tell her she does not know whom she's dealing with. Tell her to mind her own business and think of her own safety. Tell her that.'

Everything in me screamed to hit out wildly at her. At a remote distance I heard my voice say, 'I'll give her your message.'

What a stupid thing to say! And then I was past her, the blessed sting of cold water waking my deadened face. When I turned later, she was gone.

I was indecently hungry. I peeked into the living room. It was still shrouded with the shapes of sleep. They were all in there, except Lalli. All, not excluding the murderer, sleeping the sleep of the just.

I returned to the library to find Lalli frowning over my notes.

'Do you think you could bear to go to the pantry?' she asked. 'Felix has sensibly moved provisions in there. Some hot toast and coffee would be nice.'

I didn't want to. I couldn't bear to. But I went.

I concentrated on making the coffee, found butter and jam, toasted bread.

I couldn't leave that easily.

I opened the serving hatch.

The kitchen stared back emptily, with the sense of death that old monuments contain. A sense of life frozen at its peak, music stilled on the top note, a laugh silenced.

The bench, still damp from Felix's scrubbing last night, looked secret and black, an altar awaiting ritual slaughter in some complicated cult of hate.

I should have seen phantoms. I should have seen the murderer in his stealthy advance, the swift brutal quietus, I should have seen that.

I saw nothing.

I shut the hatch halfway as Felix had. The bench and its ghostly occupant were now out of my field of vision, all I could see was the floor, an acute angled wedge of gleaming tiles, not a trace of the stains of death remaining.

I returned to the library in a daze. Lalli bit gratefully into the toast. The hot sugary scent of pineapple stung the air. I forced the coffee down. It tasted vile.

'Rafiq was here a moment ago,' Lalli said. 'He'd remembered something Tarok had told him – about Dr Sane. It made no sense to him, but he wanted to tell me. Tarok had told him he'd known Dr Sane "before the silver". He hadn't asked Tarok to explain, and he didn't have a clue what it meant.'

'They'll all be doing this now,' I said. 'Pointing fingers at each other.'

'Oh do you think that's what Rafiq intended? Any way, I got lucky. I often do, you know. Here, look what I found.'

She pushed a small volume at me. I recognized the book I had been reading yesterday morning. *The Collected Browning.* I'd forgotten it on the window seat.

'Luck is a large part of detection,' she laughed. 'And am I one lucky detective!'

I was mystified. What did Browning have to do with this?

'Didn't you hear Tarok quote Browning?'

I had, actually.

'I heard him quote Browning at least twice, so I asked him if Browning was his favourite poet. He laughed and said Browning was his *only* poet. In his flight from Dhaka, one of the few treasures he'd salvaged was his father's copy of Browning's poems. It was his most precious possession. For years, the only book he had to read. "I know every one of those poems backwards, so I feel I know the man backwards. And the strangest thing, when I was in London, I found out about his life, his marriage, and do you know, none of that had any bearing on the man I knew," Tarok told me. Then of course, once I saw this book, I made the connection.'

'With Dr Sane?'

'Aha. *Just for a handful of silver he left us, just for a riband to stick in his coat ...*'

I remembered that one. I had learnt it tediously in school.

'*The Lost Leader*, persistently anthologized.'

'So that's Dr Sane's story. The mustard oil matter. He lied about it. I asked him if it was in 1985, because there was a spate of deaths from a dropsy epidemic that year, argemone posioning from adulterated mustard oil. He quickly said no, it was in 1988. He said it too quickly for 1988 not to be an important year for him. It was. He got married that year, Ujwala told us. She also told us that by that time he had quit Kalbadevi and set up a society practice in Opera House. She said he had saved the life of

Mirajchand Sethia – of Taj Oil Mills. It's easy now to read Dr Sane's story!'

'I still don't see it.'

'Tarok's friends were not small shopkeepers as Dr Sane suggested. They were Dr Sane's *patients*. Mirajchand Sethia had to answer for the adulterated oil he marketed. When the matter came up in court, Dr Sane was to present medical evidence. The victims considered him their champion – till he accepted that handful of silver from Sethia. Dr Sane probably changed his story on the witness stand, and said there were no signs of argemone poisoning in his patients.

'The impoverished young doctor, philanthropic and dedicated, could help his poor patients no further. He couldn't tell a lie. He couldn't say the mustard oil that maimed and killed them was adulterated because there were tests to prove it was not.

'Sethia must have fixed that. The oil had FDA clearance, bought, no doubt, at an astronomical price by Taj Oil Mills. I wonder what Dr Sane called the mysterious illness that had smitten so many – viral fever, probably, that convenient clothe shorse for undiagnosed illnesses. The victims were poor, faceless, obscure. Dr Sane was ambitious. Mirajchand Sethia was prepared to be generous.

'The Sethias went free on Dr Sane's evidence. The victims got no compensation. A year later, Dr Sane had turned his back on Kalbadevi and got the Sethias to buy him swank rooms in Opera House.'

'But that's criminal.'

'You can't get lower than that, I agree.'

I thought of the anger in Tarok's voice as he presented Dr Sane his mustard fish. I remembered Tarok's contempt: 'Never pity him,' he'd said. 'Wait till you hear my story.'

He had died without telling it. Now I would learn it piecemeal, by happenstance, puzzling out the missing pieces.

Lalli picked up the tray.

'I'm going to be busy for a while. I'll be upstairs in my room if you need me. If Mr Bajaj wants to venture out, keep him waiting with the others and let me know.'

And with that, she was gone.

I picked up the Browning and read *My Last Duchess* with an aching heart.

29

Everybody slept late. At ten o'clock the living room still seemed full of bodies, torpid, inanimate shapes. Mr Bajaj picked his way across Rafiq who had fallen asleep after his brief lucid interval and now lay like a tree uprooted on the rug.

'I will freshen up,' he announced. 'After a cup of tea, I will start my car. Then let us see how to get out of this situation.'

'See' was an optimism. Visibility was near zero, with thick grey rain still blowing in gusts.

'We must do something. Look how we all slept. As if drugged. It's the tension. I am a man of action. I can't sit here doing nothing. Luckily the Pajero is a tough vehicle. Let me see if we can make it.'

Remembering Lalli's instructions I said, 'I'll get you some hot breakfast here in ten minutes.'

I ran up to Lalli's room.

Lalli said, 'Good luck to him. And it's best he goes alone. If Felix or Rafiq volunteer, tell them I need them here.'

I made tea, and returned to the living room hoping I had enough cups on the tray. They might all be awake by now. They were. Mr Bajaj vetoed Felix's offer of help. Rafiq glowered silently. Felix said he'd fix breakfast for everybody, and took himself off. In a while we heard the roar of Mr Bajaj's car as the headlamps cut bright arcs in the blinding rain.

'These men of action, how they tire me,' Alif Bey sighed.

'At least he's doing something,' Ramona snapped.

'Yes, I'm very grateful to Mr Bajaj,' Hilla said in subdued tones. Her tea stood untouched.

Mrs Sane said, 'We don't have to wait here anymore. Devdutt will get a taxi.'

Devdutt didn't move.

Rafiq sprang up, towering over us.

'Finish breakfast quickly, children. Ramona, you are not allowed to cry now. First practice, then I will make you cry. Come on! After lunch you must rest, so this is last chance for practice. Show starts six p.m. on the dot.'

'Show?' Hilla's voice rose in a wail. 'You can't have a show today Rafiq! It isn't decent!'

'Children have practised Rain Dance,' Rafiq said firmly. 'While we are waiting, why not watch? After that I perform Annapoorna, dedicated to my friend Tarok.'

We stared at him.

Rafiq said with a hard laugh, 'All Breach Candy ladies want me to do special show for Somalia. One full hour they talk to me about Somalia. So I make this dance, Annapoorna, for hungry people. And I ask, why for Somalia when children are hungry in Govandi? I tell them here children in slums, on footpath, look worse than Somalia children on TV. You want to make charity show, go tell your sponsors all the money will go for slum children, footpathia, station children, every paisa – food, medicine, clothes, maybe school also. Big publicity for sponsors, big publicity for Breach Candy ladies kind heart. But they say – NO! Somalia or nothing. So I say – nothing.

'Now they say Rafiq is only after money. What he cares if children are dying in Somalia, his stomach is full, no? I made this dance for children who have no food. Now I dance it today for this footpathia who gave everybody food. It is justice.'

Hilla nodded and Ramona put in a quick appeal to go to her room as the celebrated bustier would have to be rescued in time for the dance.

Around noon, Mr Bajaj returned – without his Pajero. He looked ready to collapse, covered so thick with mud even the pelting rain hadn't been able to wash it all off. We heard his sorry tale after he was revived by Felix, and generally detoxified with hot water and soap. He was alarmed at discovering the coffee had a generous tot of brandy in it.

'Nonsense, you need to sleep it off,' Hilla said firmly. 'For once I'm all for booze.'

He had got as far as halfway down the hill when the brakes failed. He tried to jam the gears and stall the brakes. The car stalled, but wedged against a rapidly liquifying mud bank and, sank without further ado. He'd tried over the next hour to extricate it – to no avail. Finally, he had attempted the impossible – to go ahead on foot. Very soon, he was close to sharing the fate of his car.

'I decided not to give you the pleasure of one more body,' he said with ghastly jocularity.

Nobody laughed.

Lalli stayed out of all this. Hilla said she was probably catching up on her sleep.

But I had seen my aunt on a case before. She was rigidly insomniac till she had the matter tied up.

I couldn't bear to be with the lot of them.

I went into the library and buried my face in a book, letting the lines blur and dissolve into my own emptiness. I could hear the dancers' feet on the parquet, adding to my distress. I was torn between my sense of natural justice and an awful understanding of the murderer's despair. Lalli had gone off on a tangent. I couldn't blame her, really, for drawing all the wrong conclusions.

She lacked the emotive force that propelled me. Love may blind you to the faults of the loved one, but it certainly turns the searchlight on your own soul. In seeing myself in that harsh light, I could, with empathy, see also – the murderer.

It was slowly beginning to dawn on me that I would have to do something about it. Besides, I didn't want Lalli to make a fool of herself.

I went to the studio to watch the dancers. They were intent on the music and took no notice of me. Finally, they came to a halt.

'You bring the sun with you. Rain Dance is over,' Rafiq said.

He was right. I hadn't noticed. The rain had thinned to a fibreglass luminance, holding in its watery mesh a furtive trace of the sun. The children ran with excited shouts to the verandah.

Rafiq turned to me, 'What is worrying you so much? Sadness, yes, fear yes, but you are not afraid, you are worried.'

'You must talk to Lalli,' I blurted out. 'It's better that way, Rafiq. She'll tell you what to do.'

He shut his eyes and shuddered. 'She has told me already. What to do, when to do, how to do. I will do that.'

On an impulse I clasped his hands, overpowered by a tumult I could not define.

'Calm yourself,' Rafiq said in a voice of ice. 'I also am learning to calm myself. It is necessary. For those who are dead and for those who must live beyond this day.'

With these strange words, he went away.

I stayed on in the studio watching the sun creep like a felon past the thinning bars of rain.

30

Felix served lunch in the dining room. Everybody ate with dedication, as though preparing for the siege ahead.

Mr Bajaj said even if the rain did stop now, it would take at least till tomorrow morning for the roads to be passable. Everything now depended on the telephone. Lalli agreed.

'We ought to prepare ourselves for one more night here,' she said. 'But one with less uncertainty and dread.'

'Do you know?' Felix asked breathlessly.

'Yes. But my work is not complete yet. Everything now depends on Rafiq.'

We stopped in mid-chew and stared at Rafiq. He turned away, reddening.

'Yes, Rafiq is helping me towards the solution,' Lalli said. 'After the dance – we must have the dance in honour of Tarok – after that, I hope Rafiq will let me conclude this matter.'

'I'm feeling very ill,' Ujwala Sane said in a high voice. 'I can't eat this food.'

'Let me get you some tea then,' Lalli said firmly. 'Come Hilla, let's make some. I fancy a cup myself after Felix's delicious lunch. Don't you just love a sparkling cup of delicate tea with a twist of lemon – oh Felix, do we have any mint?'

Ujwala went like a lamb.

'This is it,' Felix whispered in an undertone.

'My wife is very delicate,' Dr Sane announced. 'I am very worried about her.'

'We're all worried about her,' Alif Bey said.

Dr Sane bristled, 'What do you mean?'

Alif Bey, coward that he was, shrugged and moved away.

'Be easy, Devdutt,' Mr Bajaj said heartily. 'Come, eat something.'

Dr Sane, who had already eaten a lot, glared at him.

The children stared fearfully, sensing danger.

Lalli was back very soon.

'Give Ujwala ten minutes to finish her tea, then you had better take her to her room and give her something for her migraine,' she told Dr Sane. 'Arpita and Darshan, let Mamma sleep for a while. You can help me make sandwiches for her when she wakes up.'

'Do you think Lalli will let me talk to her?' Felix whispered urgently as we carried the dishes back to the pantry.

'No. Looking for copy, are we?'

'I'd like to do a scene with the kids, actually. You know, the good mother as opposed to the bad mother.'

'You keep the kids out of this,' I said angrily, not realizing how sharply I'd spoken.

'Hey! Cool it, sweetheart.'

'And don't you dare call me sweetheart!'

Before I could help it, I had slapped him hard. I was horrified, but Felix was shaking with laughter.

'I'll have my revenge yet,' he giggled. 'I'll put you in my book.'

Now this had me really mad, and if Rafiq hadn't appeared, I would have burst into tears.

'Why you are not learning to dance, Rego? Come I show you how to dance, you show me how to make like this bhurji, very tasty.

Then I surprise my ammi when I go to G'ondi, see here is French food taught by famous French cook.'

Felix turned red, but Rafiq's manner was so inoffensive, his scowl turned into a grin and he wiggled his hips in an exaggerated dance. Suddenly I was dragged into that mad caper and when Hilla arrived she found us helpless with laughter.

'Hysteria,' she said crisply. 'First Sane Bai and then the three of you. God give me patience!'

Patience, though, was in short supply.

Alif Bey and Dr Sane were snarling at each other. Mr Bajaj, ever the man of action, was angrily taking his cellphone to pieces. Arpita and Darshan quarrelled loudly, then joined forces in being mean to Ramona. Hilla, at screaming pitch, tried to make herself heard above the din. Dr Sane was summoned to his wife's bedside. Alif Bey was offered a drink – which he refused. He took to his Recamier pose again, glowering malignantly at the world. Mr Bajaj threw the fragments of his cellphone in the bin and went to sleep on the sofa. Ramona and the kids patched up in the interests of a card game.

I met Felix and Rafiq in the corridor with Lalli.

'I don't think either of you can help with this,' she was saying.

The men turned worried eyes on me.

'Lalli wants to go down the hill right away,' Felix said. 'It's stopped raining, but there's a strong wind ...'

'Don't worry, I shan't get blown off the hillside,' Lalli retorted. 'She's coming along with me.'

I followed Lalli upstairs.

To my surprise, she went up to Framroze's eyrie. She had the telescope directed north, over the steep hill face, down over the rocks.

'Take a look.'

The field came slowly into focus. A blur of rock and scrub. Then a black shapeless mass. The light was too poor to discern more.

'What is it?'

Lalli shrugged.

'Let's find out.'

We left silently through the back gate.

Lalli kept to the green embankment, knee deep in slush. There was no other way, the road was an eddying swirl of water pitching itself urgently downhill. We fought our way around the hill. I followed Lalli who trekked expertly, finding handholds in branches and crags that I would have considered impediments.

The black bundle had either washed up on the rocks or had been flung there.

'Hurled down!' Lalli shouted above the howling wind. 'From this point, look!'

To our left was a jut of rock like a promontory. Beneath us the sea boiled angrily, just short of the bundle which had fallen inward, deflected by a sharp shoulder of rock. It lay curiously tumbled about fifty feet beneath us.

The road was lost in the slurry of muddy water. Somewhere beneath us sunlight winked lazily from the chrome headlamps of Mr Bajaj's submerged Pajero. There was no way we could get to that bundle.

'Wait here. I'm going down.'

Before I could protest she had clambered down.

I watched her, terrified, reminding myself she was sixty-three, an age when bones snap at a nudge, and if she fell now …

She didn't.

I didn't even want to think of how she would climb up again. She was crouched over the black bundle. She straightened up, made a throat-cutting gesture at me, drew a pair of scissors from her pocket, held them up for me to see.

A thin current of corruption wafted up. I could see nothing but her back bent over the rock. Then she straightened up and stepped away.

On the black spread of wet plastic, lying face down was the body of a woman.

From this height, the short spiky spill of hair seemed oddly unkempt, the rest of her so decorously robed in uniform black. I knew the black blouse, the black trousers now bunched around bulging thighs. And I knew, without looking, that one swollen foot was still held in the jewelled clasp of a flashy shoe.

It was Lola.

It was Lola, and she was dead.

I watched as Lalli turned the body over. I did not see Lola's face. I did not see anything more. I was too busy being sick in the bushes, heaving and retching till a hand rested on my shoulder, and magically, Lalli was there with me again.

31

We sat down on a flat rock. Lalli was out of breath. I felt curiously cleansed. Beneath us, the sea still clamoured for Lola.

'I told you I'm a lucky detective,' Lalli said. 'I thought we'd have to wait a week to find her.'

'You knew she was dead?'

'Obviously.'

Nothing obvious about it, as far as I could see. We sat in companionable silence, oddly at peace.

'You've known too, all along, ever since you found that shoe. You just didn't want to face it.'

She was right.

I had known all along that Lola was not coming back, that the violence that had pursued her all her life had caught up with her at last. But what is knowing? If it's a feeling deep inside you, a wordless conviction, then yes, I had known Lola was dead.

'In a way, you suppressed the truth,' said my aunt slowly. 'You made light of the shoe. You dismissed the earring. You just didn't want it to be true. And why? Because you never could like poor Lola? Unlikely. You suppressed it because you were protecting somebody. Somebody whose feet of clay you were intent on not noticing.'

'Alif Bey, yes. I was disgusted with him. But I couldn't understand it either, Lalli. After that awful fight where they almost killed each other, they were strolling in the moonlight cooing like lovebirds.'

'I rue the hour Hilla gave you that room. Now I want you to do one thing. Go over that last conversation you overheard. Try to recall the exact words. Try.'

I tried.

I couldn't remember a darn thing they'd spoken, except Lola's strident 'No!'

I couldn't recall a single word he'd spoken.

'There's only one way to find out, isn't there? Let's ask Alif Bey.'

'We can't just leave her there,' I protested.

'I've bundled her body back in that tarpaulin and pulled it as far inland as I could. It'll have to wait there till help arrives.'

As we toiled back towards the house, my mind raced with questions. I stopped Lalli. 'Why did she come back? When did she come back? Where was she all that while?'

I had a picture of Lola wandering the streets aimlessly, locked out of the flat, with no money, perhaps, in the sane light of morning, regretting the quarrel. Making that phone call to judge her ground. Then, like a beaten animal, dragging herself back to him, to die ...

Then suddenly I remembered Rafiq, waiting for reprieve.

Had she surprised him in the act?

If she had, then she had waited for an entire day and night before coming back to Ardeshir Villa. But she couldn't have. It was raining too hard by then, she couldn't have made it up the hill.

Perhaps Lola's death had nothing to do with the others. Perhaps she had died of natural causes and Alif Bey had panicked and bundled her in a tarpaulin and flung her down the cliff.

'Don't try,' Lalli advised, reading my mind as usual. 'Lola was strangled, like Tarok. A cursory look did not tell me much about the ligature – there's too much swelling, but I think it was done the same way.'

'With that nylon cord?'

'Not necessarily. He might have used anything. But she was garrotted from behind, swiftly. A man of iron nerve, swift, decisive, opportunistic.'

'That's not him at all.'

'Who?'

'Alif Bey.'

'It isn't. But all those features belong to the man I know as the murderer.'

'I know why Tarok died, why Chili died,' I said slowly. 'But why did Lola have to die?'

Lalli looked sharply at me, pushed open the gate and wading through the back garden, ran up the steps to the house. I followed. We walked quickly past the sealed-off kitchen and the storeroom. We walked slowly up the spiral staircase, across the terrace.

Lalli pointed to the pile of tarpaulin sheets neatly folded under the eaves. We went indoors and up to Framroze's eyrie, and squinted through the telescope.

Lola was no longer in view.

Lalli did not announce the discovery of Lola's body.

Instead, she sent me to call Alif Bey to the library.

'What new torment do you bring me now?' he asked theatrically.

Lalli said, 'I must insist on your telling me what your quarrel with Lola was about. It's more important than you can imagine. Let me assure you, most earnestly, you will not be betraying her in any way.'

He looked startled at her serious tone. He said, 'I-I can't be very precise, I'm afraid. There were things that had upset me. I was not my usual self. It was not going well between us.'

'Perhaps you will be able to tell me more if I showed you Ujwala Sane's statement. She made a formal statement this morning, in which she has mentioned your relationship with her. I must also tell you Dr Sane is at present ignorant of that week in Silvassa in 1988. He will have to be told in the event of his wife being charged.'

'For murder?'

'Possibly. So you see, I know already you were in an unhappy state of mind with the reminder of an old affair constantly before you. One that, I think, influenced you deeply.'

'It wasn't an affair. I married her. We're still married, I guess in the eyes of the law. We lived together for a week. She eloped with me. We married at the registrar's, lay low for a week at a tatty resort at Silvassa – it was all I could afford, those days! The first few days – and nights – were heady. And then she left me. Everything went wrong. She could not bear me, she said. I was too – strange.' His face twisted with either bitterness or contempt. It was some time before he spoke again. 'She was everything to me,' he said simply. 'For years and years I lived off the memory. And it was all a lie.'

'You made no attempt to reclaim her?'

Alif Bey smiled. 'Her father set a couple of goondas on me. They beat me up – very lightly, I must say. I'm a coward, but they couldn't intimidate me. I was young, and not easily dissuaded. When the old man realized that, he got her to send me a wedding card. She married Sane, a big society wedding. After that ...' he shrugged and fell silent.

'You didn't tell Lola about her, did you?'

'Good heavens, no! Lola would have laughed. Lola will laugh if the thing becomes public and I shall have to survive that. I am a fool, but not that big a fool. Our quarrel had to do with Lola, not with me. It had to do with that whole sordid mess in her life. You know about it, right? The lawyer?'

'Yes. I busted that.'

'You did? Then this should interest you. Lola always was soft on that lawyer. I couldn't get over that. Had you noticed it too?'

'I was not in a position to judge that. I never spoke to Lola about the matter. I got to the lawyer by what you could call a parallel route. My client was a different woman, one more of the man's victims.'

'Then let me tell you Lola feels the lawyer was the fall guy. She insists that the racket will go on despite the lawyer being behind bars. She's quite obsessed with the idea. She said the people or the *person* who really matters remains untouched by rumour or scandal. I'm uneasy with this paranoia of hers. I can't even honestly call it paranoia after what she's been through. But I don't take this dread seriously. Well, that night it all came up and I was sick of it.'

'Why did it come up? Why then?'

'Oh some foolish fancy of hers. She said she was certain now who had put the lawyer up to the whole thing. Something Chili told her, I gathered. Now that she had the name, she was going to make good on it.' He stopped abruptly.

'Go on.'

'No, that's all.'

'No, it isn't. She meant she would go to the police with the name?'

'Probably.'

'Probably not. That wouldn't have infuriated you. Lola had another quality that baffled you. You simply couldn't stomach her brand of morality. I rather think she wanted to "make good" by selling her silence.'

'I don't know, Lalli. I don't know. It sounded like blackmail to me. I didn't like it. I was out of my depth. I realized I didn't know her at all. Hell, it begins to look like I don't know anybody! I hit out! I wanted out! I didn't want this dangerous bitch hanging around me. I still don't. I'm sorry. I know I'm being a cad, but the moment we can leave here, I'm making certain Lola doesn't get within a mile of me again.'

'Why then did you make up to her later that night? Even within intimate relationships, anger like yours isn't resolved so fast.'

'We didn't make up. I told you I passed out. I was pissed. And she walked out. I certainly hadn't lost any of my anger then, and I haven't now.'

'Then you didn't stroll in the moonlight on the terrace shortly after midnight?'

'With Lola? After that? Look, for one thing I was dead to the world. If I hadn't been, after that kind of quarrel, the usual ploys simply don't work with me. I have a kind of visceral disgust.'

'I understand.'

'You do?'

'Yes. Anything else would be out of character. Tell me, was Lola telling the truth, you think?'

'About finding out the truth? Or about using it for blackmail? Both, I think, were true. She had an edgy quality of excitement that night which was certainly no pretense. And I don't think she's above a spot of blackmail. She probably thinks it's a neater form of justice.'

'You're not very fond of her, are you?'

'No, I'm not. But then I'm not fond of many people.'

'And fewer still are fond of you?'

'Touché.'

Lalli was still not giving away the truth.

'I suppose you'll tell her all I said,' he said lamely. 'She'll dine out on me for a month. She can get really gruesome on detail.'

We had nothing to console him with, so he left.

'He throttled her in rage,' I said. 'I'm sure it's him, not Dr Sane. Ujwala's accomplice.'

Why was I pushing her down that blind alley?

She looked sharply at me.

'Let's see what Rafiq has to say,' she said.

32

Once more we were gathered on the terrace. Surprisingly, the weather held its truce, though the wind blew throatily and the sea menaced unceasingly. We were a bedraggled lot, made shabby somehow by suffering.

Ujwala Sane still slept, but the rest of us adults had flocked to the terrace on Lalli's command. Ramona, in the celebrated bustier at last, radiated the joy of being seventeen that not even two murders could quench. Some of her joy was reflected in Hilla's tired and swollen eyes. The murky dusk would not hold for long. The lanterns that had lit Tarok's tandav were back in attendance, strung gaily in a row. I tried not to notice the nylon cord that held them up, and to ignore the pile of folded tarpaulin, now diminished by one.

The Rain Dance was sprightly and vivacious.

Arpita was a leaf and Ramona, in white diamante, had a true raindrop sparkle. Rafiq was a storm-tossed cloud. Darshan whooped and cavorted, turning cartwheels to his heart's content in his role of the wind. The music was eerie and haunting, and while it lasted, all of us forgot the murder.

Then we were all clapping and hugging the children, and it was over.

Not quite.

Lalli introduced Rafiq's Annapoorna.

She said he had choreographed this dance for his friend Tarok Ghosh, and would like it to be a tribute from all of us to his many talents. After the dance, Rafiq had something important to say. It would solve the mystery that baffled us, put an end to the tragic happenings of the past few days.

As introductions went, it was pretty lame.

I was momentarily distracted from the words by Rafiq who materialized near my left shoulder. He had quickly changed out of the slate-coloured fatigues he had worn as a storm cloud. He was dressed now in a black bodysuit. His eyes were outlined startlingly against the stark white paint on his face. They focused on me for an instant, then withdrew again to some inner anguish. He put out a hand in a gesture that reminded me eerily of Chili's as I had passed her that night in the vestibule. Half greeting, half avoidance. With a shudder, I mirrored the gesture. His eyes held me for an instant. Then he was gone.

Night had stolen in while we shuffled beneath the eaves, anxious and uneasy.

The lanterns had been taken away.

The terrace was almost pitch-dark.

Rafiq walked on stage, a dense shadow against the fuming dark.

All at once a flare of light sprang up and died.

The grave voice of the rudra veena welled up, dense, heavy. The first deep notes of Raag Jinjhoti trembled in augury. The slow unfurling of the dhrupad began as the terrace lit up around the central black pillar, tense, immobile. A pool of light lapped around him. Turning, I saw Hilla directing a large flash lamp. The beam of light travelled up Rafiq's still form, halting at his shoulders. He was, once more, headless, a torso of might, devoid of life. He waited as the music completed its preliminary cycle of notes. In the pause I listened to my dread.

This is a raag that plucks at the heart, constricts it with anguish, crushes it in the compelling fist of melody till there is no resisting pain any more. The music rushes in and floods you then, with unnumbered sorrows. All the devastation of loss is encompassed in its harmony, the bitterness of melancholy and the unbearable sweetness of remembrance. It is not a raag of yearning. There is no expectation in its narrative, there is no hope. There is no mourning. Pain is not history. Through it pain becomes your geography, familiar, cherished, no longer the suppressed doppelganger, but an equal, coeval with joy in its place in the sun.

The music broke me, fractured the hard armour of my calm and the tears came at last, hot, bitter, burning. Either they blinded me, or else I had my eyes closed for I missed the first few minutes of the dance.

When I began to look again, Hilla was managing the flash as a spotlight very cleverly. Now only Rafiq's face was lit. The white mask swam in the dark. Now Rafiq's eyes were Tarok's, quicksilver in their tremulous glitter, now narrowing in that 'seeing' look I knew so well. He had it down to perfection. He sprang lightly, his eyes seeking out a face in the audience each time. Now the light illuminated all of him and he danced a mime of a hungry child holding out a bowl. Hilla's job, I realized, was quite simple. She switched a black shade back and forth every five minutes (I timed it on my watch). *Sh*e set the rhythm. Rafiq improvised.

Now Rafiq was back to being Tarok. This was Tarok challenging us, conjuring up dishes that provoked us. Here now was Tarok. Seated on a bench of air, his back to us as the music sank lower and lower in timbre till it was a deep throb in the air. What was Tarok doing with his back to us?

The light went out.

When it came on again, Rafiq sashayed up and down, swivelling his hips, staring in fury at the darkness in the centre where we all knew the seated figure waited ….

He was no longer Rafiq, he was Mohini enraged. He erupted in one magnificent leap – and disappeared.

The spotlight now returned to the seated figure. No longer was he sitting upright. He had fallen forward, his arms clutching at the darkness, still magically levitant. With the next pulse of music, the light shifted again to his head. It turned slowly towards us, its movements reflecting each slow drawn-out note in the descant. It turned, mirroring the anguish in the music, struggling, distorting, straining until in the unbearable rush of pain it stilled abruptly and fell forward limp.

The music ceased.

The audience sighed.

The light went out, and came on again, almost at once.

Now Rafiq danced that last movement fully illuminated, his trunk exaggerating the torque of injury.

The dhrupad began its second descant, quicker, more insistent, throwing away veil after veil of pretence, edging closer and closer to the white-hot centre as Rafiq leapt in a wide arc and landed frozen in mid-fall, one arm outstretched, the other balancing him on the floor, making a perfect triangle with the line of flank and leg. The perfect geometry stayed unmarred as his head, lost in the darkness, waited out the last anguished note on the scale. As the music plunged and plummeted from the top note and funnelled down to plutonic depths, he turned his face in the spotlight once more in the slow grimace of death.

It was horrific. It was obscene. It was compelling. One simply could not look away.

The next descant began, quickening subtly, and Rafiq played the line again.

Once more we watched his shoulders disappear, and the death mask slowly reappear in its uneasy arc of pain.

Another descant, this time quicker, wilder, more urgently

insistent, we were almost there, almost at the incandescent burning core, almost as his shoulders disappeared in the dark.

And now, once more the white grimace of death would turn its hateful visage on us.

The music was plunging, plunging to its lowest note.

The spotlight fluttered like a moth on emptiness.

One heartbeat.

Two.

Then Lalli's voice roared 'LIGHTS!' and all was confusion.

The flashlight skidded, dazzling us with its bounce as Hilla and Felix rushed. The light steadied, and we saw.

Rafiq was stretched on the floor, Hilla bent over his face.

I noted that in passing, for the light had swept over the figures and was pouring into the deep pit of the staircase. Lalli was staring up at me, her gaze blank, blinded by the flash. Her arms were twisted around something that lolled against her, black in the glare. Slowly, as Felix steadied the flashlight, my eyes took in the scene.

Lalli's arm was crooked about a man's neck. Flail against her, his large frame wedged against the iron railing, his neck nearly broken, was Mr Bajaj.

Lalli released him and he fell in an ignominious heap on the stairs.

'Tie him up!'

She flung a length of cord at Felix. It was the same nylon that had garrotted Tarok.

Lalli gave me a tired smile.

'Poetic justice,' she said.

Rafiq had begun to breathe again, Hilla said, but his colour was not good.

'You took a terrible risk,' she shouted angrily. 'You could have killed him.'

Lalli did not reply. She looked deathly tired.

I dragged her away into my room, pushed her onto the bed and shut the door. She offered no resistance. Her passivity frightened me.

Damn Rafiq, *Lalli's* colour was not good. I had lost Tarok. I could not afford to lose her as well.

Perhaps I had shouted out the words, for her hands were on my face, on my wet cheeks and gibbering mouth.

And here was Hilla, her arms around us both, laughing and crying in relief.

'Those darn guys are right every time,' Hilla said. 'Women are lousy at this game.'

Rafiq, under the able ministrations of Dr Sane, soon sat up, looking bizarre in his white death mask that had come so close to the real thing. His neck showed a red weal where Mr Bajaj had made his mark with the nylon cord.

'He was very sudden,' Rafiq rasped hoarsely. 'Perfect timing.' He sounded almost admiring. 'How is he, do you know?'

I hadn't asked.

The last I heard he was still knocked out. Lalli had worried a bit over his game heart. 'We can't afford to lose him now,' Lalli said coldly. 'Spare no effort to keep him alive. Every luxury, please.'

Ironically, it was Rafiq who carried Mr Bajaj's inert form to his room, it was Rafiq he first saw as he regained consciousness. He struggled to get up, then fell back vanquished. He shut his eyes again quickly as Lalli spoke the formal words of arrest, charging him with the murders of Tarok Ghosh, Chili Divadia and Lola Lavina. Rafiq loomed over him till he was forced to open his eyes again.

I watched Rafiq with dread. A convulsion of hate swept his face, then, just as quickly, it was wiped away. He turned on his heel and strode out.

He looked up blindly when I joined him on the stairs. He said, 'Lalli says you thought I was the murderer? How could you?'

I could have lied, but I owed him the truth.

'Because you heard Tarok and Chili too that night on the terrace,' I said. 'But I was wrong to think you felt the same way as I did.'

He shook his head.

'You were not wrong. I did feel that way. But not for long. The anger went away.'

'Yes, the anger goes away.'

We sat together in silence, listening to the rain.

33

It was past midnight when Lalli emerged from Mr Bajaj's room. He had asked for a meal and, preferably, a cup of tea.

Ramona suggested rat poison sandwiches to go with it.

'I can't bear it, I called him Uncle,' she burst out. 'Oh I'll never live that down!'

The rain kept up its grumble, but the wind had quietened. There was every hope of the morning bringing release.

Mr Bajaj had been locked in. Rafiq sat guard outside. He said it gave him some peace to be separated from his enemy by nothing stronger than a door. A thick four-panelled teak door, I might have observed, but I let that pass.

We sat at the long table in the dining room eating the rather dispirited sandwiches. 'I can't be a cook just now,' Felix explained. 'I'm on the job. I've got to keep my mind on crime.'

Surprisingly, he had shown no inclination to probe the murderer's mind.

Two doors away from Mr Bajaj, Ujwala Sane snored in Valium bliss.

Lalli stared at her sandwich as though she couldn't bring herself to take a bite. I remembered how she had coaxed me to eat and drink in those first brutal hours after Tarok's death. Now the rest of us felt relief, but for Lalli the burden had to be carried still further.

'You owe us an explanation, Lalli,' Hilla said.

'Yes, I didn't dare ask, but I second Hilla,' Felix put in quickly.

'I hate explanations – they go on for pages in your books, Felix. I must confess I skip that entirely!' Lalli said wickedly.

'I promise to make him condense it into one tight paragraph if you'll only tell us,' Alif Bey said. He looked ravaged. The news of Lola's death had percolated slowly through the group. As yet, Lalli had made no announcement about it.

'There are two ways of looking at what happened here,' Lalli said. 'The first is the obvious chain of events. Let's consider that.

'Some time between Saturday night and Sunday morning, somebody tampered with Chili's vitamins. That was the first event.

'Some time between eleven-thirty a.m. and three p.m. on Sunday, Tarok Ghosh was murdered. That is the second event.

'But there was a third event unknown to us that happened before these. I am going to exclude that for the moment.

'Tarok's murder was a crime of opportunity. The opportunity was provided by an attack on Tarok that left him injured, but did not kill him. The murderer saw the fallen man as easy prey. He stepped in and garrotted him. It was simple. There was a coil of cord at hand, the door was open, the victim offered no resistance. If he were quick, he might escape unobserved. If he were observed, he could raise the alarm. If he were seen, he could raise the alarm of finding Tarok injured and take it from there. It was a win-win situation. As for the act itself, he was so sure about it because he had done it before.

'How did he happen to be there when Tarok was attacked? The best lies are always the ones closest to the truth. He went to the pantry to keep his promise to Hilla. He went there to pick up the picture cord. When he was there, either curiosity, or a suspicious sound made him open the hatch. He saw Tarok's assailant flee in fright. He saw Tarok slumped forward and bleeding. He knew the injury might not be fatal, but that he could make it so. He cut off a piece of cord, went in through the open storeroom door and garrotted Tarok. Then he walked out quickly. The storeroom door was still open.

'Shortly after that, Felix sneaked into the storeroom, pulled out the garbage bin, examined it, replaced it and sneaked away again.'

'Good God! You mean he was already dead then!' Felix cried out. 'If only I'd gone in!'

'You would have found him dead, Felix. Mr Bajaj is an able worker when it comes to murder.'

'But ...'

'Yes, I was coming to that. Mr Bajaj started building up an elaborate smokescreen beginning with the lie that Tarok had met him in the corridor with the coil of cord.'

'How did you know that was a lie?' Alif Bey asked

'Let's say I thought *everything* that led up to the coil of cord was a lie,' Lalli said. 'I took that as a given.'

'Why?' Felix persisted.

'The murderer had flung down the ligature, Felix, you forget that. He *wanted* us to find it there.

'Why would he want us to find it? It was planted there to establish a point of reference. It came from the coil that Tarok had handed Mr Bajaj, and Dr Sane had later carried back to the pantry. Therefore, it's easy to conclude that it could only have been used to kill Tarok *after Dr Sane had taken it back to the pantry.*

'That is what the murderer wanted us to believe. The moment I saw that as the point of reference, I knew who the murderer was.'

'It was meant to frame me,' Dr Sane said heavily.

Lalli shrugged. 'Who shut the storeroom door?'

'I did,' Dr Sane admitted startled. 'You knew?'

'I wasn't the only one who did! Mr Bajaj knew that once you went upstairs to your wife, you would discover what she had done. She would turn to you for help or consolation. Your first impulse would be to come downstairs, bolt the storeroom door on the outside. You'd lack the nerve to go in and look. Illogical, but in perfect keeping with your personality. Felix nearly queered Mr Bajaj's pitch by opening the hatch before lunchtime – but he didn't see very much.'

Felix looked grateful at the reprieve.

'After Tarok's body was discovered, Mr Bajaj only had to sit back and watch us all blunder over time schedules and that coil of nylon.

'As for Chili's death, there was nothing at all to connect him to that. At three p.m. on Sunday afternoon, Mr Bajaj was sitting pretty for the first time in thirty-six hours. There was still the small matter of Lola's body in his car, but as long as the weather held, he had a plan for that too.'

This was the first mention Lalli had made of Lola's death.

A sigh swept the room.

'The third event, the one I have left for the last, was actually the first to occur. I discovered Lola's body this afternoon. She was killed some time in the early hours of Saturday, soon after midnight, perhaps.

'Mr Bajaj and Lola were overheard on the terrace. His voice was mistaken for Alif Bey's – a natural error considering what had passed earlier that evening.

'Lola bargained with Mr Bajaj. What was she trying to sell? Her silence, probably. She knew something about Mr Bajaj and was willing to use that knowledge for gain. She was excited, even triumphant. When they were overheard, she appeared in control. Shortly thereafter, he killed her. She was killed somewhere here, either this room, or in the living room because they went down the staircase together stealthily, for a clandestine tryst.

'Once she felt secure that she had him in her power, he garrotted her. An easy crime. He then took her body to the garage, went back to the terrace for a sheet of tarpaulin, bundled the body in it and thrust it in the boot of his car. He was seen crossing the drive as he returned to the house. Unfortunately for him, one of Lola's shoes fell off. He discovered that on his way back, perhaps he stumbled on the shoe. He must have been worn out by then. He dumped the shoe in the little pond in the back garden. That bit of laziness cost him his neck.

'Once again, circumstances brilliantly fell in with his actions. The quarrel between Alif Bey and Lola was the perfect explanation for her disappearance. But he overplayed his hand with that phone call. We can check that, you know.

'When the rigmarole over that coil of cord started, it had a familiar ring. I couldn't really place it till I learnt of Lola's shoe found in the pond. Then I remembered the phone call, and it all fell in place, it was the same ploy, wasn't it? The phone call too was a false point of reference. It established that Lola was still around somewhere.

'He had planned to dump Lola's body on Saturday morning, on his way to pick up the flowers, but you, Alif, scuttled that by insisting on accompanying him on that trip to Malad Station. The flowers and the plants were stowed over the tarpaulin that wrapped the body. Who was to notice? But there's always something, isn't there? Her earring, one of those distinctive Calder mobiles, got caught in a tangle of fern from a potted plant. I learnt that only when I heard about the shoe,' she gave me a severe look.

'I knew the body was still in the car. I knew that he would soon try again to dump the body. Luckily for me, the weather forced his hand.

'This morning he ventured forth gallantly to find help. He went alone. He threw the body off the promontory, certain it would fall into the rough sea beneath. It would have too, if it hadn't been deflected in its fall by a projecting rock. I couldn't have anticipated that. I just got lucky. The weather changed. It cleared enough for me to see something big and black on the rocks. Without that bit of luck I would still be trying to piece this together. He drove the car on a little further, turned it off the road and left it there. Then he came back, quite the hero.'

'If he killed Tarok earlier than we thought, wouldn't it have been evident when you examined the body?' I asked.

'Half an hour at the most? No, not really. Especially with ice and cold water soaking him. I put the time of the murder at eleven-thirty or a little later. Again, remember, it was Mr Bajaj who fixed the time with his little fiction of the clock striking as he tried single-handed to hoist the picture.'

'If you knew all this already, why did you risk Rafiq's life?' Ramona demanded.

Lalli smiled.

'That had as much to do with Rafiq as it had to do with me. I made a bargain with him. We each kept our part in it. The dead are gone, Ramona. I have responsibilities towards the living. So I was willing to use Rafiq.'

'True, I knew all this, but I needed proof. So far, I had none. If this went on till we were rescued, even if charged, Mr Bajaj would get away. He'd have a safety net of lawyers waiting for him. Chances were that I would not be able to charge him. I had to push him into revealing himself.

'The dance and the lighting were Rafiq's idea of course. It was, you will admit, brilliantly choreographed. I hope to see him perform it again – with happier results! I was waiting for Mr Bajaj on the stairs. He was a desperate man, and he had very little time to try his last trick. Rafiq was supposed to reveal something after the dance, wasn't he? Mr Bajaj couldn't risk thatt!

'We expected him to act in that instant of Rafiq's head disappearing into the dark. Rafiq played the line again and again, luring Mr Bajaj into grabbing the opportunity. And he did – on the third occasion! He was quick as lightning I must say, and I'm glad I was able to nab him just as he was tightening the cord ...'

'What did Tarok mean when he gave Mr Bajaj steak tartare?' Alif Bey asked. 'I know he breeds horses, but Tarok's comment seemed a little more pointed than that.'

'Indeed it was,' Lalli smiled. 'That's what gave me the answer to the puzzle. Tarok made the distinction between horse flesh and human flesh. He was trying to tell Mr Bajaj he knew he was in the flesh trade.'

'As Lola knew,' Alif Bey sighed.

'As Chili knew too. Which brings me to the reason why Mr Bajaj went to all this trouble.

'Because of Tarok's magnetism, his artfully contrived dinner, I, like you, made the mistake of seeing Tarok as the central figure in this tragedy. His murder was simply a side effect, as Dr Sane might like to term it.

'The tragedy hinges on Chili. For those of you who haven't heard it, I will tell the story of Chili's friend Payal. She has been dead a couple of years, but this tale begins with her story.

'Payal was in college with Chili. They were friends. Quite without apparent reason, Payal hanged herself. In the aftermath it was discovered that she had been leading a very active and very lucrative double life as a call-girl. It came as a shock to Chili who had not suspected any such thing about her friend. Payal was a quiet girl, with few friends. But she had often told Chili how much she relied on her uncle. Chili had met this uncle too, once when he came to pick up Payal from college.

'Payal's family knew of no such uncle. Neither could the police trace him. The uncle was dismissed as a fiction on Chili's part. You can imagine how Chili must have suffered through all this. Sadly, two years after Payal's suicide, there's still an active traffic among college students. The police know about it, there are occasional raids, but they are no closer to clearing the mess than they were two years ago. In situations like this the small fish netted at every raid don't really matter. They're replaceable. After a lull the racket takes up where it left off.

'Chili was an intelligent kid. She was also an angry woman. She hadn't got over Payal's death. She hadn't forgotten the mysterious uncle.

'And then, on the night of Tarok's Millennial banquet, she met him again. Do you remember how drawn and tired Chili looked that night? Everybody thought it was her plain dress. That's nonsense. Chili would have looked stunning even in sack cloth and ashes. No, she was frightened out of her wits. She recognized Mr Bajaj. And he recognized her.

'You see she had met Mr Bajaj before. In the company of her ill-fated friend. He was the mysterious uncle, the one who disappeared without a trace, the only link between the college student – and the double life she led as a call-girl. It's a link Chili made. She wanted to tell me about it, but Lola dissuaded her. She wanted to tell me *before* she met Mr Bajaj, before she knew he was the sinister uncle. She simply wanted to tell me what she'd seen and known of this mysterious figure in Payal's life. Chili had made the connection. She might even have known other girls in the racket, since she knew the traffic still went on.

'But Chili didn't tell me. Because she told Lola first, and Lola knew at once what she was talking about. Lola had recognized Mr Bajaj too. She had met him before in her professional capacity. She knew the lawyer who had used her so shamefully was only a small player in the game. Lola, you see had her own plans, and we know now how they ended.

'To return to Tarok's banquet, and the game he played – Tarok knew a lot about us. Each of you knows the precise significance of what he said about you. I do too. Tarok was an angry man. He had been hurt and distressed by some of you. He offered you the only brand of justice he understood: the moment of introspection to contemplate your guilt. In that, he was too generous.

'At first his murder seemed an act of retribution for the truths he had revealed at the banquet. But if you think a little you'll see that's impossible. There could be little point in silencing him *for what he'd already said.*

'The moment I realized that, I knew I had to look for something that Tarok had learnt or seen *after* that dinner.

'Tarok had comforted Chili at the dinner table after her angry comment on Mrs Sane's remark about Lola. What could he have said to her? Knowing him, I think he would have asked her to talk to him after dinner. Which I now know she did.

'I think Chili told him all she knew about Mr Bajaj. I think Mr Bajaj saw her talking with Tarok.

'He had to act, and quickly. Probably while Chili was talking with Tarok in the kitchen, he nipped into Chili's room, lifted the bottle, worked on the capsules in the security of his own room and, when the chance arose, put it back in her room. That would not have been difficult. Chili stayed a long while talking to Tarok, and he probably knew that. He must have watched her. He was a desperate man by then.

'And then next morning, quite without planning it, Mr Bajaj was presented with another sitting duck. Tarok, knocked unconscious and bleeding from what was essentially a mild head injury. The assailant was Ujwala Sane. The assault was unpremeditated. She has made a statement.'

Lalli stopped, exhausted.

Dr Sane cleared his throat.

'My wife would like you to hear her statement.'

Hilla said, 'Really, Devdutt, it is not necessary.'

'No. We both feel it is. At least when I tell her I have read it, there is no argument possible.'

For a man who had made his fortune out of adulterated mustard oil, he was remarkably righteous.

Lalli said, 'The decision is not in your hands, Dr Sane. Unless Ujwala decides to tell us, we do not want to know about events as ancient as 1988. Or indeed – 1985.'

A delicate silence quivered till Ramona broke it.

'But she hit him, right? She hit Tarok because she lost her temper? That's what you told us at first. That the back of his head had been beaten in. And then we heard that no, he was strangled with that picture cord. So what did she hit him with? A hammer?'

'A piece of ice. It cut his scalp, he bled a bit, but he would have recovered.'

'She is truly sorry about it,' Dr Sane said. 'Because of the migraine, you know, it was not voluntary, she couldn't help it.'

'I certainly hope she gets her migraine cured completely,' Ramona said.

'It is a consummation devoutly to be wished,' added Alif Bey.

'And now it's time somebody relieved Rafiq,' Lalli rose briskly. 'Let's take a look at the dawn, shall we?'

I stood watching the uneasy light approach the sullen tide. Alif Bey walked up to me. He carried a book. The Browning I had once again abandoned in the library. He opened it at random and read in the growing light:

Round the cape of a sudden came the sea
And the sun looked over the mountain's rim
And straight was a path of gold for him
And the need of a world of men for me.

Afterword

Things cleared up surprisingly fast. It wasn't till the police arrived and Mr Bajaj was taken away that I remembered Lata Sandeha. How trivial all my troubles seemed compared to the terrible burden she must now carry! I hated the thought of how she must regard my presence – a jinx, a catalyst for tragedy, if not something worse.

I needn't have worried.

She barely noticed me. She met Hilla – once – to promptly and completely discredit her husband. She refused to see him in custody. He was served with divorce papers within twenty-four hours. She 'cooperated fully with the police' as they put it and was out of the country on a long overdue sabbatical within the week.

I guess she's going to be away for a long long time.

Lalli has been busy with Mr Bajaj since the arrest. He has grown quite fond of her and admires her proficiency with knots. He's had a thing about rope, apparently, since his rodeo days in Texas.

As for my aunt, she despairs daily over what she calls in Lola terms 'crimes of patriarchy'.

Lola's ex-lawyer gladly identified Mr Bajaj as the mastermind, and drove Lalli into a spitting rage by stating his racket was purely philanthropic, a long-term project against AIDS.

'Prostitution is the oldest profession, we cannot stop that,' he said. 'But by providing respectable women from good families, we can protect the health of our country.'

Savio said Lalli had to be restrained from inflicting grievous bodily harm on the lawyer.

For a woman who spends her free time working out strategies to abolish the death penalty, Lalli has little sympathy for Mr Bajaj and his kind.

'Hang a murderer and you're one yourself,' she often says. 'But condone with him, and you're worse.'

In her view, there are no extenuating circumstances.

Mr Bajaj's reach proved further than she suspected: several suburban colleges were on his payroll. Young women, like Chili's friend Payal provided a discreet and loyal service. His clients paid well for youth and innocence. For the girls, if money was not lure enough, there were small attentions and luxuries that made it worth their while. Few of them apprehended any danger. Lalli spared no details when she spoke with them. She carried a grisly album of autopsy pictures when she met them.

Most days she returned home saddened.

'There's only so much one can do,' she sighed.

The truth about Lola depressed her even more. Lola had kept up contact with some of her ex-clients. She had, as Alif Bey told us, identified Mr Bajaj as the brain behind the lawyer, recognizing him from a previous encounter. She had tried to persuade Mr Bajaj into giving her what he called 'a piece of the action' in exchange for silence.

'She was difficult to resist,' Mr Bajaj told Lalli.

Before Rafiq's dance that night, she had made her stand known to him. He had agreed to meet her to talk things over. When they met, Lola drove a hard bargain. She told him she knew about the college racket as well, and one of the guests here might well have enough information to threaten him. She would persuade the girl to be silent – for a price. Meanwhile, she was prepared to be generous with him on the living room couch. Whereupon he killed her.

We will never know the extent of Chili's distress, or her helpless anger against what she knew as a certainty. She had trusted in Lola, or she would have been alive today. She had trusted in Tarok – if she hadn't he would be alive too.

And so it went, the endless chain of circumstance.

I am still picking up the pieces.

Last week, Savio brought home a visitor. Lalli was away, and Savio left me to discover what R. Sadashivam wanted to talk to me about. Mr Sadashivam, dressed in immaculate shirt and veshti, redolent of sandalwood paste and vibhuti, placed his small cloth bag carefully between his feet and sat in grave silence, like a man paying a condolence visit. Which, in a way, was what he had come for.

He was the brother of the late Nataraj Iyer. Perhaps I had heard of him?

Thus I learnt one more fragment of the interrupted tale of Tarok's past, of his years as an apprentice, and of his hope after his years in Europe, of widening Nataraj Iyer's enterprise. But he had returned to a failing business, doomed to bankruptcy. Nataraj Iyer himself was too ill to take care of it. Tarok had spent the last year salvaging what he could, enough to recover for his mentor's widow a small income for life. 'He left our lives as suddenly as he entered,' my visitor mused. He could have been speaking for me.

I have the teapot and Tarok's tattered Browning. One day I shall open the small parcel of his belongings that Lalli gave me. One day, perhaps. But not yet. Not yet.

Hilla will soon sell Ardeshir Villa. Ramona has taken seriously to karate. Her new boyfriend is a black-belt. The Sanes have passed out of memory. Alif Bey has got over Lola, and if Page 3 is to be believed, is shacked up with the Bidri Bitch. Rafiq is in Paris, staging his new ballet, Annapoorna,

They were all on Page 3 last week, with Felix centre stage at the launch of his new thriller – you guessed it – *Carrion Cook*. 'A gourmet murder,' the caption says. There's a picture of Felix biting into a (hopefully) live lobster. Sonia Sorabjee, leggy in a wetlook designer loincloth rather overshadows Ujwala Sane who is trapped like a fleshy fish in webby chiffon and a blouse like a wonderbra worn back to front. She must be the only woman in the world to flaunt a cleavage at the back.

Ramona is blissful in her white bustier and Hilla is *not* wearing a catsuit.

Felix sent Lalli an advance copy of the book, nestled in a basket of carnations. The cover is a cubist frenzy of egg yolk and bloodstains, and the copy much as expected. The book is dedicated to Lalli. Tarok is not mentioned in the book. His Millennial menu appeared without acknowledgement on the invitation to the launch.

Naturally, we did not attend.

Meet Lalli again in 'The Gardener's Song'

It's a Carrollian summer at Utkrusha. Lalli's flat on the second floor is no longer the haven it used to be for her niece. The staid lives of their neighbours aren't exactly what they seem, and she's so caught up in the dizzy whirl of events that it's some time before she sees the fantastic pattern in their random spill...

It all begins with the Adventure of the Banker's Clerk ...

That is scarcely explained when they're startled by the curious behaviour of the Sister's Husband's Niece...

A brief distraction is provided by a Bear Without its Head...

And then the new resident meets a Rattlesnake that Questions Him in Greek.

And the estranged husband gets a Letter from his Wife...

After an Excursion on a Damp Night, Mr Rao encounters a most peculiar Vegetable Pill...

All of which leads Lalli to consider the argument of a Bar of Mottled Soap...

But it is not till the baffling incident of the Gardener's Song that Lalli reads the Double Rule of Three...

Available to you in 2007
An IndiaInk/Roli Books title